NOVEMBER'S DAWN

NOVEMBER'S DAWN

C.T. MOSHAGE

Cursed Dragon Ship
PUBLISHING

For V

CHAPTER ONE_

The only constant to living at the bottom of the ocean was the darkness that dwelled at the edges of even the brightest light.

But these shadows were new and should not have been there.

They shrouded the cramped metal passageway when Josie left her family's cabin for the morning. Inside, her mom and little sister still slept. Josie liked to be the first one awake. That way she avoided any chance her mom would lecture her on things like respecting authority.

Josie glanced up. The light fixture above the cabin's hatch had finally failed. That was no surprise, and she was almost happy it had gone out. Watching it grasp for life over the last few days had been infuriating. Now two more fixtures down the passageway started to flicker the same way. That made her smile. One flickering light could be the cause of any number of electrical issues. Two or more, and she knew exactly what to do about it. It was part of her training as an engineering apprentice. Faulty wiring made them fail in succession and she could fix faulty wiring. Working out the problem would also be a welcome distraction, especially today—the anniversary of the worst day of her life.

Josie eyed the access panel under the fixture. The game was about to begin. In one practiced motion, she twisted her red hair into a bun and secured it with a worn pencil. Then she took a small screwdriver from her pocket and removed the panel. A thick mess of wires in every color and gauge branched in several directions inside. She pushed the wires to the side and found what she expected. A screw holding the wire connection had come loose. A few turns of the screwdriver tightened the connection, forcing the fixture back to life above her.

"Nice job, Josie," she whispered with a smirk.

Just as she replaced the access panel cover, a deep vibration rumbled up from the metal grate floor. She frowned and steadied herself against the wall until it subsided. It was strange to feel a tremor like that aboard the submerged, thousand-meter-long ark *November's Dawn*. The ever-present swaying caused by the ark's colossal metal legs walking across the ocean floor was a central part of life. It was so much a part of life that many people didn't realize *November's Dawn* never stopped walking. But this tremor was nothing like the slow, steady pace she was so used to. That was the second unusual thing about today.

"Josie? What're you doing there?" a low male voice asked.

Josie spun around and jammed the screwdriver into her pocket. "Miles?" Her face flushed. "Nothing. I'm on my way to class."

Miles looked at her with the same hazel brown eyes and impish grin she stole glances of in class. She often caught herself admiring the way his smooth brown skin captured the low light and the way his eyes squinted when he was thinking hard. He wore a standard-issue apprentice jumpsuit like hers.

"Wait. What're you doing here?" she said.

"Going to class, same as you."

Josie huffed at his perfectly reasonable answer. Every kid on the ark took general education courses. Josie would much rather be working on her engineering training, but she didn't have a choice. Today their class had been invited to the Observatory for a special demonstration by one of the ark's higher ups.

"It's weird, isn't it? That they changed where class is being held today? I'm not complaining though. Our usual classroom gets so stuffy sometimes." Miles chuckled and waited for Josie to respond, then shifted uneasily when she did not. "I could have sworn this light was going out."

"I fixed it," she said, declining to elaborate further.

"Really?" In two steps, he spanned the distance to examine the fixture. For sixteen, he was more muscular than most and a good head taller. A slight smile crossed his lips. "I'm not going to lie, that's pretty cool you managed it without another engineer's help."

Josie watched him for a moment. Nobody ever complimented her, and if they did, it followed some other cruel comment. But Miles kept smiling.

"Thanks," she blurted out as her face turned hot again.

"We should get to class," Miles said. "Or else we won't make it to the Observatory in time. Instructor Hale would be furious."

"Yeah," she said, eager for the shift in conversation. "You'd think with all the pressure they throw on the engineers, they'd ease up every now and then. Especially since we're all that's left."

"Maybe that's the reason. It's up to us to make sure humanity survives." He shrugged. "We won't be kids once we formalize our work assignments and you know what they say,

'In the darkness below, *November's Dawn* will provide.' Can't provide if people are slacking off."

Her eyes flicked up to the wall behind him.

Bright orange and yellow neon letters burned against the metal wall. *In the darkness below,* November's Dawn *will provide.* Down the passageway were two more sets at regular intervals.

"Yeah, engineers provide," she said under her breath.

Ever since her dad's accident five years ago to the day, Josie and her family had struggled to get by. Her mom did what she could, but it definitely never felt like they were in the *provided for* category. They survived though. Maybe that was what the promise really was—survival.

Josie and Miles were silent the rest of the way to the Observatory. She didn't know what to say anyway and was secretly glad to be spared the anxiety of trying to make small talk. Their class passes got them past the guarded checkpoint between decks without incident. The Observatory was a cavernous chamber with a system of catwalks and supports which made the place look like a steel jungle. Miles whistled as he took in the complexity of the catwalks. He pointed to something across the way, but Josie stopped him and motioned straight up.

"What's that?" he whispered.

Josie grinned. She had heard the stories and knew exactly what it was. "That's the Observatory Dome." Together they looked at the inky-black, ocean water canopy held at bay high above their heads by a glass dome, reinforced with wide steel beams as thick as their legs. The dome was vast but still trivial when compared to the engulfing emptiness beyond. Survival on the ocean floor meant adhering to two principles: respect for the water and reverence for *November's Dawn.*

"It's all so calm," Miles said.

"It's hard to imagine that just a few thousand meters above

us the whole planet's surface is just raging waves and endless storms."

"What do you think *November's Dawn* looks like from out there?" he said. "I bet it looks like a gigantic lobster walking on the ocean floor, only without the claws in front. I mean, it has to have over a hundred legs."

Josie knew there were in fact over two hundred legs, but she didn't correct him. The description of *November's Dawn* as a lowly lobster was the last thing she imagined him saying.

"What?" he said sheepishly.

"Nothing." She smiled and looked away. "I just think it looks like home."

"Miss Owens? Mr. Thomas? What are you two doing down there? Come up here at once," a woman's firm voice called out from a high catwalk.

Josie recognized the voice as Instructor Hale's. That location must have been what Miles pointed at earlier. More students gathered on the catwalk suspended high in the air across from her. Her ears burned as they made their way up the stairs to join them.

"Sorry, Instructor Hale. I was only admiring the dome's construction," she answered, much to her instant regret. Most of her classmates weren't training to be engineers and they didn't understand.

"Oh look. Scrawny Josie Owens, with grease on her hands and obnoxious red hair, is going on about stupid math and metal again. How dreadfully Bottom Bay," a girl named Odette quipped.

The insult was echoed by throaty laughs from Odette's friends, Nila and Triss. Each dressed in a summer park outfit too nice to be seen outside of Olympus Deck—the section of *November's Dawn* where the rich and powerful lived—and their blonde hair was done up in the latest fashions their mothers decided were now in style.

Josie glanced at Miles, wishing he did not have to hear that. She was not a Bottom Bayer. In fact, there really was no such thing as a Bottom Bayer as it wasn't a residential part of the ark. Josie lived on Aegean Deck, where most people and workers on *November's Dawn* did. But it didn't matter to her classmates who laughed to avoid Odette's wrath. Even a poor insult was still an insult and getting called a Bottom Bayer meant you were worthless.

Miles looked at the ground and stuffed his hands in his pockets. But he did not join them. That was enough for her.

Normally, Josie backed off when Odette lashed out, but she could not hold it anymore. "If you had any brains at all behind that huge forehead, you'd know Aegean Deck is not the same as Bottom Bay. Nobody lives in Bottom Bay."

Odette yelped and covered her forehead. Josie's classmates joined in on the laugh this time. Odette looked at Theodore, a boy from Olympus Deck who Josie knew Odette had a crush on. Theodore snickered with his friends too.

Guilt crept through Josie. She had taken a cheap shot and did not like being mean, but it was a split-second decision and Odette was the worst. She was just thankful to not be the one being laughed at for once.

"It's not true, Odette. You know you're the prettiest in class. Everyone says so," Triss comforted.

"Oh, shut it, Triss. I hate coming down to the poor people decks. It's no wonder they're not allowed on Olympus. I don't know why they don't have separate classes for us," Odette said. She stepped toward Josie as the catwalk groaned beneath them.

"Ladies! Ladies, please," Instructor Hale begged. "Tradition dictates that children from all decks have class together to encourage cooperation. So enough of this. We have a most esteemed guest today, and he will not tolerate this disunity."

Odette sneered and gave one last foul look before turning to Instructor Hale. As if by cue, the heavy boots of two fully outfitted and masked peace-and-compliance officers thundered down the catwalk from a higher level. The hulking figures demanded respect.

The entire class held its breath for what was coming.

CHAPTER TWO_

Josie watched the two peace-and-compliance officers step onto the platform and flank the entry. A tall and poised man came behind them. He wore the pressed gray vestments of a cleric from the Order of Scientific Discovery. Jet black hair slicked back around his ears, and high cheekbones made him look very serious. Josie thought he could have been handsome, but his sharp eyes reminded her of the little rats she had seen scurrying around the Engineering Bay. As a rule, she avoided anyone involved with the OSD, but even she knew who this man was. Everyone had seen his face on the holoscreens that lined the passageways at one point or another.

Instructor Hale beamed, as if she had just received an extra ration card. "Class, please give a warm *November's Dawn* welcome to First Vicar Adrian Frost."

Odette and the other students from Olympus Deck clapped and cheered for the First Vicar. He was an almost divine figure to them and responsible for the ark's continued prosperity, which was precisely what the Order of Scientific Discovery wanted them to think.

Josie didn't buy it. While she was fascinated by the ark's

engineering, in her mind the OSD encouraged devotion to an unhealthy degree.

The students from Delos Deck, where the moderately successful lived and where the Observatory was located, clapped in a light and hopeful manner, eager for the opportunities *November's Dawn* offered their station. Josie and the others from Aegean Deck made a small show of enthusiasm. It was hard to be hopeful when they had little chance of improving their status in life.

First Vicar Frost closed his eyes and smiled as he took in the applause. Josie rolled her eyes instead.

"Children of *November's Dawn*, thank you. This is a most special day Instructor Hale arranged for you. Welcome to the grand Observatory," First Vicar Frost said while opening his arms. He gave a slight nod to Instructor Hale who nearly fainted at the praise.

"In the darkness below, *November's Dawn* will provide!" a student from Olympus Deck shouted.

The First Vicar's mouth twitched up slightly, but he quickly masked it. "Yes, children. Words more important today than ever before." His voice was low and clear, like he had never once doubted his purpose or message. "Today marks an important day in our history. Today, and the week that follows, will be replete in celebration and reverence. It has been many years since the last time we commemorated the Great Turning. But today we begin this honored celebration once more. For in one week's time, the great legs of *November's Dawn* that carry us across the ocean floor will turn their course and we will walk a new path, away from the Obsidian Trench abyss. A maneuver made possible by the stalwart helmsmen of Olympus Deck and the OSD's guidance, of course. But no less important are the Aegean factory workers and the historians and instructors of Delos." He glanced at Instructor Hale who responded with beaming pride.

Josie moved closer to Miles. "He talks like he's giving a sermon," she whispered.

"I'll say," Miles joked but then frowned.

Josie rolled her eyes, not in a bad way. She knew Miles was much more reserved than she and did not feel quite the same animosity about the OSD as she did. Instructor Hale's gaze cautioned Josie from saying anything else. Hale would be furious if she interrupted the First Vicar.

"Seventy years ago, when the War Above flooded our world, all that was left of humanity came aboard Cornelius Graham's great ark, *November's Dawn*. It has sheltered us, fed us, brought us light and heat, and given us hope for a better tomorrow ever since. Let our celebration and reverence begin, for in seven days, the mighty machinations of *November's Dawn* will carry us ever onward to a new frontier."

"In the darkness below, *November's Dawn* will provide," the class responded in unison.

Josie sighed. Loudly. She couldn't help it. It just came out. Everyone on the catwalk turned to stare at her, and Instructor Hale looked as if steam might erupt from her ears. Nobody spoke, not even Odette and she always had something to say.

"You wish to speak, child?" First Vicar Frost said smoothly, his eyes fixed on Josie.

Josie froze. She had no idea what to do. She could run and maybe jump from the catwalk, but she quickly decided against it. She might survive the fall.

"The First Vicar asked you a direct question," Instructor Hale seethed.

Her mind raced, unable to come up with an excuse. The scoff was loud; everyone heard it. There was no going back now. Then she did the unthinkable. "It seems foolish, doesn't it? People on Aegean Deck are starving. There's no medicine. A celebration won't fill their bellies. It won't help them in the end."

Josie should have stopped after the first sentence, but she didn't. Now the words were spoken. They hung over everyone on the catwalk like an immovable weight bearing down on their chests.

First Vicar Frost stood eerily still. Josie could almost feel the gears of his mind turning.

"Such enlightened words from one so young." First Vicar Frost waved off Josie's attempt to reply. He looked at the whole class. "We all must sacrifice. But this celebration is a shining exploration of the hope *November's Dawn* provides us when we stay united. And as long as there is order, *November's Dawn* will continue to provide."

After another moment, he turned back to Josie. "Tell me your name?"

She held her head up high. "Josie. Josie Owens."

The First Vicar stopped, and his face turned curious. "Owens? As in the daughter of Dominic Owens?"

The mention of her dad caught her off-guard. "Yes."

First Vicar Frost's black eyes never left hers. He studied her. It made her stomach feel uneasy. "No doubt you will make a fine engineer one day, just like your father was."

Instructor Hale stepped forward. "I'm so sorry, First Vicar. I'm mortified you've been treated this way. I will escort Miss Owens back to Aegean Deck immediately."

He turned to face Instructor Hale. "Speak no more of it. This is a joyous day. I would not take the spectacle we are about to see away from a child. Shall we proceed with the show, Instructor Hale?"

"Yes, of course. Excellent idea, First Vicar," Instructor Hale said, casting a dark look at Josie. "Everyone come close. You're about to see one of the most magnificent sights on *November's Dawn*."

The First Vicar took over. "Children, when you look above, what do you see? Darkness, nothingness, the abyss. But no longer. *November's Dawn* gives us the gift of life!"

As the First Vicar's words trailed off, the low lighting and holoscreens in the Observatory dimmed, replaced by a light Josie had never seen before. Around the dome's exterior, glowing blue lights made to mimic the natural bioluminescence of the ocean's many creatures pulsed in soft waves, illuminating the watery world around them.

"Did you see it?" Nila called out, pointing straight up at the dome. "Right there, you see?"

"What are you talking about? I don't see anything," Odette shot back.

"Look! There it is again. That streak of greenish—maybe whitish—I don't know. The light outside the dome. In a circle. Something's moving!"

Some others were now saying they saw it too. Josie's gaze followed Nila's finger. After a few seconds, her eyes adjusted, then she saw it.

It stopped her breath and made her forget her brewing anger. She had never seen something so captivating before. Maybe in pictures on the old databases from before the world flooded. The knowledge of life before the War Above was something not restricted by the OSD. She guessed learning about it was allowed because it was a world no longer possible.

After all, who cares about something that can never happen again?

Still, Josie often read everything she could from the terminals, but this was something special. The pulsing lights had attracted a swarm of jellyfish. Each one tens of meters long from body to tentacle tip and each one responding in kind with a ghostly light from their bell.

"I never knew such beauty still existed in the flooded world," Josie whispered to Miles.

He responded with a low whistle, as he stood with his head cocked back and his eyes wide open.

Josie giggled—it looked like he was about to topple backward—before she turned back to the pale brilliance of the jellyfish.

"I ate a jellyfish once, but it was small. My father spared no expense to have Chef Holcomb make it for me," Theodore remarked with his mouth open.

"You all might just think these are regular old jellyfish, but they're not. These are *Aequorea*, more commonly referred to as crystal jellyfish. Their tentacles can grow to over thirty meters long," Nila said, on a roll now.

Josie smiled to herself at hearing Nila talk about something she cared so much about. For a brief second, it made her believe things were different between them. That it wasn't all insults and bad feelings.

"There's a whole other world out there, and this is just the start," Miles said.

Before Josie could respond, the low humming lights and holoscreens kicked back on. Several students shouted as they were blasted by the returning brightness.

"That will be all for today, children. Remember to tell your families about the start to our week of celebrating the Great Turning." As soon as First Vicar Frost finished, he spun around on his heel then disappeared back up the metal stairwell he had come from.

Josie caught his eyes one more time. The way they fixated on her made her stomach do flips. After what seemed like minutes, he continued on his way.

Miles must have noticed the sick look on Josie's face. "You okay, Josie? You look like you swallowed a jellyfish."

"I'm alright." Josie smiled. "The First Vicar just creeps me out."

His smile disappeared. "Josie, what you said earlier, about the celebration and mocking the OSD. You shouldn't talk like that. It's going to get you in trouble. It's better to keep your head down."

Josie turned. "Thanks for the warning," she snapped but immediately regretted her words. "Miles, I—"

"Miss Josie Owens. Oh, do I have something to say to you." Instructor Hale marched straight toward her.

"I know what you're going to say. I can't fight the system. We all live thanks to the generosity of Olympus Deck. So on and so forth." She waved her hand dismissively.

Instructor Hale's face turned bright. "No, Josie. Not this time. I can stand the rest. But your disobedience today, in front of the First Vicar no less. . . I want you out of my class. I don't even know if that's possible. But something must be done. I will be sending a holomessage to your mother tonight."

"My mom won't care."

"Well, I hope you're happy with the way you present yourself. You must be such a model big sister for Rose. You'd make your father proud. Look where that got him." Instructor Hale snorted before turning to the class.

Josie's throat felt tight as she tried to find the right words to hurt Hale. She could take people talking poorly about her, but she would not stand for someone's foul words against her dad. A sidelong glance from Miles made her think twice, but she couldn't just remain silent. "Fine, it isn't as if you know what it takes to be an engineer anyway."

She stormed across the catwalk before breaking into a run, unwilling to listen to anything else Hale had to say.

She wanted to see one face, her dad's, the one face she would never see again. So, she went to the only place with any memory left of him. A passageway deep in *November's Dawn*, far away from the Observatory and the harsh words of people who did not understand her.

As always, the passageway was cold, and the dry, recycled air tickled her throat and left a stale taste on her tongue. Her destination was ahead, an access inlet cut into the side wall. Thick pipes and wires twisted along the wall, and fluorescent lights overhead cast shadows across the inlet as if hiding it from prying eyes.

The inlet was a few meters wide with panels allowing access to a section of the complex electrical network that ran throughout the entire ark. Dust and grime covered everything. Her eyes shifted to the cast metal plaque, lit haphazardly by a lamp fastened to a panel. She knew every word on the plaque from memory, but her heart still hammered as she got closer.

In memory of Dominic Owens. An engineer. A man for the people. A friend.

She reached out to trace the crudely formed letters but stopped when her eyes drifted to two words scratched into the hard iron by an unsteady hand. *My dad.*

Her chest tightened the same way it had when she had chiseled those words into the plaque all those years ago. After his accident, a few of her dad's engineering colleagues had cast the plaque as a memorial to him. Of course, they had not been granted a permit to put the plaque up, so they chose a spot that meant something to the engineers and no one else, an access inlet they so often worked in.

There had been a small ceremony. Some people said a few words and that was it. That night, she snuck back to the passageway and scratched the words into the iron using her dad's old tools.

"It's my birthday again, Dad. Sixteen. Folks say it's a big one, but it doesn't feel that way. One year closer to being the engineer you always said I could be, though. I guess that's something," she whispered.

From the corner of her eye, she watched a speck of dust settle between two letters. She stuffed her hand in her pocket and pulled out a coarse rag soaked with streaks of machine oil.

Gently, she reached up to polish the metal. The action helped keep the memories alive for her. The rag slid effortlessly across the raised letters, which was odd. The rough metal should have offered much more resistance. Running her finger across a different section pulled up newly applied oil. That made her stop. She was the only one who ever came to see the plaque anymore, and this oil was fresh enough someone must have applied it a few hours ago.

Well, there was one person who might have come to pay his respects to her dad—Felix, an old engineer who had been close friends with him. But Felix would have told her he was coming. Doubt began to gnaw at her. This was supposed to be her space and the thought of a stranger happening across her dad's plaque made her heart sink. She shoved the rag back into her pocket smearing grease across her palm like it did every time she visited.

She had to find Felix to know for sure.

CHAPTER THREE_

Before long Josie reached the familiar passageways of Engineering Bay. She stopped against the bulkhead to catch her breath in the humid air of the lower levels. There were not as many holoscreens in the deep reaches of *November's Dawn*, but the OSD's propaganda was always present. The shining neon signs bolted into the passageways at regular intervals each had the same message. The eternal promise that *November's Dawn* would provide.

"The OSD sure love their words, don't they? And now this celebration. Just another chance for them to distract folks from the fact every year there's less and less to go around," a smooth, deep voice mused from just behind her.

Josie jumped and turned to meet the voice. "Felix! You scared me half to death."

"Sorry, Josie. I should have made myself known."

Josie studied him. His gray and navy-blue engineer's jumpsuit looked dirtier and more battered than usual. His weathered face, which usually always bore a smile, was solemn, but he was the same Felix she loved.

"I'm sorry, Felix. I've just been out of sorts today." She slumped against the wall.

Felix moved closer. He was over sixty-five as near as Josie could tell, but he still moved well. "Ah, little fox. Tell me what happened? Was it the other girls again?"

"No," she said, embarrassed. "Well yeah, but that's not what's wrong."

Her eyes brimmed with tears at hearing her old nickname. Since her dad died, Felix was the only one she let call her little fox and normally adored it. Today it brought up more memories. She turned and buried her face in Felix's waiting chest, the smells of oil and grease comforting her. The engineer held her close.

"It's five years to the day since the accident, and it hasn't gotten any easier. It doesn't hurt any less, and I still miss him like he was here only yesterday."

"Shh, here now. I know today has always been a hard one, but you know what he'd say? He'd say 'One day, little fox, you'll look back at the problems you have today and know it all gets easier. Because things will be better. The future can always be better.' That's what he'd say."

Josie smiled as she pictured her dad speaking the words. She clung to the image. "Felix?"

"Yes?"

"You didn't go and visit his memorial today, did you?"

Felix frowned. "No, I meant to go today, but I haven't had a spare moment yet. Why?"

"No reason," Josie lied and looked down. The uneasy feeling in her stomach came back stronger.

He smiled. "Ah, I almost forgot. I have your cut from the work you did last week on the radiators in my office. Not much, but that's just how it is these days."

"Thanks, Felix." Josie tried to sound cheerful. "Maybe it'll be enough to get one of the seamstresses to make Rose a new stuffed animal. She's been talking about the extinct animals she learned about in class for weeks now."

Felix chuckled. "That would be nice. Come, I have something else for you. There are still reasons for a little happiness."

"What is it? Did another steam valve break?" Sometimes, whenever something different or complex broke aboard *November's Dawn*, Felix would take Josie with him so he could teach her the ways of an engineer. She worked with other engineers as well, but nobody knew their stuff like Felix.

He smiled. "Better."

No matter how much Josie pestered him, he said no more as he led them deeper into Engineering Bay. Other engineers hurried past them focused on various duties and paid them no mind. Finally, they stopped outside a large metal hatch.

"The engineer's common area? There isn't anything in there interesting enough to fix to warrant a special surprise." Josie tried to mask her disappointment. She had been looking forward to something to take her mind off the anniversary of her dad's death.

"You'll see, little fox. Come," Felix said as he worked to open the hatch leading into the common area.

By the look he had on his face, Josie knew there must really be something special. He would not get her hopes up otherwise.

The common area was unusually dark. As soon as she stepped through the threshold, all the lights flicked on.

"Surprise!" multiple voices shouted.

Josie rubbed her eyes, trying to adjust to the light. She could not believe it. A few engineers were gathered in the common area. Among them she saw Mags, the head of Engineering, as well as Bruce, an engineer a couple years older than Josie who came from Delos Deck and got the position because of his smarts. Josie smiled at them all. Each one wore an engineer's gray and navy-blue jumpsuit with dirt and oil smears on them, making a ragged but lively group. Across the bulkhead of the room, they had hung a handmade sign that read *Happy Sixteenth, Josie!* One last person moved out from behind the others.

"Miles," Josie said. "I thought you'd go home after class."

Miles only smiled. "Thought you'd like me here. Afterall, we'll be working together someday."

"And a damn good engineer he will be too," Mags interrupted. "He has a quick eye and a strong hand."

Josie looked over at Miles who grinned from ear to ear.

"Between you two, the engineers will be in good hands," Mags said as she turned. "Your mothers must be proud. Speaking of moms, Miles, how is yours?"

Miles's grin faded and he looked down. "Doc said the sickness is spreading. But she'll beat it, I know she will."

Josie grimaced, having heard about Miles's mom but not the extent of her sickness.

Mags's eyes softened. "I'm sorry, son. She's a strong woman." She looked at Felix, who had settled in a chair. "Felix! You old sod. What are we waiting for? Show Josie the thing."

Felix looked puzzled. "The thing? Oh right!" he exclaimed as he walked over to a refrigeration unit. "We got you something. It's not much but I hope we got a good one."

He stepped back to reveal the most beautiful cake Josie had ever seen. Well, the only cake, besides pictures in the old databases. It was small and covered in a smooth white frosting, with little candles fashioned from leftover wax.

"Not much?" Josie turned. "This is too much. You're all just too good to me." She jammed her hands into her pockets and looked down.

"Nonsense, Josie. You're family. That's what engineering is, a family. Don't you think nothing of it," Mags said.

Josie sighed as she looked around the room one last time, thinking her own mom might have come down for the party.

Somehow knowing exactly what she was thinking, Felix put a hand on her shoulder. "I'm sorry. I told your mom about the party, but she said she couldn't come."

"It's okay. Her work comes first. I know that. I have everything I need right here." Josie smiled, but she could feel her ears getting hot.

"Well, let's eat!" Bruce said, walking toward the cake.

"Hold it, Bruce," Mags barked. "Josie gets it first." She handed Josie a slice.

The inside was as white as the outside and Josie could smell the sweetness. She had never had cake before, and it did not disappoint. It melted in her mouth in a rush of sugars and cream. Every bite was as pleasant as the last.

"How did you guys even get something like this?" Josie said, in between bites. The only thing that eased her guilt was watching the other engineers enjoying it also. From the looks on their faces, she doubted they'd ever had cake either.

"That's where we thank dear Bruce. He knows a baker from his time on Delos Deck. The baker needed some equipment fixed. Bing, bang, boom, we got a cake," Mags said, grinning.

"A Delos baker? But they only bake for Olympus. He wouldn't risk sending one down here."

"Normally yes," Mags said. "But for some reason the companies weren't sending him the parts he requested to fix an industrial mixer. A few of us went up there and jury-rigged something together. All very hush-hush. We wouldn't want Olympus to start thinking those below them were capable of new ideas, would we?" She winked, but her tone betrayed frustration.

Olympus Deck and the companies were the intellectual center of *November's Dawn*. They viewed any development they did not oversee as a threat to their margins. And that could never be allowed.

"When you're done out here, come to my office. I have something for you," Felix said before walking to the back of the room where the offices were.

"I'm sorry about earlier, Josie," Miles said quietly. "Instructor Hale is hard on you. Some people just really believe in the OSD."

"It's okay. I need to learn to think more before I talk. Sorry I ran from you."

"Well, I still beat you down here, so—"

"Only because I ran into Felix!" She playfully punched Miles's arm and turned to follow Felix. Then she looked back at Miles and smiled again. He was laughing with Bruce. She was so glad he'd come to her party.

Felix's office was cramped, every spot on the few cabinets and shelves was home to some piece of broken machinery or scrap metal. Felix squeezed behind a rickety metal desk. Before him sat a small dusty brown package, tied up with loose string. "Close the door," he said.

Josie did and stepped closer to the desk. "What is that?"

"Sit down, little fox. You'll see."

She did as she was told, watching Felix and the box intently.

Felix placed a hand on the package. "This is something that has been yours for a long time now."

"What? Then why—"

A hand quieted her. "As I was saying. This package is from

Dom, your dad. I don't know exactly what it is, only that it is yours."

Josie's mouth opened slightly. Her dad? Felix was giving her a package that he had held onto for five years. Something important. So many emotions built up, it became hard to say anything and all she could think was *why?* Why give it to her now? Why keep it a secret? She tried to not let Felix's secrecy hurt too much.

Felix noticed her hesitation and walked to the hatch. "I'll give you some time. Happy birthday, little fox."

Josie stared at the package for a little longer, until the hatch closed again and she was alone. Then she picked it up gently, as if worried it might crumble to dust at any moment, and she would lose her dad's gift forever. Unwrapping the package revealed a curious contraption. A bundle of various tubes and knobs came together on a little metal disk. Her dad had recorded a holomessage for her.

Using the utmost care, she placed the holomessage on the desk and turned it on. Her chest tightened. The holographic face that greeted her was like a punch in the stomach. She could not hold back the tears at seeing her dad. Not just a picture of him, but him speaking and moving. Seeing him alive. His hair was tousled and unkempt, just as she remembered, and his glasses were at the tip of his nose, just as they'd always been. Josie reached out and cursed as her fingers swiped through the hologram. She wanted so bad for it to be real. Hearing his voice brought back so much happiness but also all the pain.

"Josie, my little fox. If you're hearing this now, it means you're ready. Yes, I told Felix to wait until you were. I wish I could tell you all the things I never had the chance to, but I fear there isn't much time left. Little fox, please listen now. I have learned a terrible

truth, something they will never let see the light. Even now I think they're coming. Cornelius Graham built November's Dawn to be a haven for all people. It has been our home ever since we were driven from the surface. But it was never meant to be our final resting place. The ark was meant to rise again and be a shining city floating upon the waves of the surface. But there are some who would never let this happen because it threatens their power.

"This is the great truth of November's Dawn. You must do everything to keep its spark alive.

"The biggest regret I have in my life is I will never be able to see the smart and beautiful young woman I know you have grown to be. Your mom and I are so proud of you. Everything we've worked for has been for you and Rose. Protect our beautiful flower as you always have. Be there for your mom, little fox, even she will not understand everything. Most of all I will miss your courage and compassion and your willingness to do the right thing, no matter the cost.

"I'm leaving you the Heart of the Dawn, a necklace I'm certain is the key to building a world worthy of my family. I wish I knew more about what it does, but things are moving faster than I ever dreamed. It will be up to you to find its meaning. Guard it well, little fox. This is a burden you should never have had to bear. I should have stopped it all sooner—"

Her dad's image jumped as someone pounded on the hatch to his office.

"Engineer Owens!" a voice shouted. "Open the hatch at once!"

"A moment!" he called, then turned back toward the message. "They're here. Remember my words, little fox. I love you. Now and forever."

The holomessage cut off, leaving Josie speechless and unable to move. Warm tears caressed her cheeks, which she did not bother wiping away. Something small and glimmering in the light caught her eye under the holomessage. She pulled out a captivating small bauble attached to a long golden chain. The pendant had small, spinning golden rings like from the planets she had seen in old photos and, suspended in the middle, sat a stunning red stone like nothing she had ever seen before. The stone gave off its own golden light from within, which amplified its red face and the golden rings around it. The whole necklace pulsed with heat in her hand.

"The Heart of the Dawn," she whispered. She pictured her dad holding the necklace and imagined what his touch would feel like now. How his voice would fall on her ears after a long day. The accident had taken so much from her.

She sucked in a sharp breath. That was it; there was no accident at all, no bulkhead pressure explosion which made recovering his body impossible. It was all a lie. Someone had been after him. Someone could not risk what her dad knew getting out.

A knock came from the other side of the hatch. "Josie? Are you okay?" Felix called.

Josie wiped her eyes clear. "Yes, I'm alright. You can come in."

Felix stepped into the office and fixed upon the flickering holomessage of his old friend. "The gift? It was a message?"

Josie stopped. For a moment she considered lying to Felix. Her dad had gone through great lengths to keep the holomessage hidden and it was likely the reason he died. But there was little she could do on her own. Felix had kept the holomessage a secret for years and been a close friend to her dad. She reasoned he might know more about what it all meant. "Yeah, he recorded this before he died. Felix, I don't think it was an accident at all."

"What? No, don't be foolish, little fox. You'll only bring more pain to yourself thinking like that. It was a pressure explosion. Everyone knew the equipment down there was faulty."

"Felix. Listen to the message yourself. It can't have been an accident. He found out a truth about *November's Dawn*."

"A truth? Play it." Felix sat quietly while the holomessage flickered to life again.

Her dad's voice came to life and all over again Josie let herself be lulled by the thought that maybe he was not really gone. She watched as the old engineer's expression shifted from cautious disbelief to stunned shock. At times tears glistening in his eyes. When the recording finished, he sat back in his chair for several long moments.

"I don't believe it. You're right, Josie, someone was after him. I don't doubt that now. This Heart of the Dawn, you have it?"

Josie pulled the chain up from around her neck. The stunning red stone immediately cast its brilliance on the office walls.

"Remarkable," Felix whispered. "After so many years, our future lies in wait. In a little box in my desk, no less." He chuckled to himself as he ran his hands through his hair.

"My dad said the Heart of the Dawn was the key. Do you think it has something to do with bringing *November's Dawn* to the surface?"

Sorrow filled Felix's eyes. It looked like all the air had been sucked from him. "I don't know. In all my time, I've never heard anything like this. I can't imagine where Dom found this information. The helmsmen pilot *November's Dawn*; engineers only fix her. And you heard your dad. If what he says is true, the OSD will stop at nothing to keep this a secret."

"But—" Josie was interrupted by a small thump outside the hatch. A sound that could only have been made by another person.

"Quick, Josie, you must go. It isn't safe." Felix stopped and his face relaxed. "Dom was the best of us, and he would never put you in this position if he had no other option. Give me time to figure this out and come back." Felix rushed to the hatch and pulled Josie along with him. There was nobody outside, whoever had made the noise had gone.

"Okay, I'll come back and then what?" Josie asked breathlessly.

"I'm not sure, but we'll do it together." Felix smiled. "Go, little fox. Tell no one about this."

Josie was already running down the passageway and past the rest of the engineers still gathered for her party. The last thing she wanted was to be stuck in idle small talk after what she had just learned.

As soon as she got to the passageway of bulkhead 254, she stopped and made sure nobody was around. Bending down, she fidgeted with a metal vent on the bulkhead. She struggled for a moment but soon heard the satisfying pop that signaled the vent was free. Josie looked around one last time before ducking in. It led to an old utility closet. Josie had found it one day while helping Felix fix an intake pipe. Near as she could tell, the utility closet was not there for any particular reason, and she set up camp in the small closet many times when she did not want to go home. There was no better place to wait now.

Josie wrestled with how long to wait before she went back to Felix. She didn't even know why Felix made her leave anyway, unless he knew more than he was letting on. She tried to be calm, but her mind raced, and it had been an hour at least. Her patience had run out, and she left the hiding spot.

It was late in the workday now, so less folks were around. She stopped right before the last turn to the engineer's common area. Voices echoed out from the hatch that did not belong to any engineer she knew. She crept down the passageway and stopped right before the hatch leading to the room.

"I told you, I don't know anything." Felix's voice carried from within.

"Old man, do you think I would have made my way down here on false information?" a man replied, cold and cruel.

Josie's heart dropped as she peeked into the room. Her knuckles turned white from how hard she gripped the edge. Felix was tied to a metal chair. His gray hair flared wildly and a dark ring around one of his eyes accompanied a busted lip.

A man stood in front of Felix, his back turned to Josie, but she knew who it was by his short crop of blonde hair and the black tactical gear he wore. Commandant Reyes, the commander of the peace and compliance officers had blood smeared across his black leather gloves. Several other peace-and-compliance officers stood at the ready, but none faced the cracked open hatch where Josie spied.

Felix looked at Commandant Reyes. "As a lacky of the OSD, I'm sure you make your way around *November's Dawn* for any number of mindless errands."

Commandant Reyes's fist came hard and fast, connecting squarely with Felix's jaw. The impact rocked the old engineer back. Felix spat a glob of blood onto the ground.

"You destroyed the holomessage in your office. Smart move. Tell me what it said, or I promise you, these moments will be your last."

Felix's eyes locked with Reyes's. Josie could see the pain and the sorrow they held, but they still flashed with a streak of defiance.

"Then I die, believing in a hope for the future that you will never know. Something I never lived with, but I am honored to die with. You will fail, Reyes. We're stronger than you know."

Felix smiled, a crooked, bloody approximation of one, but a smile all the same.

Commandant Reyes scoffed. "Enough of your babbling." He studied the old engineer for a moment more. Then, in one swift move, he drew a pistol and fired into Felix's chest.

The crack of the gunshot split Josie's ears. Time seemed to stand still. She took one last look at Felix as his eyelids fluttered closed. She focused on Commandant Reyes. Through the storm of her emotions, one impulse rose above the rest—rage. This man had taken everything from her. She wanted to make him feel as she did. To feel the same loss. The same pain. She clenched her fist around a screwdriver in her pocket.

Just as she was about to spring through the hatch, an arm wrapped around her chest and pulled her back. Josie squirmed wildly to break its hold. The grip relaxed as she turned and recognized Miles. With one hand he held her close and the other he brought to his lips in a gesture, begging her to be quiet. Josie struggled for a moment more before giving up. He pointed back to the hatch, back to Felix's lifeless body.

"The old man was working with a girl. Josie Owens. Find her. I want her brought to me at once," Commandant Reyes ordered the P&C officers gathered. The officers saluted and walked toward the hatch.

"Run, Josie. We have to run," Miles whispered.

She took one last look at Felix's lifeless body, then at Reyes, and swore she would never stop until he paid for what he did.

But Miles was right. There was no other choice now than to run down the dark, cold passageway. She was always running, only now it was for her very life.

CHAPTER FOUR_

THE COLD PAINTED eyes of the founder of the Order of Scientific Discovery looked down on First Vicar Adrian Frost who stared squarely back at them. The artist had captured Cornelius Graham's serious demeanor perfectly, and for that reason Adrian always admired it. It was part of why he had hung the portrait behind his desk in the office of the First Vicar. The unnerving hardness of Graham's eyes had demanded obedience in life, and his portrait lent its power to Adrian's own voice and authority now in death.

The office of the First Vicar was a stately one, filled with fine plush couches and intricately inlaid oak and mahogany desks and chairs. Cornelius Graham would accept it no other way. The trillionaire energy tycoon had spent a small fortune on acquiring furniture and decorations from some of the most splendid estates and palaces around the world. That is, before the world flooded. Adrian never approved of the excessive nature of the office, but Graham told him it was more than just about expensive things. It was about tenacity and the courage to continue on—and the power that emanated from the office. It was about hope. A hope people would feel when they stepped into the office of the First Vicar, seeking direction and salvation, for they stood before the leader of *November's Dawn*, the last bastion of humanity. *And in the darkness below,* November's Dawn *will provide.* Everything was built upon that simple promise.

For those reasons and more, Adrian had not changed the office much upon his ascension to the office of First Vicar. He had been Graham's protégé and the most versed and accomplished deacon the Order of Scientific Discovery had ever had. For nineteen years, he had shepherded the people of *November's Dawn* according to Graham's vision, and he would not lose control now. Adrian clasped his hands together and turned away from the painting. There was business to attend to.

In the center of the room stood a man in black security gear. He had not moved a muscle since assuming his position.

"Commandant Reyes. Tell me again how this gross incompetence was possible?"

The commandant's back stiffened. He was a man of professionalism and poise, the last male in a long line of military heritage, and utterly devoted to the teachings of the Order of Scientific Discovery. "The old engineer's insolence could not be excused. Subversion to the OSD and *November's Dawn* must always be stamped out, no matter where the spark may rise, sir."

Adrian eyed Reyes closely. Reyes was using Adrian's own orders against him, and Adrian would need to handle this with tact. "Truly you are a man of action and ability. But this will not stand. The engineer knew secrets. Secrets we now know nothing of. Tell me, Commandant, how will you stamp out the spark of subversive thought when it has crawled into bed with you and lit your sheets on fire? You should never have killed him. Not without my express authorization."

Reyes remained motionless until he was sure the First Vicar had finished. "There is another, sir. The informant spoke of a young girl who also heard the holomessage."

"A girl? You're fortunate, Commandant. She must be found at once. I will not allow the celebration of the Great Turning to be marred by the whisperings of some girl. Who is she?"

"She comes from Aegean Deck—" Commandant Reyes started.

"Undoubtedly," Adrian remarked. Some sheep were harder to shepherd than others and the lowly folk of Aegean Deck were the hardest of all.

Reyes said, "Josie Owens is her name."

"Miss Owens?" Adrian asked. "Interesting. Do you know who her father was, Commandant?"

Reyes looked like he was about to say something but then thought better of it and shook his head. Adrian was not surprised, there was no real reason he should know after all.

"Engineer Dominic Owens."

The corner of Reyes's mouth twitched at hearing the name, but he still stayed silent.

"The stakes have never been higher. All your efforts must be toward the apprehension of this girl before stories of her defiance give any ideas to those who work against us. Speak with anyone close to her. Send out notices, plaster her face on the holoscreens. Fifteen thousand souls live on *November's Dawn*; someone will know something."

"What about the Directors? Should they be made aware of the situation?"

The Directors were the heads of the most powerful consortiums and companies on *November's Dawn* who were supposed to advise the First Vicar on matters of governing. As it had been since Cornelius Graham first brought the companies together to forge *November's Dawn*. Adrian disliked most of them. They were pompous men, born to inherit much they never worked for, and with no sense of duty to the greater good. "I see no reason they would need to know at this time."

The office intercom buzzed. "Sir, Helmsman Ido is here as you requested."

"Send him in."

A short man, with long black hair bundled together in a knot poked his head through the office doors. Ido used a mechanized wheelchair, the result of an infection at a young age that had gone unnoticed for too long which limited the effective treatments even those on Olympus Deck had access to. His green leather jacket and calf-height black boots distinguished him as one of the helmsmen. "First Vicar? Are you indisposed? I was told to come in."

"Yes, Helmsman. Come." Adrian had been told on many occasions that nobody knew the computer systems and piloting better than Ido.

Helmsman Ido chuckled and moved forward. "Yes, First Vicar." He spoke to Adrian, but his eyes never left Commandant Reyes.

Reyes had that effect on many. Like a cat, he appeared ready to pounce on someone without a moment's notice. Adrian had seen him do it. Afterward, the victim of Reyes's brutality was barely recognizable to his family.

"Do you have an update on our little problem?" Adrian asked.

"I'm afraid not, First Vicar. My crew has been working twenty-three hours a day trying to solve the navigation issue, but I fear we are no closer to fixing the computers than we were a month ago. *November's Dawn* will not be able to turn from the course it is on now."

"Then work twenty-four," Adrian sneered. "Is piloting our ark not the duty of the helmsmen? And by extension Olympus? The same as those in Aegean who work our factories, we too must provide or the whole system fails. The celebration of the Great Turning has begun. The Obsidian Trench lies a mere week away. I will not fail now. *November's Dawn* must be ready to turn."

Ido wrung his hands together. "First Vicar, I know it is not my place to question the word of the Order of Scientific Discovery. But might it be prudent to cancel this celebration? People from Olympus Deck are touring the bridge daily and disrupting my crew. Without the navigational computers working, *November's Dawn* is a week away from falling into a twelve thousand-meter-deep trench. The outer hull will not survive that. No one will survive that. I just, well it seems like our efforts might be better focused if we were left in peace."

Adrian had not expected Ido to speak so purposefully. "Do you know the story of how *November's Dawn* came to be, Helmsman Ido?"

"Well, yes, of course. Everyone does."

Adrian waved him off as he rose from behind his desk and circled the room. "Let me remind you." Cornelius Graham's painted eyes continued their ever-watchful gaze. "The world ended in the year 2052. Decades of resource tensions flared hot, fanned by the insatiable greed of corporations. Warmongering was common. By October 2052, their influence on the weak leaders of the time paid off. Bombs tore apart the surface and deep-sea mines destabilized the very foundations of the world. What was once a lush and fertile planet was reduced to a flooded waste. The world started over in November and with it—and so aptly named I might add—Cornelius Graham launched *November's Dawn* and assumed the role as the First Vicar of the OSD, the spiritual heart of humanity. *November's Dawn* was our last and greatest beacon of hope, and it has remained that way ever since. Hope, Helmsman Ido, is why the celebration will continue. Hope for another tomorrow is no power to scoff at. It must be tempered and controlled, or it will spread and consume all order, but it must stay alive. Without it, anarchy reigns. You will fix the navigational computers, Helmsman Ido. It is our duty to ensure this ark's survival. I will not be another worthless leader who watched humanity fall and you will not take my hope from me."

Ido gulped and looked down. His hands were still pressed together and his knuckles stark white. "Yes, First Vicar. I see your vision now."

"It doesn't make sense," Commandant Reyes said. "If the threat is *November's Dawn* walking off an underwater cliff, why don't we just shut her down? Cut the power till we fix the problem?"

Helmsman Ido cleared his throat as he pulled at the collar of his jacket. "It's just not that simple, Commandant. *November's Dawn* can't merely stop moving, the results would be catastrophic."

Reyes's eyes narrowed. "Do you care to tell me why?"

"It's a matter of power you see. *November's Dawn* is the largest mechanical construct ever built and as such, the power required to bring it alive was unlike anything ever harnessed before. Its state-of-the-art fusion reactor took fifteen years to design and fund by Cornelius Graham before the world flooded. But the reactor's power is not enough to keep *November's Dawn* fully functioning. The perpetual movement of each of her 214 legs also generates power and makes up the needed difference. If *November's Dawn* ever stopped, the reactor would not be able to produce enough power to get her moving again." Helmsman Ido stopped to take a breath. "Sure, we might survive a few years, maybe even a couple decades. But it would only be a matter of time until seismic movement tore us apart. We would be stuck, without power or purpose, under the crushing dark abyss of the world's oceans." His words trailed off as fear returned to his eyes.

"And that is why, in one week's time, our great ark's navigational systems will be working again, and the Order of Scientific Discovery will lead *November's Dawn* into a new future," Adrian interjected. "Isn't that so, Helmsman Ido?"

Ido bowed his head slightly. "Of course, First Vicar."

"That will be all," Adrian said, waiving him off.

Commandant Reyes pushed the door closed after Ido had left. Then returned to attention in front of the First Vicar's desk.

"For you too, Commandant. Don't you have a girl to catch?" Adrian said.

Reyes stood silently for a moment. His eyes flickered and mouth twitched. "Yes, sir." He turned to the door then stopped and looked back at Adrian with a curious look. "Is that oil on your hand, First Vicar?"

Adrian set his cup down and slowly turned his hand over. Sure enough, a shiny black smear of machine oil streaked down the side of his palm. He swallowed hard then glared at the commandant. "Don't fail me, Reyes. All our futures will be decided this week."

As soon as the commandant had left, Adrian sat in one of the great leather chairs in the office. He could not bear sitting underneath the eyes of Cornelius Graham any longer today and worked some of the buttons of his vestments undone. A long sigh of relief followed. He had devoted his whole life to *November's Dawn*, and it had been good to him in return, but now, in the span of a week, everything stood to be taken away.

He prayed silently that some good fortune might befall him, and Commandant Reyes would move swiftly with the case. Adrian hated leaving variables unaccounted for.

He needed to know what the smashed holomessage said. He needed Josie Owens.

CHAPTER FIVE_

THE DEEP SECTIONS of *November's Dawn* were known for their secret parts and mazelike design. Normally, that never bothered Josie as the Engineering Bay was in the lower parts of the ark and she had practically grown up there. But now her mind raced, and the passageways looked a little less familiar.

"Josie! Come on. We have to keep moving," Miles said as he encouraged her along the dark passageway.

"We've been running all night, Miles. I have to stop." Adrenaline had kept her alert, but she could feel the fatigue setting in as the morning approached.

"Okay, fine. But only for a moment."

Josie put her hands on her hips and stared at him. "And what are we going to do? Run forever? I can't just run the rest of my life." Running had made sense at first. There was nothing else they could do. But now she was tired, and frustrated. She needed to do more than just run.

Miles ran his fingers through his tight, curly hair. "I know, Josie. But with everything going on, the only thing we can do now is keep our heads down. Maybe then the OSD will forget about us. I mean, we didn't do anything wrong. It was Felix."

Before Josie knew it, she had sprung across the passageway close to Miles's face. "Don't say that! Don't you ever talk like that about him. Felix didn't do anything wrong."

Miles flinched and looked down, but he stayed quiet.

A moment passed before Josie realized what she was doing. Her heart hammered. Then the tears came. "Miles, I'm sorry. Please, I'm so sorry." She buried her face in her hands.

Everything was going wrong. She wanted to run to engineering, to Felix. She could imagine his calming voice and gentle eyes, waiting to comfort her. But Felix was gone. He had been taken from her, just like her dad. Each thought was accompanied by a choked sob and her throat became hoarse.

Miles hesitated before he pulled Josie into an uncertain hug. She could feel his body tighten up, only to relax when she returned his embrace. And she did, fully. He did not try to stop her tears or ease her pain. He was only present and there for her—the one thing she needed. She pulled back and wiped the tears away. Miles let out a slight laugh.

"What?" Her stomach sank like a rock.

Miles wiped her cheek. "There, just some smeared oil." He looked at her for a moment more. "Josie Owens, with her red hair and grease on her cheek."

"Why would you say that?" She stepped back from him. All her troubles circled around her, and now Odette's mocking words circled too.

"What? Oh, shit, no. I didn't mean it like that. I'm sorry."

Josie blushed and pushed her hair back. He seemed genuinely sorry, like he somehow meant it differently. "I'm sorry. I just . . . I don't know what to think right now. Everything is so wrong. Felix. He's just gone. And you. You saved me and I haven't even said thank you yet. You didn't have to do that." She looked down while she thought. "Why did you? Save me, I mean."

Miles looked down now. "I don't know, I just . . . Well, I heard people shouting in anger. And then I saw you there. After the gunshot, you were about to run right into it. I just couldn't let that happen."

The gunshot rang in her ears all over again. She pictured Reyes's face, heard his cruel words, and the trembling fear coursed through her all over again. "They're after us now," she whispered. "After me. You should go. You still have a chance to get away."

"What? No, I'm not leaving you down here. Not like this."

"Miles, please go. My whole world just got turned upside-down and I have no idea what to do from here."

Miles stepped closer and brought his eyes to hers. "What about your mom? Your little sister? Anyway, I'm not leaving. Not now."

"My mom . . .? It's just complicated. But you're right about one thing. I need to make sure Rose is safe; she's all I have left."

"Wait, Josie. Are you sure? We should be finding somewhere safe. Your home will be the first place they look." Miles's face scrunched in a curious look. "And won't she be okay with your mom anyway?"

"Miles, my mom works on Olympus Deck. She works for the people who killed Felix. I can't rely on her right now. I'm supposed to take care of Rose. I won't let anything happen to her."

"Then what?"

"You heard Reyes. He ordered them to find me. How long before that order includes my family? And if you're with me, that means you too."

Miles ran his fingers through his hair. "This is so messed up. You have a plan?"

Josie nodded. She didn't want Miles to think she was foolish, but she knew what was next. Stopping Reyes and getting justice for Felix, even if she didn't have the faintest idea how to do that. Then there was her dad's message. She wouldn't forget what he'd told her even though she had no idea why he had decided to tell only her. There had to be more capable people her dad had known. If only he had told one of them, this wouldn't have happened, and Felix would still be here.

No, she couldn't think like that. Moving forward was the only real choice and right now, that meant figuring out how to make *November's Dawn* rise to the surface and making Reyes pay for what he did. She hoped the OSD's celebration would distract some attention away from them, enough to give her time to come up with a real plan.

Miles looked up and down the passageway as he wrestled with the situation. "Are you sure you want to go back to your cabin? It's just so dangerous."

"What choice do I have? It's my family," she said, losing her patience. "You saved me. That was definitely dangerous, and you still did it. I can't let them get away with what they did to Felix. You can run if you want, but I'm going to do something about it."

Miles leaned against the bulkhead and put his hands on his knees.

Josie took a deep breath. He was probably just as scared as she was, even if he did a better job of hiding it. "Well?" she asked, harsher than she meant.

Miles sighed. "You're right, we have to make sure your sister is safe. But that's it, okay?"

"Mhmm," Josie mumbled and turned. "Come on, we've got to get to Aegean Deck before it's locked down." Deep down, she was relieved he was not leaving, even if it only added to her guilt.

They walked in silence on their way to find an elevator that would take them to Aegean Deck. After a bit, Josie stopped and studied a directional map that showed where they were at. Josie knew a lot about the ark, because she worked with the engineers who saw life outside Aegean Deck with some regularity, but she was not completely sure where the nearest elevator would be. The elevators ran vertically and horizontally throughout the entire ark in a complex system making the directional maps vital, even if many sections of the maps were censored off. Aegean Deck folks had no need to know the layout of Olympus Deck after all.

November's Dawn was divided into thirds, making three decks from bow to stern, with Olympus being closest to the bow and Aegean falling near the stern. Engineering Bay ran the full length of *November's Dawn*, below the other decks. She traced her finger across the map until she found where they were and where the nearest elevator up to Aegean Deck would be.

"We ran farther than I thought. I've only been this deep in engineering a few times, but we shouldn't be too far from an elevator," Josie said.

"Great, the sooner we can get up there, the better."

"We're going to have to be careful, this elevator comes up right to the middle of the Galley Markets. P&C officers are probably swarming it right now."

Miles sighed. "What choice do we have anymore? They're going to search Engineering Bay just as thoroughly. At least on Aegean, we can try to blend in."

Before long, they arrived at the elevator and were quiet as it ferried them up. The elevators ran slow, and they had to climb hundreds of feet to reach the lower levels of Aegean Deck.

She spent the time watching Miles. He leaned against the small elevator cabin, and Josie tried her hardest to make sure he did not notice her glances. She could not help but wonder why he had put himself and his family in such danger, just to save her. And now they were on the run with no idea what was coming. She liked Miles, and she wanted to trust him. But life on *November's Dawn* had taught her that folks don't needlessly help others unless they were family or close enough to know no difference. The familiar elevator bell signaled their arrival and shook her from her doubts.

"Okay, we have to be quick. I don't want to be in the market for any longer than needed," Miles said as he stood up and brushed his pants off.

"Fine by me," Josie said. She turned and waited for the elevator doors to open.

They could already hear the marketplace clamor through the metal. It was early in the day, but life in Aegean started early and ran late in accordance with the factory schedules. That was how people survived. Extra work today could mean a little more food provided by the companies tomorrow. They were greeted immediately by the heavy odors of fish and burning oil permeating the galley.

"How are we playing this?" Miles asked. "I'd put a day's rations on it that P&C officers are already at your cabin."

"I know. I'm working on it," she whispered back. In truth, she had no idea what they were going to do. She just knew she needed to make sure Rose was safe.

Miles grunted and nodded his response. Josie was glad he did not press her on it this time.

Galley Marketplace was in an expansive chamber and was the heart of commerce for its passengers. Ramshackle structures, built layer by layer over the decades using every bit of sheet metal scrap and waste imaginable, clogged every alley and avenue. It was one of the few places on Aegean Deck where metal walls were not within an arm's reach away, which made it very desirable to many. Hundreds of voices echoed between the two-meter-thick outer bulkheads of the market, fervently pursuing the bartering that was the lifeblood of their world. Here, anything was possible for the enterprising individual.

Josie and Miles walked quickly between the cramped stalls and merchant stands.

"We have to find stairs to get to level C. Hurry, Miles," Josie said.

Miles looked at a merchant stall that was selling fresh biscuits. "I'm starving. I haven't had anything to eat since your party yesterday."

"Get down," Josie said as they ducked behind the stall. Two P&C officers talked with a merchant ahead. Thankfully, there were enough people in the market that nobody noticed their sudden movement.

They were just close enough to hear the officers.

"If you have any information regarding the missing girl—" the officer began.

"Newly stitched clothes for sale! Only been stitched five times before!" a shop owner shouted over the crowd.

"—or else the commandant is going to march through here with a hundred of us and you don't want that, do you?" the officer finished.

The merchant stood his ground. "I wouldn't tell you nothing, even if I knew."

"We'll see about that." The officer wagged a gloved finger in the merchant's face.

Josie let her head fall back against the shack. Hearing the officer's threat made her stomach feel like it was tied in a thousand knots. They were after her, and these folks would suffer for it. The window to get to Rose was closing fast.

"What is it? What did he say?" Miles asked.

"Nothing we didn't already know. Come on," she lied, not wanting to tell Miles. He had family on Aegean Deck too.

Josie scanned the outside of the galley and found the nearest stairwell. All of the different levels of Aegean Deck had outlets to the Galley Marketplace and were connected by stairwells.

The residential passageways were emptying out as people went to work. Josie's mom was one of the few on Aegean Deck who worked on Olympus and she did not talk about it much. Her job provided enough to get by but no more. Once, years ago, Josie had given some rations to a neighboring girl whose family was struggling. Nila had been with her. They were closer then. When Josie's mom found out, she said Josie didn't understand the way things were and made her promise she would never do it again. Josie had tried to explain the girl was hungry, and she was only helping, but her mom would not listen. Nila didn't question it, and Josie fell out with her not long after.

"Okay, my cabin is around the next passageway." She stopped as soon as she peeked around the corner.

Two P&C officers stood guard right in front of the hatch to her cabin. Josie spun around, looking for any sort of cover or outlet in the passageway. A couple of abandoned crates were stacked against one side of the bulkhead, she jumped behind them with Miles.

"What are we going to do?" Josie said, as she pulled her hair into a ponytail.

Miles glanced over the crates. "There isn't any way we sneak past them. The passageway is too narrow. Maybe wait till the shift changes?"

Josie slouched against the crate. "We can't sit here for hours. Someone is going to see us. Or worse, a patrol will come the other direction and we'll be stuck."

"Josie? Is that you?" a high-pitched voice squeaked behind them.

Miles and Josie jumped at the same time and spun around. A girl of about five stood clutching an old and worn plush rabbit. Its once-white fur covered by black and gray soot. Rose's hair was light blonde, unlike Josie's deep red, but they shared their dad's blue eyes.

"Rose? Oh, Rose! What are you doing out here?" Josie pulled her sister in while Miles kept an eye on the P&C officers down the passageway.

"I was playing with Mac down the hall." Her bottom lip trembled as she pointed to the officers. "Then I got scared."

Josie pulled her back and looked Rose in the eye. "Are you okay? Did the officers hurt you? And Mom? Where is Mom?"

Miles put a hand on Josie's shoulder. "Give her a chance, Josie," he said softly.

"Right, you're right. Oh, Rose, I'm just so glad you're okay." Josie pulled her sister back into a hug. She could feel her shoulders loosen and the relief wash over her from seeing her sister safe.

Rose's eyes brimmed with tears. "Big men were talking with Mom when I came back. Mom was looking for you. She yelled and went with them. Those two stayed, but I was scared to go home. Then I saw you."

"It's okay, Rose. You're safe. Nobody's going to hurt you, I promise."

Miles leaned down. "It doesn't seem like they were out to hurt your family. I think they already would have if they wanted to."

"Yeah, then where is my mom now? Why's my sister wandering around with nobody taking care of her? I mean, does Mom even care? She had her chance. I'm done."

Miles's eyes sharpened. "We just need to be more careful. We've already had some close calls."

Josie looked back at her sister. "Come on, Rose. We're going to get you somewhere safe."

"And you too, right? You'll be with me?" Rose asked with glossy eyes.

"I'm going to make it so we're all safe, from now on."

"And Mom?"

Josie looked down. She was not sure how to answer her sister. She wanted so badly to be able to say yes and it be the truth. "And Mama," she said with as much hope as she could manage. "You hold Lewis close, okay?"

Josie smiled and pointed to the worn-out bunny, then took her sister's hand as they went back toward the galley.

Miles walked close to Josie, near enough that only she would hear what he was about to say. "Where are we going to take her? She won't be safe with us," he whispered.

"I know. I think I know where she'll be safe."

"Where?"

"Mags, from engineering. She lives close. And I trust her."

"Well, yeah. That might work." Miles's brow furrowed. "For now."

CHAPTER SIX_

Josie ran as she towed Rose and Miles behind her. Mags's cabin was many levels higher than hers, on level F, but still reasonably close. She just hoped the engineer would be there and agree to take Rose in. Mags was no friend to the OSD and always seemed to watch over Josie—much like Felix had done—so Josie was hopeful. But now that Felix was gone, she didn't know what to think anymore. What if Mags didn't believe her? Or worse, what if she turned them in?

"Hey, Josie. Are you okay?" Miles said with a gentle hand on her arm.

"I'm okay, just tired," Josie replied. "Oh, look. Level F. We're almost there." She zipped up her jumpsuit and pulled Rose closer.

Josie eyed Mags's cabin hatch as they got closer. Nothing seemed to be out of order, but she was wary all the same. She knocked against the metal hatch three times. There was no answer. She did it again. Boots shuffled on the other side. Then the locking mechanism on the hatch opened and Mags's face appeared between the hatch and frame.

"What? Who is it?" Mags said. She looked back and forth

between the three of them as her eyes widened. "Josie? And Miles? What's going on?"

"Mags, please. Can we come in?" Miles asked.

"Well, of course! I'm sorry, lad. I just wasn't expecting anybody this early. And who is this little one?"

Rose hid behind Josie's leg. "My sister, Rose," Josie said.

Rose smiled but focused her attention on Lewis. The cabin was very similar to Josie's. Three small rooms enclosed by stark metal walls. One with bunks stacked high, another for a bathroom and the last, an area for living, cooking, and any other needs a family may have. Even though Mags lived alone on account of her being the head of engineering, the cabin was meant to fit as many people as possible, not to provide comfort or luxury.

"So, what can I do for you?" Mags asked. "I must say, I have seen you in better shape."

"Mags, have you heard about Felix?" Josie looked down as the memory flashed before her.

Mags walked over to a small table and poured a cup of tea from a beat-up metal pot. "What? No, I've not seen him since your party yesterday. I got a holomessage that he wasn't feeling so good today. Is he alright?"

Josie's throat tightened as she sat on a small metal stool. Mags stood unmoving as Josie told her what Commandant Reyes had done and parts of her dad's holomessage. She could not bring herself to say the words that Felix was dead, so Miles did. Mags's lips trembled and her eyes glistened a little more in the low light when she heard. Rose quivered next to Josie but stayed silent. Mags was a strong and proud woman, Josie had seen it all her life when Mags dealt with many issues and challenges being head engineer, and she carried that same strength now.

"Josie, Dom's message? You're absolutely sure of what he told you?" Mags said.

"Yes. He said the ark had the ability to rise to the surface. He knew the OSD would stop at nothing to hide the truth and it's now my responsibility to make sure people know." She left out the part about the Heart of the Dawn; the necklace her dad had left her was too personal to tell anyone else about. At least not now when she knew so little about it. "Mags, we're being hunted. Rose isn't safe at home or with my mom. I didn't know where else to go. Please, will you hide her?"

Miles followed her lead. "I don't know what's going on. But I know what I saw." He looked over at Josie. "And I trust Josie."

"Dom Owens was one of the best men I ever knew," Mags said. "No doubt you've heard that before, but if it wasn't an accident what took him, then I'd say folks ought to know the OSD isn't what it's cracked up to be. I'll do what I can to keep young Rose safe. For Dom and Felix."

Josie stood and walked over to Mags, then wrapped her arms around the woman. "Thank you," she whispered. Then she bent down to her little sister and held her close. "I have to go now, Rose."

"But why? You can stay. Please will you stay?" Rose looked down. She had Lewis pushed tightly under her chin.

Josie gently lifted her little sister's chin. "I know. I'm sorry, Rose. It's just that some other people need my help right now. I'm the only one who can help. Just like Lewis helps you. I have to go, but I promise I'm coming back, and we'll be a regular, happy family again." A lock of hair fell across Rose's blue eyes and Josie hooked it back behind her sister's ear.

Rose bit her lip to stop it from trembling. "You promise?"

"With my whole heart I do." She hugged Rose one last time before standing.

"She'll be safe with me, lass," Mags said. "It's about time

someone put their foot down to all this nonsense. But this is dangerous. What're you going to do?"

"I don't know. It's all I can think about, and I still don't know. All I *do* know is that Reyes and the OSD have to pay for what they did. People must know. We should be free. My dad talked about bringing *November's Dawn* to the surface . . ." She stopped and felt the Heart of the Dawn beneath her jumpsuit. "Mags, have you ever heard anything about a key? Or something like that? Something to trigger the ark's return to the surface?"

"A key? No never. Why do you ask?"

"I'm just trying to think how this all might work," Josie lied. "It must be something on the bridge then." She was disappointed, but she still had time to figure it out.

Mags let out a low whistle. "That's a beast of a different nature, lass. I've never even been allowed near the bridge. No one outside of Olympus Deck are given access."

"I know. I'm hoping during all this excitement from the OSD's celebration, we can get close. First Vicar Frost said it will be a celebration like nothing ever seen before." Josie had been thinking about it for a while. With the OSD after her, the best chance she had was now. If she tried to hide until after the celebration, the entire focus of the OSD and Olympus would be on finding her. At least on the bridge there might be some clues about returning to the surface.

Mags spat at hearing Frost's name. "I always figured him to be a weasel. But still, lass. You don't know anything about Olympus Deck or the bridge. You'd need full directional plans for the front half of *November's Dawn* and access codes to get an elevator to take you there."

"Exactly like the kind engineers would need to do their job," Josie said.

Mags shook her head and looked down. "I wish it were that

simple. We haven't had access to those documents since before I became an engineer. It was deemed unsafe by the OSD. And you can bet I've never been given access codes before. We're always escorted by P&Cs."

Josie slumped up against the wall and closed her eyes. "We'll find another way then."

"If you're not giving up, lass, I've heard rumors of others who won't give up either." Mags had a sly smile on her face. "They've been fighting for us little folk for a long time now."

Josie looked up excitedly. "Who? Maybe they can help us too?"

"I don't know about all that, but I can tell you how to find one of them. I warn you though, if you go this way, there isn't no going back to your old life."

"My old life is gone," Josie said as she lifted her head high.

"I wasn't talking to you," Mags said looking at Miles.

Miles sat on a metal stool with his head down and hands clasped together. Mags's words hung in the air, but Miles said nothing, and Josie started to think he hadn't heard.

Right as she was about to say something, Miles looked up and their eyes met. "With what happened and what I know now, I don't think my life could go back to what it was before anyway. I have to see this through."

Josie's shoulders eased and a faint smile crept across her lips.

"Well, it's settled then," Mags said. "We've got to get you two out of here. If someone sees you leaving my cabin, P&C officers will come knocking."

Mags walked over to a small metal cabinet. After fumbling around for a moment with something inside, she pulled out a small, worn envelope.

"I can't tell you much for your own good—and mine. But inside you'll find something that can help." Mags handed the envelope to Josie but did not release it right away. "It never sat right with me what happened to your dad. More secrets are webbed around this place than in a nest of spiders, and I think it's about time someone shook them all out. Don't let them get away with it, Josie. Don't let what they did to Felix be forgotten."

"I won't. I promise." Josie looked at the envelope and back at Mags before opening it. The piece of paper inside only had two words written on it. A single name.

Marcus Abbott

Josie frowned and looked up from the paper. "Marcus—"

"Shh, not out loud, Josie. It isn't safe," Mags whispered. She rushed over and crumpled the paper into Josie's hand. "We can't risk anything now. Go to the Garden of Tomorrow, on Delos Deck. Be there tonight."

Mags stopped and looked past Josie. She was not looking at anything in particular. It was the look someone gave when they were deep in their own mind. Then she smiled. "I've heard tales about it, you know. The sun. About how you could once feel its heat on your skin. Wouldn't it be nice? To feel that?" Her smile faded and her eyes turned serious again. "Go, go now, lass. Remember what I've told you. And trust no one." Mags turned the metal latch that held her cabin hatch in place and ushered Josie and Miles out.

Josie grabbed Mags's hand as she stepped across the threshold. "Thank you, Mags," she whispered. Mags smiled in return.

As Josie closed the hatch behind them, she heard Mags talking with Rose. "Come, little Rose, let's find you something to eat. Then you can tell me all about . . . Lewis, you said his name was?"

Josie could not hear the response, but a small giggle from Rose filled the cabin and spilled into the passageway. She prayed Rose would be safe till it was all over.

CHAPTER SEVEN_

Josie and Miles stood outside Mags's cabin for a moment longer. She felt conflicted about leaving Rose, but she knew it would have been more dangerous bringing her with. Still, Josie wished there was another way.

"You did the right thing," Miles said.

"Yeah, I hope so," Josie said. "Now about what Mags said, we have to get to Delos Deck. To the Garden of Tomorrow. Have you ever been?"

Miles shook his head. "No, besides yesterday at the Observatory, I've only been to Delos Deck a handful of times. And that was always for big events or celebrations."

"I just hope we can get through the checkpoint into Delos."

He scoffed. "The checkpoint officers don't like letting Aegean folk into Delos. Have you ever tried to get through? Well besides for class."

Josie shook her head. "Never wanted to."

"I tried once. They said I didn't look like the quality of citizens that belong, even if we're supposed to be allowed there."

Josie looked down at her own dirty and battered jumpsuit, then at Miles's own clothes. She ran her fingers through her hair, and they were immediately met with knots. Her face flushed as she saw Miles's eyes on her. "Well, we really don't look very presentable. We'll need to look the part if we're going to get through to Delos."

"Have you got any money? That might be an easier way to get through. The checkpoint P&Cs don't like us, but they've never said no to our money," Miles said. "Or at least that's what I've heard."

Josie jammed her hand in a jumpsuit pocket, pulling out everything in it. Miles eyed her as she opened her hand, revealing a pocket wrench, a loose red wire, a forgotten bolt, and other odds and ends.

"Why do you have so much thread?" Miles pointed at the tangled sewing thread.

"Ah, wait one second." Josie stuck her other hand in a different pocket. "See?" She pulled out a button that had fallen off her jumpsuit. "I was going to fix it. Never got the chance. No holocoins though."

It was Miles's turn to rustle around his person for any holocoins. His pockets were far less interesting. But three square holocoins spilled out. Dull blue holographic light, contained in a ring of metal, danced against the passageway. Miles smiled but it faded fast when he realized he only had three.

"Not even the most desperate guard would risk his skin for only three holocoins."

"No, they wouldn't," Josie shot back. She threw her hands up and leaned back against the bulkhead. "If only there were no P&Cs at my cabin, I could get into my stash. I don't know what to do now."

Miles leaned right next to her. "We'll be okay. I have some savings too."

"I can't ask you to do that. You shouldn't have to. All of this is just so wrong."

Miles started walking down the passageway. "Josie Owens, nothing is hopeless. This is easy, anyway. I have the money we need. This is the right thing to do."

Josie cocked her head and slowed down. She had not been expecting him to say that. It made her realize there was probably quite a bit more to Miles than she knew. After all, everything she knew about him was from school. She wanted that to change, to know all about him.

"Okay, okay. So, let's say we do the right thing. You're sure that's going to get your money? What about your family? Wait, do you have any brothers or sisters?" Josie asked before her face flushed. "I'm sorry. I just feel bad that I really don't know much about you."

A pair of men pushed a large trolley down the passageway, interrupting their conversation. Josie and Miles squeezed themselves up against the bulkhead and lowered their eyes as the men passed.

Miles turned to Josie's ear. "I want to help however I can, Josie. And that's just what I'll do." The men were nearly past them now. "Also, it's just me and my mom at home. Now you know a bit about me." He smiled and watched the men with the trolley.

Josie nodded. She knew from class that in the beginning, every person was assigned a cabin. But in the years since, the people living on the ark had spilled into every nook available, leaving some cabins cramped and others empty. Olympus didn't care to make sure those on Aegean were housed properly.

"Lead the way then. But I'm going to pay you back."

"I wouldn't expect it any different," Miles said. "Come on, we need to have time to make it to Delos Deck. Who knows what'll be going on once we get there."

Josie nodded her head and followed Miles as they wound

through the many levels of Aegean Deck. They climbed up several flights of stairs before emerging on level H.

Miles stopped right before coming to a hatch leading to cabin 2732. Before he turned the lever, he looked at Josie, his lips moved as if he was going to say something, but he then looked back at the door and shrugged. "Eh, it'll be fine."

Josie eyed him. "What? What is it?"

Miles had already turned the lever and stepped through into the cabin. The inside looked similar to the rest of Aegean Deck, but there was a makeshift bed pushed up against the far wall. A small pile of clothes lay on top of it. The kitchen faucet ran a trickle of water. Miles jumped to turn it off and pushed the pile of clothes into a small basket. An orange ball encircled with a pattern of thin black lines sat on a ledge.

"Sorry about the mess," Miles said as he ran fingers through his hair.

"What's that?" Josie asked, pointing to the orange ball.

Miles squinted back at her. "You don't know? It's a basketball."

"A basketball?"

Miles picked up the ball and spun it on his finger. "Yeah, a sport. The greatest athletes of the old world played it." He tossed the ball to Josie. "I've watched every game in the database."

Josie ran her fingers over the strange material the ball was made from. A small blue and yellow metal fetterball sat right next to where the basketball was. "You like fetterball too?"

Miles looked at the ledge and his eyes lost their excitement. He took the basketball back from Josie. "Yeah, it's alright I guess."

His answer surprised Josie. "There are some great fetterball players on board. You must like them."

"Sure." Miles squatted by his bed and pulled a metal box from under it. "Let's just get the holocoins we need."

Josie fidgeted with her hands as she watched him work on getting the box open. Something she said clearly had upset him, but she didn't know what.

Miles pulled out a brown pouch that jingled when he shook it. "Ah, here we go."

"Miles! Miles, is that you?" An older woman's voice rang through the cabin.

Miles jumped up, and his eyes locked onto the bunk room hatch. "Yes, Mom! I'm just grabbing something, then I have to go again."

The lever on the hatch started creaking as it opened. Before Josie could do anything, Miles's mother poked her head out. She wore a brightly-colored headscarf that contrasted against her dark skin. The fingers wrapped around the frame of the door were thin and fragile, and the woman's face was gaunt, but her eyes were sharp. They met Josie's with a fierce and curious gaze.

"Miles, you brought a friend home?" she said as she shuffled into the room. "I didn't know you had a girlfriend."

Josie's face flushed fast. Miles's did too.

"Mom! She's not my girlfriend. She's my . . . friend."

Miles's words did little for Josie's embarrassment. She rushed to introduce herself to Miles's mom. "Hello, I'm Josie Owens." She held out her hand in introduction.

Miles jumped over and touched Josie's outstretched hand. "No, she can't—"

Miles's mother laughed. "It's alright, child. I won't break." She shook Josie's hand with force. Miles walked over to get a chair for his mother, who beamed as she watched him.

"Are you feeling okay, Mrs. Thomas?" Josie said.

"Oh child, please, call me Edith."

Josie nodded and placed her other hand on Edith's. "I will."

Miles placed the chair behind his mother and moved to help her sit. Edith took her son's guiding hand. After she was situated, she brushed her hand across Miles's cheek.

"My boy. He takes such good care of me. Not like his older brother." Her eyes turned dark.

"Mom, please. Not today."

"Not today?" Edith asked. "I could be in my grave and Joshua wouldn't even know. Lord knows I'm only feeling better because of the medicine you scavenged."

Josie frowned. She knew a lot about *November's Dawn*, and the chances of scavenging medicine were about the same as Olympus opening to the rest of the ark. Medicine was something tightly controlled by the OSD.

Miles's panicked gaze darted to Josie and then to the ground. He leaned down. "Mom, Josie is a guest. She doesn't need to know our business."

Edith sighed. "Fine. Then why are you here?"

"I told you—" Miles started but was interrupted by the low and yet joyful chimes over the *November's Dawn* intercom that signaled an announcement.

Josie froze at hearing her mom's voice echo throughout the many speakers on the decks and passageways.

Citizens of November's Dawn. *The Order of Scientific Discovery and the Directors welcome you to enjoy these pleasant comments. Look around yourselves, to those you live with, to those you work with. Every one of us is a vital part of our continued life and prosperity. As long as we remain dedicated and in union, we will endure. Today marks the second day in our week-long celebration of the Great Turning. At the end of this week,* November's Dawn *will turn its course and carry us into the new unknown. Remember, citizens, all we have, we owe to our great ark. Tonight's celebration will be marked by a much-*

anticipated match of your most beloved sport, fetterball. Join us tonight to witness the next legendary clash between the undefeated Olympus Swords and the Aegean Flatfoots. All are welcome tonight in the Garden of Tomorrow. As always, in the darkness below, November's Dawn *will provide.*

The chimes sounded again, ending the announcement. Josie's hopes faded with it, but at least her mom seemed okay. Her voice had been clear. It had been her show voice, the one she used in her official role as the voice of *November's Dawn*, not at all like the tired voice she used when speaking to Josie.

Outside of the cabin, chants supporting the Aegean Flatfoots rang throughout the deck.

"'In the darkness below, *November's Dawn* will provide,'" Edith recited and put a hand on Josie's sleeve. "Oh, I do love that woman's voice. She speaks of hope to us all. Wouldn't you agree, child?"

Josie could only nod and give back a half-hearted smile. Edith beamed and Josie didn't have the will to speak her mind. Josie moved closer to Miles, out of Edith's earshot. Miles looked more serious now, with good reason.

"Miles we have to go now," she whispered. "The game tonight—in the Garden of Tomorrow—that's where we are supposed to meet the contact!"

CHAPTER EIGHT_

"I hope this works," Miles said as he ran his fingers through his hair and looked back around the corner.

There it was. The checkpoint between Aegean and Delos Decks. The P&C officers on guard were not supposed to stop people from Aegean from going to Delos, but there was nobody to enforce those rules on the officers. Or at least nobody with any power cared to. Only direct authorization like they had yesterday for class was enough to get past unscathed. The small pouch of holocoins sat silently in Miles's hand. They were the only option.

Josie reached over and took the pouch, carefully dumping half its contents into her palm. It was way more than she had been expecting. "Miles, where did you get all this? This is over a month's wages. You can't risk it."

"I've been saving. I can make it back."

Josie swallowed. The guilt was growing more and more. She put a handful of holocoins back in the pouch and showed Miles how many she took.

He looked at the holocoins and then back at the officers. "Okay. Yeah, that should be enough."

Josie pulled the cap she wore further down. They had decided her red hair made her too conspicuous, so she had bundled it up and stuffed it under the short-brimmed hat those in the cannery factory wore.

The passageway lighting was dim, but she could see Miles's smile when he looked at her. "What?" she asked in a hushed tone.

He jumped. "Oh sorry. It's just, that was my mom's hat, from when she could still work." Then anger flashed in his eyes. "Before we had to rely on charity to survive."

Josie's stomach clenched. It hurt to hear the anger in Miles's voice. It hurt even more to think about the suffering he and his mom had endured, and she could not do anything to help. And now she was making them more vulnerable by using Miles's savings.

Before she could say anything, he had already started walking toward the checkpoint. She fell in beside him and held her breath. The checkpoint was five meters away. Pressure in her chest grew with every step. The small hairs on her neck stiffened and goosebumps crawled across her body. The P&C officers noticed them now. She eyed their batons and security vests, the way their hands moved to grip their weapons. Officers like these had killed Felix and they were after her now. With one meter left, the breath finally escaped her. The holocoins shook in her hand.

"Oy! What's going on here?" one officer called.

His two companions stood from behind the makeshift table they had been sitting at, the remnants of the card game laid bare, revealing the suits they each possessed.

The holoscreens behind the officers flashed through advertisements for the upcoming fetterball games before moving on to news. The anchors, the clean-cut and smiling duo of OSD deacons Jack Burlesque and reporter Donna Albert, detailed reports of a criminal gang. Josie tried to focus on getting through the checkpoint, but the voices coming from the holo-screens kept thundering through her thoughts.

"The group some have come to know as Hades Fist are outlaws and any signs or sightings of them should be reported to your nearest peace-and-compliance officer," Donna Albert said through the holoscreen.

"Are you deaf?" the officer demanded again. His security baton twitched.

Miles tapped his foot against Josie's, willing her to pay attention. Her eyes snapped back to the officer. She smiled and tried to act like they were supposed to be there, but she couldn't help but wonder if the gang was the same group Mags had told them about. There wasn't any time to think about it more though.

"I'm so sorry, officer. I heard the report on the criminals. I got scared," she said and lowered her head. Miles followed her lead.

The officer relaxed as he glanced over his shoulder at the holoscreens. "No need to worry, young miss. There ain't no criminal on *November's Dawn* that'll get away with it. You got the best of the P&Cs right here." He grinned a toothy smile and opened his arms toward the other two officers. "Now, what're you here for?"

Josie stepped closer. "We need to get into Delos Deck," she said with as much firmness and determination as she could.

The officer looked at Josie and Miles for a moment before laughing. "You? Why would you need to go and bother our friends in Delos, huh?"

Josie stopped and tried to remember the plan. The voices of Jack Burlesque and Donna Albert crowded her thoughts again. The officer watched her, his eyes narrowed ever so slightly.

"The games!" Miles stepped forward. "We're going to the games tonight."

The officer's attention shifted to Miles. "The games you say? Well then get lost. We're not letting you people through for another four hours." He turned to go back to his post.

"Shouldn't even let them through at all," another officer remarked.

Miles urgently nodded toward Josie's hand clutching the holocoins.

"Wait!" Josie called. She reached out and opened her hand. The square coins imprinted into it. Light bounced off the clear plastic visor of the officer's helmet.

"Well, isn't this something else altogether," the officer said. "We might be able to make something work now. What do you say, boys?"

Jack Burlesque's voice dominated the silence. "In another development, the OSD is looking for a lost teenager from Aegean Deck." The news anchor described Josie, and a picture of her lit up the holoscreen.

"There's more!" Josie yelled. She needed to distract them fast. The guard turned back to her, before he had seen the holoscreen and pictures that would have doomed their mission before it started. The other two officers' eyes fixed on her as well. Josie pulled out the pouch and emptied the rest of the holocoins into her hand. "Please, we've been saving."

The images on the holoscreen turned back to promoting the celebrations going on throughout the week. But now her hand was filled with the rest of the holocoins. She couldn't hide them now.

Josie was breathing hard. Miles too. The P&C officer was silent as he looked between the two of them and the pile of money as if going through the calculations, weighing the risks. After all, Miles had saved up quite a bit, and these officers knew they could attract attention from higher ups by taking too large a bribe. It all depended on how much they wanted it. Guilt started to gnaw at the back of her mind. This was a lot of money. Then the guard smiled and beckoned them forward.

"Alright, you two. Hey, Mike, open the door. Let them through," he called back.

It was too late. If Josie backed out now the guards would likely still take the holocoins. She silently cursed to herself and dumped the holocoins into the officer's outstretched hand as they walked by.

"Keep your head down," Miles whispered as they walked down the passageway. Josie did just that, knowing there was still a chance the officers would recognize her. Then, no amount of holocoins would help.

The two officers hooted as their fellow came back with the holocoins. "What do you say we get this game going again?" he asked as they grinned and laughed.

"No, I'm betting big on the Olympus Swords tonight," one replied. "They're going to crush those Flatfoot junkies. Nobody can stop them."

Josie didn't hear the rest as the metal double doors hissed and closed behind them. They were enclosed in a small elevator, which would take them to the main level of Delos Deck. They stood in silence as the car rumbled ever higher. But after a while Josie could not take it.

"Miles, I'm sorry about the money. I didn't mean to give them all of it. I just panicked." She watched him, he was doing the thing where he looked off at something, neither very far nor very close, and was consumed by his own thoughts.

"I brought it all, because I thought we would need it. It turns out we did."

"But it was so much. I mean I don't know where you could have even gotten that much money." Josie wrung her hands together. Miles's mom was sick, and she had just given away his entire savings.

"Josie Owens, what have I been telling you all this time? We're in this together. It was only a couple holocoins."

"Hmm. More than a couple," Josie mumbled. "At least tell me where you got it and when this is over, I can help you earn it back."

Miles gave her a sidelong look and his mouth twitched. Before he could speak, the elevator bell dinged, signaling their arrival on Delos Deck. An automated voice came over the elevator speaker.

The OSD welcomes you, citizen, to Delos Deck. In the darkness below, November's Dawn *will provide.*

Josie had been on Delos Deck before, but like Miles, it had been for things like their class trip to the Observatory or a couple engineering jobs she had accompanied Felix on. She had never been there alone. And she had certainly never been there as a fugitive before.

Miles gave her a playful smirk. "Another time, I guess," he said before stepping out.

Josie had to bring her arms up to shield her eyes as she adjusted to the new light. They had emerged into a passageway, somewhat similar to those on Aegean Deck but noticeably cleaner. The walls were not covered with pipes and electrical cables, so the familiar noises of the waterworks and steam were gone, replaced now by an eerie silence and a much brighter lighting system.

"That'll take some getting used to," Miles said, squinting.

Josie nodded. "Let's see if there is a directional map close. We have to find this contact before the celebration. Or else we'll never find him."

Miles nodded and they started down the passageway. They passed several hatches leading to other passageways and rooms as they continued. These hatches were quite different from the ones on Aegean Deck, being just two seamless metal plates with an entry keypad on the side. The hallway was well lit, and its corners and outlets were not filled with forgotten junk and rubbish.

Miles laughed to himself. "It's amazing really. There's so much light and power, I have to shield my eyes from it. Can you imagine Odette, or one of the others from school, trying to survive on Aegean? There are folks living in Bottom Bays, with no light, no power, nothing."

"No, I can't. But wait, Miles, there are really people living in Bottom Bays? I thought those were rumors."

Miles nodded. "You've seen how folk on Aegean are forced to live. All it takes is one accident in the factories. Or one illness," his voice got very quiet. "My mom and I almost lost our cabin. I don't know where we would have gone."

Josie cringed. She was only really starting to understand how fortunate her family had been, even if they still lived on Aegean. And that was all thanks to her mom and the sacrifices she made. Maybe Josie had been provided for much more than she knew. "That's why we're doing this, Miles. Once everyone knows the truth, we won't have to live under the OSD anymore. On the surface we can make sure the rules are different. We can make sure people are cared for and resources aren't hoarded by Olympus."

"Yeah, I know," he said, resigned, and kept walking. "Oh look!" Ahead on the wall was a directional map for Delos Deck.

"Finally, some luck," Josie said as she ran to the map. She traced her finger around the map. There was no telling when they would find another so she tried to commit as much to memory as she could. Delos Deck was much larger than she thought, and fewer people lived there than on Aegean Deck.

Miles released a low whistle. "Look at the space between

cabins, they must be at least twice the size of ours. And look, they don't seem to have any factories or industry levels on Delos either." He planted his finger on the map. "There's the Observatory."

Josie nodded but kept looking. They needed to find the Garden of Tomorrow. Her eyes were drawn to a front section of the directional map where Olympus Deck should have been shown. But it was blacked out. "It looks like there are some secrets even those on Delos are not allowed to know. Oh! And there's the Garden of Tomorrow. Wow, that chamber must be one of the largest on *November's Dawn.*"

"Well, they play fetterball there. They need a lot of space for it."

"Right, I didn't think of that," she replied. In truth, she didn't know much about fetterball. The game always seemed barbaric and needlessly brutal, but the people worshiped it and those athletes who performed were well rewarded. "Well let's get there before the celebration turns Delos Deck to chaos."

It was a straightforward path to get to the Garden of Tomorrow. Delos Deck was not nearly as labyrinthian as Aegean. They tried to keep as quiet and natural looking as they could to avoid detection. Risking anything now would be foolish.

By the time they reached the entrance to the Garden of Tomorrow, some residents of Delos Deck were already flocking there, enthusiastically awaiting the night's celebrations. Josie and Miles stopped before the large doors that opened into the garden. Josie pulled out the small piece of paper Mags had given her and read the name again.

Marcus Abbott.

"How are we going to find him?" Miles asked.

"I'm not sure. Mags just said to be here tonight. We bought

extra time with the guards. Let's use it to look around and be ready."

"Yeah, you're right. I don't want to be here when every eye on board is focused on the Garden."

An officer stepped in front of the crowd and raised his hands. "Listen up you lot. By the grace of the OSD and Directors, the Garden of Tomorrow is open to all tonight. But if you so much as step on a leaf, you'll be finding a couple of P&Cs at your door tomorrow morning."

The people from Delos gathered started cheering and clapping. They dressed in the colors and costumes supporting the Olympus Swords. Some had shiny white and gold capes. Some wore traditional fetterball helmets, making them look more like the spacemen from the old world. The excitement and energy hummed through the air.

A rush of fresh, clean air blasted them as the great doors opened into an expansive space. Josie had never seen the Garden before, and it was extraordinary. The directional map had done little justice for the sheer size of the chamber. Large light fixtures lined the room and both sides of the path were bordered by lush, green trees and bushes. Flower beds crept right up to the trunks of the great trees. Josie let her hand slide across the leaves gently waving in the artificial environment that allowed life deep in the darkness of the flooded world. The five-pointed tree leaves were the size of her palm. Vines criss-crossed the trunks and spilled onto the pathway, tumbling over the fences built to constrain them. She breathed deep the earthly scents of nature. It was clean, and damp, and she could not get enough of it. There was nothing of any comparable beauty on Aegean Deck or likely anywhere else on the planet for that matter.

Further still, the pathway expanded into a sunken arena of sorts, with all manner of greenery surrounding it, making it look like a jungle clearing from the old pictures. But what caught Josie's eye was a colossal sphere suspended high from the chamber's reinforced rafters, positioned directly above the sunken arena. Metal support beams and glass made the hollow sphere transparent so the game inside could be seen from the outside. All told, the great sphere was over twenty meters in diameter. It looked like a giant version of the fetterball she had seen in Miles's room.

"That's a fetterball sector? They play inside of that? It's much larger in person than it is on the holoscreens," Josie said.

Miles grunted a response and turned away. "This place is filling up. What's our plan?"

Josie put her hands on her hips and tapped her foot as she looked around the cavernous chamber. "Well, we're here and we're early. I think our best bet is to look for someone who isn't here for the celebration. Maybe they'll find us too."

A mighty cheer went up from the over-excited fans. Josie spun around and looked at the fetterball sector. A ramp leading to an opening in the side had been revealed and two lines of fetterball players made their way into the sphere. Josie looked everywhere, scanning the room for the man they were supposed to meet.

"It's already starting? We'll never find him in this," she groaned.

"No, this is just a preliminary match for the upper decks. The big game starts later," Miles said. "Let's start looking."

Josie nodded and together they walked around the perimeter of the arena. She tried to act natural but sweat tumbled down her back. They were exposed here and the worry of it made her head throb. She kept scanning the multitude of faces gathered, and with every minute that passed, more of them showed up from all corners of *November's Dawn*. It was easy enough to discern those from Aegean Deck to those from Delos. Most people from Aegean wore similar worn-out jumpsuits that identified what section or industry they worked in by the colored insignias on their collars. Those from Delos Deck wore brightly colored ensembles with pleated pants and garish tunics. Others, like she had seen outside of the garden, were dressed head to foot in the ornate fan gear of their favorite fetterball squads. The eyes of those gathered fixed on the fetterball sector now that the preliminaries were starting. A face caught her attention, but not for the reason she wanted. She blinked twice and the person was gone, obscured again by the moving crowd. "Miles, did you see that?" She tugged on Miles's sleeve.

Miles stared at the fetterball sector. The two squads inside were now lined up. A low horn signaled the start of the match. As soon as the horn's final note ended, the fetterball sector erupted in a flurry of movement. A small fetterball dropped from the top of the sector and both squads jumped to catch it with their long sticks. Each stick was topped with a cradle the players used to throw the fetterball around. Electromagnetic boots allowed them to run around the entire inside surface of the sector sphere. The crowd gathered roared their approval.

"I never understood this game. It just seems so brutal to me," Josie said. As soon as the words left her mouth one player ran full force into another on the opposing squad, sending him crashing to the bottom of the sector. "What's even the idea here?" she asked, cringing.

"The goal," Miles said in a low voice, eyes locked on the match, "is to keep possession of the fetterball for longer than the other squad." He pointed to a neon countdown timer flashing in the sphere. There was just over twenty-nine minutes left. "Whoever has the fetterball longer when that reaches zero wins. Players can shoot the fetterball through that ring in the center to add to their possession time. But there has to be another player from their squad on the other side to catch it or it doesn't count."

His words were drowned out by another roar from the crowd. A player had been knocked down while he was upside down at the top of the sector and was not moving.

Josie's stomach turned over, but there was also a small sense of excitement growing in her. "I guess I can see why people like it."

Miles spun around to Josie. "I don't like fetterball." His face was set in a heavy frown. "I hate fetterball."

Josie stepped close to him. "Why have a fetterball in your room then? The one by that basketball thing."

The clamor of the fans is all that greeted her. Miles looked back at the match, watching the violence unfold amongst the players. These were not even professional players. Josie had a feeling the real demonstration of brutal strength was still to come.

Miles looked at Josie. She could clearly see the pain in his eyes. "My dad played fetterball. He was one of the greats, or so I've been told." He turned back toward the match. "Fetterball broke him, and all he got was a few short years of glory. And all I got was a family without a dad."

Josie swallowed hard, feeling foolish for prying. "I'm sorry, Miles. I didn't know."

"Yeah," he said. "Let's just do what we came here for."

Before Josie could answer, something caught her attention. It was the same person from earlier. Only this time he was closer, with less people between them and she could now clearly see what had confused her before. The man looked strikingly similar to Miles, if perhaps a bit older, with the same frame and facial features.

"Miles, look. That man over there. Do you know him?" She pointed.

"What?" Miles said, looking over. His eyes widened. "No." He sprinted toward the man without giving Josie warning or explanation.

Josie sprang after him, but it was hard to keep up in the crowd. "Miles! Miles, wait!" she called. But there was no answer, at least nothing she could hear over the roar of the crowd.

With everyone so focused on the match, most people didn't bother looking at her, let alone move out of the way. After one final shift in the sea of fans, she was able to squeeze through a small crack. She had ended up at the outer edge of the arena. Looking around, she soon found what she was seeking. Miles stood under the canopy of great trees around the edge next to another man, the one who looked like him. She couldn't hear them, but the man had a hand on Miles's shoulder. They had to know each other.

"Miles! Finally," Josie said, as she got closer to them.

The two had stopped talking and were watching her. She looked up at the stranger and gasped, eyes flickering back and forth between him and Miles. The stranger wore a gilded tunic and black pleated pants, something only those on Delos would wear. He was tall and carried himself well. His dark skin tone was almost the same as Miles's. The hard lines and strong cheekbones of his chiseled face a more mature version of Miles's features.

Miles smiled slightly, seeing Josie's confusion. "Josie, this is my brother, Joshua."

Joshua's eyes hardened. "Shh! I said no names. I told you it isn't safe. You shouldn't be here, little brother. You need to leave. It isn't safe."

Miles stepped up. "Yeah? Tell me something I don't know." He waved his hand toward Josie. "We've been on the run for two days now. Josie's face is on the holoscreens."

"I don't have much time for holoscreens these days." Joshua's brown eyes studied Josie for a moment then flicked back to Miles. "You're on the run? Why? And why would you be here then, this is the worst place you could hide from the P&Cs."

"Well, one of Josie's friends, an engineer—"

"We're looking for someone." Josie cut in. She gave Miles a determined glance. Even if this was his brother, she still did not trust him with the whole truth. Nor was there the time for that anyway. Josie lowered her voice. "Someone that will be here tonight. Someone who knows secrets about *November's Dawn* that could help get us onto Olympus Deck."

"I can't help you. You both need to get out of here, now," Joshua answered quickly, turning away from them.

Miles put his hand on Joshua's chest. "Hang on. Why are you here?"

Joshua winced when another player got hit. Josie could tell he didn't like fetterball either. Miles eyed his brother's clothes. "And why are you dressed like this? You don't live on Delos, do you?"

Joshua sighed and looked back at his brother. "No. Look, I wish I could help you. But the people I work for don't want a couple strays."

"The people you work for," Josie whispered harshly. "And who is that? Someone named Marcus Ab—?"

Joshua's hand immediately shot up and covered Josie's mouth, before she even realized what he was doing, then he leaned in close to her ear. "If you know what's good for you, you won't say that name out loud again." He released her.

Miles stood with his eyes wide.

"Mags sent us. He's expecting us." Josie held her head high.

That softened Joshua's demeanor. He ran his fingers

through his hair, just like Miles always did. "Mags? Shit. Well, okay. I guess—"

His words were cut off by chimes signaling an announcement. They sounded through every speaker in the Garden of Tomorrow and the crowd immediately turned their attention to it.

Joshua looked up and cursed. "It's starting."

CHAPTER NINE_

Adrian listened as Serena Owens, in her official capacity as the voice of *November's Dawn*, delivered the welcoming announcement.

Citizens of November's Dawn. The Order of Scientific Discovery and the Directors welcome you to enjoy the great games marking the second day in the celebration of the Great Turning. Now please, give your attention to First Vicar Adrian Frost as he delivers this message. As always citizens, in the darkness below, November's Dawn *will provide.*

As she finished, Adrian cleared his throat and brought the microphone close. He looked out from the enclosed viewing platform over the Garden of Tomorrow, toward the crowd that had amassed. Serena had delivered her address from the communications center on Olympus Deck, and he wished he was there now, far away from this chaos. But he had to be present, the people needed to see their First Vicar, so he was here, willfully showing his support for the fetterball games. Adrian never liked the game—he thought it low that players would sacrifice their bodies and health for sport—but it had been around for as long as *November's Dawn* had walked and served a vital purpose. Fetterball was a symbol of hope; entertainment diluted the woes of life in the people's minds; its violence sated their demand for spectacle. After straightening himself in the chair, he gently tapped on the microphone.

"Good evening, citizens. Tonight, you will witness the next clash between the Olympus Swords and the Aegean Flatfoots. As you watch these games, I want you to remember. Remember the strength, the ingenuity, the courage we all have to endure and to build a better future. In our lifetime alone, *November's Dawn* has walked through the sunken cities and wrecked monuments those in the old world created. Their decadence and desire for power cracked the very foundations of our world. But we rose from the ashes. London. Tokyo. New York. These were the monuments of the old world, yet all were flattened, and *November's Dawn* has walked through every one of them, unscathed, still bearing our spark of hope, still ensuring our future. The leaders of the old world failed to protect their people. But we have learned. The OSD welcomes and provides for all. *November's Dawn* demands our unity, for in the darkness below, *November's Dawn* will provide. Let the games begin!" Adrian clicked off the microphone and sat back.

The people cheered and Adrian watched as the title fetterball match began.

"As always, a great speech, Adrian." A weathered hand clapped Adrian on the shoulder.

"Thank you, Director Clarke. But you must share some of the praise as well. Without your company keeping the Aegean cannery factory running and staffed, we'd have run out of many basic foods long ago."

Director Clarke smiled. He was an older man, with a kind and wrinkled face, but Adrian knew that under his charming exterior, a cunning and relentless force lay in wait. "Your acknowledgement is most appreciated, Adrian." Clarke smiled and leaned in. "Now if only my workers weren't given so much time off for this celebration, I could increase my yields even further."

Adrian sighed. "Your concerns are well noted, director. But this celebration and time off will do more to boost your yields in the long run than you realize. You must trust in the OSD."

Clarke sat back. "Perhaps."

Adrian nodded and waved him off. "You know, there is another way to increase your margins even further."

"Oh? I'm interested."

"Startup the fishery operation on Aegean Deck once again. How many years has it been idle? Surely there are enough hungry mouths in the lower decks to finance an increased food production."

Clarke chuckled. "You know I can't authorize that."

"Can't or won't?"

"Both. Schmidt tried to undercut my company. And until that fool agrees to sell me the uniforms and provisions I need to staff the fishery at the agreed price per unit, the fishery will remain closed. If he cannot sell any uniforms at all, he will break eventually."

Adrian considered it for a moment. "I will speak with Director Schmidt again on reaching a compromise. With your continued support of our leadership, you have my word."

He knew he could force Clarke to open the fishery and Schmidt to agree to any terms. He was the First Vicar after all; his word was law. But the two directors would never forget their anger. Anger that would now be directed at Adrian for interfering too much with company affairs. And Director Clarke was a useful ally in persuading the other directors on issues when needed. Risking his support when they were days away from the Obsidian Trench was too dangerous.

Clarke nodded in agreement. "But of course, First Vicar.

You know I have always been a pious man. I believe such humility and virtue to be of great value."

"Thank you. We will speak soon. Are you staying for the celebration?"

Clarke laughed and waved his hand at the huge fetterball sector outside the viewing platform. "As much as I love a good old-fashioned show of strength, no, First Vicar. I think not."

Adrian watched the officers show Clarke out. "Commandant Reyes, your report?"

Reyes stepped from the shadows and sat behind Adrian. "We've been tracking the girl, First Vicar. We believe she is traveling with a boy. Their intentions are still unknown, but we've put a bounty on them. It will not be long now."

"Good. Our problems would be dear indeed if she joined this . . . What do they call themselves now?" Adrian's hand swayed in the air.

"Hades Fist."

"Yes, Hades Fist. You've been after these terrorists for some time, commandant. Tell me, why am I still hearing of them? You know how much our futures depend on this week."

Reyes leaned forward and put his elbows on his knees. He didn't want anyone else in the viewing platform to hear. "First Vicar, I believe some of their members may be in positions of power. Or else someone is feeding them information. Nothing else could account for how they've been able to hide from my men for so long. If you would but authorize more force to be used, I know I could—"

"I will not condone more violence against our own people, Commandant. I will not have a reoccurrence of what you did with that old engineer." Adrian grimaced as a particularly vicious fight between the fetterball players broke out. The fans roared their approval. "Find these terrorists, that is your task. The OSD will take measure of their guilt and punishment."

Commandant Reyes stood and saluted Adrian. "It will be done." He saluted again and turned on his heel.

The commandant was always one for formalities, Adrian mused to himself. He unbuttoned the top of his vestments and took a long breath. Finally, he would have some peace, even if it had to be while watching such a detestable display as fetterball. He looked again into the crowd. Someone was looking right at him, a girl in a hat, standing next to two boys. Unmistakable red hair tumbled out of the hat.

Josie Owens was here.

Adrian smiled and was about to signal one of the officers behind him. Before he could, the chamber erupted in a daze of fire and light that blocked out all else. The explosive force rocked the viewing platform and the Garden of Tomorrow below. Adrian flew back in his chair and tumbled to the floor. Shattered glass blew in all directions. His head slammed against the metal floor. The screams of those below pierced the air. His vision faltered in and out. The last thing he saw was the huge fetterball sphere swaying back and forth, full of players suspended high in the air. The metal groaned under the stress. Every second becoming more unstable and more dangerous.

It was ready to fall.

CHAPTER TEN_

THE EXPLOSION that rocked the Garden of Tomorrow sent Josie, Miles, and Joshua flying back into a flower bed which broke their fall. Most were not so lucky. Josie blinked and tried to understand what had happened.

People were scattered everywhere. They all had cuts and bruises, broken bones, and tattered clothes. Some were on the ground unmoving, their faces frozen in abject terror. There had been no warning, just a blinding light and sudden flash of heat. Several seconds after the explosion, the giant metal rivets that had held the fetterball sector in the air screeched and finally sheared, sending the immense sphere and all the players within it tumbling down to the deck.

The impact shook *November's Dawn*, and the ark groaned and buckled under the added stress.

Josie tried to turn over and get to her knees. Miles was next to her, but he wasn't moving. "Miles! Miles, wake up!" she shouted as she shook him.

A cut above his left eye was bleeding. She had no idea what other injuries he might have. Joshua lay next to him, holding his arm and groaning but at least he was awake. She crawled over to Joshua. "Joshua! Are you okay? Miles isn't moving. Joshua, help me!"

Joshua grunted as he rolled over, still clutching his wrist. He grabbed Miles's face and held his hand on the side of his neck. "He's alive!"

Josie could barely hear him over the chaos and screams around them.

"Help me get him up. We have to leave now," Joshua said.

Josie nodded and slung Miles's arm over her neck. Everywhere she looked, people emerged from the green growth of the Garden of Tomorrow. Their groggy and confused faces quickly turned to horror as they realized what had happened. A flashing warning system activated throughout the garden. The intervals of blaring horns made it hard for Josie to even think, let alone try to talk to Joshua.

"One, two, three!" Joshua shouted as the two of them lifted Miles.

Pain shot up Josie's right leg as she put pressure on it, but there wasn't time to stop now.

The uneven terrain of the flower bed made it hard to walk. More than once, Josie accidently stepped on a person who had not gotten up yet. The thought of stepping on dead bodies was too much for her to bear. Every scream and agonizing cry echoed through her head.

After several moments, they made it to the edge. Now all they needed to do was circle around until they found an exit. Josie had never wanted anything more. She turned toward Miles. The gash above his eye bled profusely. A stream of blood ran over his eyelid. She tried to wipe it away.

"Joshua, the explosion. What was that?"

Joshua looked at her but didn't answer, instead pulling them farther along the edge of the wall toward the exit.

"Look at your brother! You knew what was going to happen!"

Joshua spun around. "Yes, I knew. And I told you to leave."

The tears pooled in her eyes. "What are we going to do?" she cried. "Miles, wake up. Wake up already!"

"He's alive, Josie. That's what matters right now," Joshua said. "He's alive."

"No! The explosion, tell me what that was, or I won't go any farther." Joshua had known the explosion was going to happen. There was only one way that was possible. Josie was sure he was involved somehow.

"You will. If you want to save my brother, you'll help me."

Josie thought for a moment and looked at Miles. Her entire body ached from the blast, but it didn't matter. Miles needed her now. "Fine," she said through gritted teeth. "What are we going to do?"

"Help me get him out of here. The garden will be swarming with P&Cs soon and they won't let anyone leave then."

"Then let's go." Josie watched Joshua adjust Miles's arm around his shoulder. She could not stand looking at Joshua now. Not with what he had been a part of.

The low and cadenced chimes of the ark's announcement system rang.

Citizens of November's Dawn. *We regret to inform you of a pressure breach in the bulkheads in the Garden of Tomorrow. If you have been affected by this inconvenience, please remain where you are until we can assess the extent of the affected and the damage done. As always, in the darkness below,* November's Dawn *will provide.*

The chimes sounded again. Josie could hardly believe what she had heard. Everywhere she looked, people were screaming, begging for help. And the OSD—her own mom—had the guts to call it an *inconvenience*.

They were close to an exit now. She could see the reflective metal doors. Two P&C officers stood on either side, their batons drawn and ready.

"There's no way we get past them," Josie whispered.

No sooner had the words left her mouth than a group of survivors stumbled out of the trees and flowers and spilled onto the path. They scrambled toward the exit and officers. Josie heard the P&Cs ordering them to stop, and threatening violent force against the people. But the survivors did not care. After what had just happened, they wanted help. They wanted out.

"This is our chance. Come on," Joshua said.

Together, they fell in line behind the group. Miles's weight shifted onto her shoulders, sending another spike of pain down her leg. She looked over. Joshua was gone.

"Let us through! We need help," survivors cried out.

Delos and Aegean Deck citizens alike begged to be let through, but the officers stood fast. A glass bottle flew past Josie's head. It whipped through the air, shattering on the helmet of a P&C officer. He fell to the ground. The crack of the glass was cut by one silent moment, before the survivors roared and rushed at the remaining officer. Josie looked over; Joshua slipped his brother's arm back over his head. He must have thrown the bottle. There was no time for Josie to object. It was now or never.

Josie and Joshua followed behind the survivors. The officer screamed at them to stop, but he was quickly overtaken by a multitude of clawing hands and fists.

Joshua ran over to the control panel for the metal doors.

It was all Josie could do to stay standing with Miles.

After several seconds, a brief alarm sounded, and the metal doors hissed to life. The crowd cheered as they watched the doors slide free. Josie nearly joined them. Joshua took back some of Miles's weight, and they stumbled into the cramped passageway beyond. Survivors spilled past them and were met immediately by more P&Cs. There were no warnings this time as officers started battering those who tried to break through. People screamed as the officers subdued them, their faces locked in expressions of confusion and terror as the officers turned against them.

"This way!" Joshua shouted as he led them past an officer who was trying to take down two people. Their ravaged and torn gilded tunics reflected their status as Delos Deck citizens.

Joshua led them to an inlet in the passageway. Miles's weight was becoming too much for Josie now. Without wasting a second, Joshua punched at the keypad next to the hatch in the inlet. Josie looked behind them at the fight still going in the passageway. P&Cs were beginning to push the crowd back into the Garden of Tomorrow. The hatch hummed and opened, revealing a dimly lit maintenance corridor. Together with Miles, they fell into the corridor and the hatch closed behind them, sealing them off from the ceaseless screams and fighting. Josie crawled and slouched up against the cold metal wall.

"I can't believe this," she whispered to herself and leaned over and checked Miles. He was still unconscious but the gash above his eye had started to slow its bleed. She put her hand on his chest, if only to feel his faint heartbeat. If only to quiet her own hammering pulse.

Joshua looked down the empty corridor. "Are you okay?"

"What?"

"Are you hurt?" Joshua said. This time with more force.

"What does it matter? Look at Miles, he's the one who needs help."

Joshua leaned down and put his hands on both her shoulders. "Look at me. The adrenaline pumping through you is going to wear off. Soon. If you're hurt, whatever pain you might have now will be unbearable. I need to know if you're okay."

Josie looked down at her open palms. They had cuts all over them and her jumpsuit was ripped in several places. Her eyes tracked down to her feet, her heart dropped as she reached her right foot.

"Oh no," she whispered. A shard of jagged metal, several inches long, was sticking out of her boot. Blood bubbled around it. Looking at it made her stomach turn. She reached down, but Joshua's hand stopped her.

"Don't," he warned. "You'll make it worse."

Josie wiggled her foot, sending splinters of pain up her leg, but the numbness kept the worst of it at bay. "What do I do?"

Joshua glanced at her foot. "Just stay still. A contact is supposed to meet me here. You'll be okay. Just don't move until you absolutely need to."

Josie nodded as pooling tears blurred his features. She relaxed her head back against the wall and tried to steady her breathing. "The explosion. Did you put the bomb there? You owe me why at least."

"I don't owe you anything." Joshua shook his head and looked down.

She looked at him for a moment more and then buried her face in her arms and brought her knees up close to her. Her foot screamed in response, but she was relieved she could still move it. She just could not bear to talk to Joshua anymore. He hardly even seemed to care about what happened to Miles, or himself for that matter.

"Joshua, is that you?" a woman's voice echoed down the corridor.

Without missing a beat, Joshua jumped up and put his back against the wall as he looked toward the voice. "Tai?"

Josie watched the dark silhouette of the woman come closer.

"Yes! I was sent to meet you," she said.

"I've never been so happy to hear your voice, Tai," Joshua said, laughing.

Tai was close now. She pulled back her hood, letting loose a bundle of dark brown hair and oval-shaped eyes. Her sharp features and even sharper eyes gave her a mischievous quality. She looked to be about Joshua's age. Josie guessed early twenties.

Tai stopped and looked at Josie sitting on the ground, then her eyes moved to Miles. "What is this? Who are they? Joshua, this isn't good." Her brow furrowed as she rubbed her neck.

"What—" Josie started but Joshua flashed her a telling look to stop.

Joshua walked up close to Tai, close enough that Josie could not hear what was being said. She cradled Miles's head close while she focused on hearing anything she could. She did not trust Joshua and had no idea what to think about the newcomer. But as terrified as she still was over what had happened in the Garden of Tomorrow, there was an undeniable draw to both Joshua and Tai, not to the persons, but to what they represented. In her whole life, she had never known any real resistance to the OSD's iron grip. Occasional groups grumbled about the way things were, but they were always silenced. But these two were proof that such a group existed, and they were organized and capable. They could help her make Reyes pay for what he did. But her need for answers about the explosion tempered her curiosity. Innocent people had died, and she needed to know why.

She looked over again at Joshua and Tai, as they discussed what to do with Josie and Miles. Josie just prayed Joshua could convince her soon, because Miles needed attention and her foot hurt more with every passing minute.

At last Tai walked over. "I don't know what's going on, but let's get you all out of here."

Joshua gave Josie a knowing smile then bent down to hoist Miles back up. As they did, Miles groaned softly. Josie nearly cried in relief; it was the first sound she had heard him make since the blast. She lifted Miles's arm around her neck, but Tai grabbed her hand.

"Let me," she said as she positioned Miles between her and Joshua. She nodded down towards Josie's injured foot.

"Thank you," Josie whispered and followed close behind. "Where are we going?"

"To Bottom Bays," Joshua answered with a sidelong glance. "You wanted to meet Marcus, now's your chance."

"And Miles? He'll be alright?"

"Aye, there're folks there who know about health and medicine."

"You seem to know a lot about medicine."

Joshua just laughed, a low and charming laugh. "If you want to survive on *November's Dawn*, you learn. That's a lesson we all know. You know that too, I reckon."

Josie needed more. "How are we getting there? I don't see how we'll even make it out of Delos Deck like this?"

"The questions don't stop with you." Joshua stopped and sighed.

"We'll take an elevator," Tai chimed in. She looked at Joshua. "She would see soon enough anyway."

"Yeah, an elevator." Joshua put his hand up, stopping Josie from cutting in. "Yes, the elevators have keypads and yes, we have the codes. Now please, can we just focus on getting there?"

"Fine," Josie scoffed and crossed her arms.

They turned the corner and continued down the maintenance corridor. The steam in the pipes on the walls made it unbearably hot. The clean, filtered air of the Garden of Tomorrow had been such a difference from what the air on Aegean Deck was like, and now that purity was gone.

"Ah, here we are," Tai said as they came to an inconspicuous door and gently put Miles up against the wall. She typed a code into a brightly lit keypad. After several seconds, the hatch opened, revealing the gilded metal cage of an elevator.

"I've never seen an elevator that looked anything like this," Josie said. Ornately laid metalwork encircled the metal cage of the elevator, serving no practical reason other than decoration.

Joshua smirked. "That's because you've never been in an elevator that can also take you to Olympus Deck."

Josie's eyes went wide. "Really? This could take me there?"

"Well, no. Not without the proper access codes. But in theory, yes."

"And there's no chance you have those, huh?"

"I certainly don't."

They spent the rest of the elevator ride in silence. Josie listened as it took them deeper into the bowels of *November's Dawn*. Bottom Bays was a derelict and forgotten part of the ark, even lower than Engineering Bay, that in the past had been used for supply and water storage. She suspected it still was, only now it had gained some unwanted tenants as well. She wondered how many others from Aegean had been forced down here because they slipped too far into poverty. That made her wonder too how Miles had known so much about it. So many had it worse than the life her mom provided them, and Josie never really knew it. But now she felt a responsibility to them. It was only after several minutes that they finally arrived. The bell sounded and an automated voice rang over the speaker.

Welcome to Auxiliary Supply Bay One.

Josie leaned on her right leg sending a spasm through it. She grabbed the cage of the elevator to steady herself and grimaced through the pain.

"We're almost there. You'll be okay." Joshua put a hand on her shoulder. "You're lucky you're wearing those clunky reinforced boots. Any normal shoe and you might not have a foot anymore."

She scoffed. "And if there had been no explosion, I wouldn't have to worry at all."

Joshua blanched. "I was only trying to lighten the mood."

"Save it for when I know your brother is okay."

"Ouch," Tai said.

"No, you're right." Joshua stiffened and slipped Miles's arm back over his neck.

They stepped out of the elevator and into the unwelcoming shroud of darkness of the Auxiliary Supply Bay. The elevator shaft opened into a large room with a low ceiling that went on as far as Josie could see, until her vision was clouded by gloom.

Tai pulled out a flashlight, revealing a tall stack of crates, some metal and some made of something else entirely. Josie realized the crates were what blocked her vision. She reached out and ran her finger across the nearest one.

"What's in these?" she asked.

"Provisions mostly, some spare parts. And that's in the crates we can get into." Tai pointed to one of the unusual crates. "See those? The smooth ones that look like shimmering glass? They're built with holotech and are impenetrable without the right codes. I'd love to see what's in one of them."

Josie watched as Tai scanned the flashlight over a multitude of the shimmering crates. "Why would the OSD just leave them down here? They must be valuable."

Tai shrugged. "We can't get into them. They know it. They're just as safe here as anywhere else on board."

Miles groaned softly, bringing them back to the job at hand.

"Okay, come on. We're close," Tai said. She led them through a maze of crates and shelves piled high with other forgotten relics of the past, eventually coming to a door outlined by a dull red light. Tai turned off the flashlight and pounded a rhythmic sequence on the metal doors. After several seconds, the door opened.

Josie let herself be guided through the room. The room was similar to the one they had just left, but smaller and less cluttered. They passed several more people, each one's face covered with a hood, and each one seemingly shocked by the newcomers in their midst.

Tai led them into another room, this one lined with a handful of cots and storage lockers packed tightly together. Metal trays holding scissors, scalpels, and other small metal tools littered many of the cots. An older woman rushed to them when she saw Miles being carried in.

"Get him over here." She pointed at an empty cot and looked right at Joshua. "What happened?"

"I'm sorry, Doc. We were caught in the explosion. I couldn't just leave him. He's my brother."

"Well enough of that. Let me take a look." Lee started checking Miles's vital signs, then looked at Joshua and Tai. "You two better go explain yourselves. He's not going to like this."

Joshua looked back at Josie. "You'll be okay. I'll be back soon. Doc, she needs help too. Her foot."

Lee leaned over Miles and looked. "Oh, child. Get on the cot over there. You need to get your weight off that leg now."

Josie did as she was told. The pain lessened immediately as she laid down. She brushed the loose strands of hair off her face and concentrated on her breathing. Doc Lee focused on Miles, checking over his body and wrapping white cloth across the gash above his eye. The bruising across Miles's abdomen made Josie cringe.

"Is he going to be okay?" Josie asked. "Please tell me he'll be alright." She was so powerless to do anything to help him and that only made her angrier. She wanted him to be okay more than anything.

Lee thought for a moment. "It's still early, and I need more time to know if he has internal bleeding. I think the blast just knocked him out. He'll have a nasty headache when he wakes, but I think he should be okay." She turned back toward Josie. "You, on the other hand. We need to address your foot." She came close to Josie's cot and started untying the laces. Her hands moved deftly and with purpose, clear signs of her training.

Josie wondered how a doctor had gotten mixed up with this group, but the thought was short lived.

Lee's eyes met Josie's as she grabbed a wad of bandages. "Close your eyes. This will hurt."

"What—" Josie began but a stark cry finished her question as Doc Lee pulled out the shrapnel and pulled off her boot. It was as if a thousand biting blades were slowly tearing at her foot. But not only the skin, tearing at the very bone. Doc Lee cleaned the wound then placed bandages on it. Josie grabbed the sides of the cot and bit down on her tongue to ease the pain.

Lee lifted the bandages slightly once the bleeding had stopped and eyed the wound. "Thank goodness for that boot. This could have been a lot worse." She put a hand on Josie's forehead. "This will take some time to heal, but I should be able to close it. Can you wiggle your toes for me?"

Josie gripped the cot tighter as she looked at her mangled

foot. Relief coursed through her when her toes still listened to her direction.

"Ah good. It doesn't seem any severe nerve or bone damage occurred. We'll need to clean it often or that'll fester." She looked back at Josie and smiled. "But I'm optimistic."

Josie let her head fall back against the cot as Lee finished her work. The sensations of the needlework made her skin crawl. It was all she could do to keep her stomach from turning over. Josie reached out and touched Lee's arm. "Doc, the explosion. This group did it, didn't they?"

Lee looked up from her work. Sadness dampened her eyes. She did not need to give an answer for Josie's suspicions to be confirmed about Joshua and this group. It was clear they were responsible, Josie just needed someone to tell her the truth as to why Miles might die.

"So, here are our wayward guests," a deep voice said from the entrance. "Weary from their journey and cleared for medical care I see."

Josie looked over. Lee turned and started bandaging Josie's foot again as if she heard nothing.

The man walked with a slight hitch in his leg, but still carried himself with unquestionable authority. Muscles pushed against the sleeves of his dark woven shirt. Dark hair brushed over his shoulders and his blue eyes lent a raptor-like gaze to his look. A long scar down the side of his face only added to his intimidating stature. He was older than the others in the group. His demeanor and poise frightened Josie. She scooted up in the cot to not look so helpless. The effort exhausted her.

Lee put a hand on her leg. "Don't move, Josie. This is delicate work."

The man walked over to Miles's cot. He brushed his hand across Miles's arm.

Lee side-eyed him. "I'd ask you to leave me to my work, Marcus. But no doubt you wouldn't listen."

Marcus chuckled, which put Josie more on edge. Everything about this man made her distrust him. "No, I don't think I would," he muttered. "Neither, it seems, do you." He walked nearer to Josie's cot. "Did I not tell you to come to me before treating people? And I meant that for our own people. Why would you think it would be acceptable to treat outsiders without my knowledge?"

Lee stood up. She was a whole head shorter than Marcus, but it was as if two titans were about to rip into each other. "I'm a doctor. I save people. It's what I do. You, on the other hand, are a killer." She nodded toward Josie and Miles. "This happened because of your explosion. Because you would not listen to reason. That's Joshua's little brother, Miles. Your grand statement did this to him."

Marcus breathed deep and lifted his head. "And who are you?"

"Josie. My name's Josie." Her voice squeaked, she coughed to clear her throat.

"A last name, perhaps?" Marcus said with a raised eyebrow.

"Owens," Josie answered. This time with more confidence.

"Ah," Marcus whispered. "The girl who stood up to the OSD. I thought I recognized your face from the holoscreens. Some people hold you in high regard for your defiance They take it as a sign the OSD is weak. There are whispers of change on Aegean." He looked at her for several more seconds, plenty of time for Josie's nerves to take over, then turned back to Lee. "Get them out of here. Now."

Josie's mind raced. The heat from the pendant around her neck, the Heart of the Dawn, radiated through her chest. It was heavier now than ever. "Wait!" She regretted saying it almost immediately.

Both Marcus and Lee looked at her. Lee with confusion and Marcus with open suspicion. "What is it, Josie?" Lee asked.

Josie clutched the Heart of the Dawn through her jump-suit. She knew what happened next could end very badly for her. But she had to. For Miles she had to do it. "After that attack, you can't expect to hide anymore. The OSD will send every P&C officer they have to find you. I have information. Information I'll bet someone like you would love to get their hands on," she said and looked Marcus dead in the eye. Part of her didn't care what he would say. She needed to buy time. If only to get some rest.

Marcus offered only a twisted smile.

CHAPTER ELEVEN_

THE FLUORESCENT LIGHTS glared bright enough overhead that closing his eyes was no relief. Bolts of pain shot through Adrian's body when he tried to raise his arm to block the glare. The unbearable heat from a memory in shades of red, orange, and yellow flashed through his mind—the blast. Adrian knew he was lucky to be alive. When he realized he was in a hospital bed, not bleeding to death in his box at the fetterball match, he closed his eyes again and tried to ease his fixation on the brightness above him—now made worse by the infrequent, but still noticeable, pulse of a flickering bulb. Adrian decided fixing the light was his newest, most pressing priority.

"First Vicar, you're awake." A woman's voice broke the silence.

Adrian opened his eyes to see a young woman rushing toward him. Her rosy cheeks and short curly hair, paired with the white uniform of a nurse, made her seem right out of a historical photo from before the world above flooded.

"I'm Nurse Marge. I need to check on you, First Vicar. May I?" she asked as she pointed to the tubes in his arm.

The particular image he thought of was an old black-and-white photo from the celebrations marking the end of an ancient world war. In the picture, a navy seaman was kissing a nurse. No doubt the sailor had little inclination that his actions in that single, time-stopping moment would become a shining symbol of the strength and resilience of man in the face of unrelenting adversity. It was a reminder to future generations that at every turn and at any cost, man has faced the storm and set his destiny ever higher. That is what Adrian remembered it for.

Marge saw his smile and chuckled. "What is it?"

"Nothing, you just reminded me of something from long ago. A photo of a nurse you have an uncanny resemblance to."

The torrent of flame and glass from the explosion roared in Adrian's mind like an ill omen. He carried the weight of the last of humanity, all that was left of the strength and fortitude that had taken man to the heavens, then deep into the watery darkness below. The legacy of human existence had led them to this moment, and by some miracle or terrible joke, he, Adrian Frost, a boy who had been taken under the wing of one of the greatest visionaries of their time, was at the helm of mankind's destiny.

"What will I be remembered for?" Adrian asked as he stared straight ahead.

"I'm afraid I don't understand," Marge said. She looked more concerned by the second. "You are our First Vicar, sir. You lead us in the darkness."

Adrian could see her worry plainly as she clasped her hands tighter together, but it was enough. This week of celebration on *November's Dawn* would not be their end. Adrian vowed he would not let the navigational problems be their final undoing. There would be no celebrated photos, no storied tales of their desperate fight to endure against the crushing darkness outside, but he would remember, even if no one else did.

The light above him flickered again, leaving its impression dancing in his vision. "I want that bulb fixed immediately."

Marge smiled again and turned toward him. "I'll have someone take a look."

Adrian calmed his voice and relaxed. "Call for Commandant Reyes as well. I must see him."

Nurse Marge nodded and finished her work. She slipped a new bag of fluids on the rack and logged her changes before leaving the room. Adrian could not decide what he wanted more, information from Reyes about the explosion or the light above him to be ripped out.

Several minutes passed before Commandant Reyes stepped into the room. His eyes scanned around and took in everything: medical equipment, shiny chrome cabinets, and holoscreens. Then Reyes's gaze flicked up to the faulty light and finally to Adrian himself. He saluted and stood at attention. His left hand was bandaged and wrapped tight.

Adrian waved off the salute. "I see you made it relatively unscathed. Tell me you have information."

Reyes nodded. His hard eyes and weathered face fixed straight at the First Vicar. "A contained explosion from a small, portable device was the source. It had been placed close to an inboard joint on the bulkhead. The blast knocked loose the fetterball sector and one of the outside legs was disabled for some time, but the blast was not powerful enough to fully pierce our hull. Director Clarke had the wit to call it an accidental pressure breach. Delos and Olympus seem to be satisfied with that."

Adrian nodded. "I must remember to thank Director Clarke for his quick thinking."

Reyes moved closer to Adrian's medical bed. "First Vicar, whoever did this had intimate details of our schematics. Schematics that are closely restricted." His voice trailed off, giving Adrian time to make his own conclusions.

"You believe this was the work of Hades Fist?"

"I do," Reyes stiffened. "I told you I believed someone was helping them. This only confirms it. If we move swiftly, we can still disrupt them before they attack again. I need your authorization to access the weapons."

"The weapons? Commandant, surely you have not forgotten our last discussion. I'm not so sure of this vendetta." Adrian sighed. He was responsible for every person on *November's Dawn*, even the ones who questioned the OSD. Sometimes the shepherd could be the greatest source of his flock's worries and fears. Adrian did not doubt the commandant's loyalty, only his ability to check his fervor on his quest to root out the wolves hidden in the herd.

"You were targeted. You hesitated, and now the people have paid the price. You should not make the same mistake again."

"Do you have evidence that I was specifically targeted?"

"Does it truly matter?" Reyes said coldly.

Adrian shifted and met the commandant's eyes. Reyes's words surprised him, and under normal circumstances Adrian would not have tolerated it, but he could not deny the truth. He had hesitated before and if Reyes's information was correct, that hesitation had cost him the lives of citizens. "How many died in the explosion?"

Reyes looked straight ahead. "Sixty-eight, First Vicar. With many more wounded."

"Then we have sixty-eight souls seeking absolution. You are authorized to use emergency force against the group known as Hades Fist."

"The Directors could prove problematic."

Adrian rubbed his neck. "These radicals might target their companies next. No, the Directors will not dare fight me on this."

Commandant Reyes saluted again, and a faint smile

crossed his thin lips. It was one of the few times Adrian had seen the man smile. The commandant would stop at nothing to see the threat dealt with. Adrian could not risk another attack jeopardizing his work to fix the navigational problems plaguing *November's Dawn.* He'd deal with the overzealous commandant after the emergency had been handled.

"I will begin the preparations immediately. I will find these traitors," Reyes said and saluted.

"I will expect a report shortly. One more thing, I saw a girl that looked like Josie Owens right before the explosion. Check and see if she's among the dead. I pray the information she had was not lost. We cannot allow it to be unaccounted for." Adrian waved him off.

Authorization to use holotech weapons by the peace-and-compliance officers had been done only once before, in the chaotic and dangerous days when the last remnants of humanity boarded *November's Dawn.* Cornelius Graham had made the call. Citizens of every country had been selected in a lottery to board the ark in an ordered manner. Yet when the world rapidly flooded and anarchy ruled, everyone felt the same terror and some unauthorized individuals tried to board. The people of *November's Dawn* unified in that moment and the weapons soon proved unnecessary after launch.

Usually, security batons were more than enough to keep the peace. Now, Adrian had just authorized the use of electro-magnetic particle rifles against his own people. The holorifles, as they were commonly known due to the dazzling display of light they produced, could stop a threat quickly but at a terrible price. There was little left of those they were used against.

Several more moments passed, time spent convincing himself he had done the right thing. He gripped the railing of the bed and sat up. On a chair lay a fresh set of vestments and boots. No doubt his old clothes had been destroyed. He combed his fingers through his hair and breathed deep before pulling the medical tube from his arm and ripping off the other monitors. No more time could be wasted.

Reyes was right on one count. Someone was leaking secrets. Someone who knew too much. He could not risk word about the navigational failure getting out. The people would erupt into a flurry of chaos and fear if they found out *November's Dawn* was walking straight toward the deepest trench in the world when it was supposed to be turning away from it. Maintaining order, even the perception of order, was his primary concern, as it always was.

After Adrian dressed, he took one last look around the room. After all he had done for the people, the thought they would turn against him infuriated him. The light flickered again. His eyes fixed on a large glass beaker. One final moment of thought passed before he picked up the beaker and hurled it at the flickering light. Both smashed into a shower of glass and sparks. The crash ushered in the officers from outside his room.

"First Vicar, are you okay?" George, one of his personal officers asked. A corner of the room was now dark, but he scanned the rest quickly, looking for any threat.

"Ah, yes, George. The light broke," Adrian said dryly and left the room. The two P&C officers followed. Adrian buttoned his cuffs as he addressed them. "We're going to the broadcast station. I have an announcement to make to every person aboard this ark."

Adrian's boots sank into the plush carpet that laid over the calacatta gold marble flooring. They were in the suite of rooms and offices marked for personal use of the First Vicar and he had spent much of his life in these passageways, although admittedly not in the medical suite he had just left. He took a mental note of changes he wanted to make.

Something about almost dying pulled him to truly notice

the exquisite beauty that was built into Olympus Deck and much of *November's Dawn*. Cornelius Graham was a man of immense appreciation for the finer things in life and as such, Graham's former quarters, the rooms Adrian now stood in, were magnificent beyond compare. Ionic-style pillars stood every five paces along the sides of the corridor with inlets that housed some priceless statue or work of art. Graham had been fascinated in life by the mystery and glory of civilizations long past. Adrian had always been more interested in the reality and trials of the present. He supposed that was why he never cared to look twice at any of Graham's treasures.

The old photo from the great war flashed in his mind again. Adrian stopped walking and stared at a small carving of a rather round and undetailed woman. But in the moment, he understood Graham's interest in the small carving, the ornate pillars, and the haunting statues. It was for the very same reason Adrian took so much meaning from the old photo. Each one symbolized the remarkable ability of humans to build, to design, to create, and to flourish, wherever they might find themselves. They were all symbols of man's perseverance throughout the ages.

The passageway outside of his suite was less splendid but all Olympus Deck passageways were wide, with high ceilings and metal floors. All the paneling was white and clean, pale light illuminated every space. But the walls were something breathtaking to behold. Running along each side were large transparent tubes, filled with water and all manner of aquatic life and terrain. Adrian watched tiny shrimp bounce through the water, surrounded by the shimmering hues of fish in every color imaginable. Coupled with the rows of holoscreens and signs on the walls, the fish highways created a lively show for anyone passing by. He was vaguely aware of the time and expense it took to maintain such an intricate display. The biome had to be carefully observed and controlled or the natural order would collapse. Adrian had once considered using those resources for more pressing needs on the other decks, but the Directors had quickly put down his plans. The fish highways were an integral part of society on Olympus Deck and removing them would be a sign of trouble. So, they remained, all for the amusement of Olympus Deck citizens.

A couple citizens, dressed in the finest clothing their station could buy, stood whispering in a group. Their ensembles imitated the most exotic and intricate schemes found amongst the aquatic animals in the ocean. They stepped back as Adrian passed, flanked on either side by his guards. Each head bowed slightly to him.

"In the darkness below, *November's Dawn* will provide," one man said in a high-pitched voice. A feathery purple plume dipped from his hat as he bowed his head.

Adrian still felt woozy from the explosion but he did his best to conceal it. He could not allow others to think he was weak. After a few more minutes of walking, he saw the bright signs above the large double doors leading to the broadcast station. The signs warned against unauthorized access to the area. Even those on Olympus had limits to where they could go. Besides the bridge, the broadcast station was the central communications hub. Officers flanked the door twenty-four hours a day and only a handful of people had access. Adrian could address the entire ark from it.

The officers opened the door when they saw Adrian coming. The bright lights of endless holoscreens and the ever-present whirring of computers greeted him. The station was a suite of several rooms housing all the equipment and machinery necessary for broadcasting throughout the ark. Adrian's eyes fixed on one of the smaller rooms. It was cave-like and sparsely furnished, except for a cushioned chair and a side table where a single microphone stood.

One of the broadcast technicians looked up from the holo-screen he was focused on. "First Vicar!" the young man exclaimed and jumped up. "I'm terribly sorry, nobody told us you were coming."

"Nobody knew I was coming," Adrian said. He looked around the room again. "Where is Serena Owens?"

"Oh Serena? Of course, of course. She left a little while ago. Sleeping in the bunk room, First Vicar. She hasn't had a moment to spare." He waved a hand behind him. "None of us have really. Not since the explosion, well, pressure breach."

Adrian's brow twitched. The rumors were already begin-ning. "The pressure breach was a terrible accident. But we will fix the problem, you have my word."

Relief flooded the young man's face, and his shoulders visibly relaxed. "Thank you, First Vicar. I don't know what we would do without your leadership. In the darkness below, *November's Dawn* will provide."

"Good man," Adrian said. "I am going to make an announcement. Find Serena. I must speak with her."

The young man nodded excitedly. "Of course. Right away, First Vicar."

Adrian turned to the other technicians in the room. "Pre-pare an all-ark broadcast, holoscreens as well."

Each nodded and started the necessary work. Adrian stepped into the small room with the lone chair and table. He looked into a mirror on one side. Dark circles ringed his eyes. He looked aged and weary, but he supposed he was. It was unusual for him to make such a broadcast, but he had no choice. The people needed to be reassured after the explosion, reassured that it was only a mechanical failure, and they were not in danger. They needed the hope the celebration of the

Great Turning was supposed to bring. But there were those among them who wanted to take that hope away. He wished he had more time to prepare. Outside the glass windows, a technician was counting down on his fingers. The fiery explosion flashed through Adrian's mind with the unknown faces of those who had died. His own face among them. The celebration was supposed to be a time of hope, but he would not let the terrorists destroy his order.

No matter the cost.

The chimes sounded and the broadcast began.

"Citizens of *November's Dawn*. I speak to you now not as the First Vicar, but as a fellow citizen. A citizen who is worried. A citizen who is anxious. A citizen who is scared. That is what the explosion that rocked the Garden of Tomorrow did last night. It stole our peace. But it was not, as you were led to believe, an accidental pressure breach. No, citizens, it was the detestable actions of the angry and disgruntled among you."

He had done it now. Adrian's gaze flicked toward the glass panels and the technicians beyond. Each one looked at him with renewed expressions of confusion from his revelation.

"The rogue group known as Hades Fist attacked you. They took your safety and your courage. They took your lives. They took your hope. But I promise to each one of you, I will restore your faith. I will restore your safety. I will bring these traitors to justice. I know your fear and your worry, and that is why I have authorized the use of deadly force in the fight against this radical group. Hades Fist will be crushed, and we will lay down these weapons when this crisis is ended. I implore you to remain strong, remain vigilant, and report suspicious behavior you see. The celebration of the Great Turning will continue and take on a new meaning. For now, when we turn into the new unknown, we will also be leaving behind the wreckage of those among us who would see anarchy rule. As always, citizens, in the darkness below, *November's Dawn* will provide."

The chimes sounded again, and the holoscreens dimmed. He leaned back in the chair and exhaled. He had not planned on revealing the terrorist group operating on *November's Dawn*. It would have been easier to go with the story Director Clarke had spun. But now there would be no hiding. Commandant Reyes was putting their plans into action. As much as it pained him to admit, Reyes had been right. His whole life, Adrian had preferred to play the game from the shadows, calculating every move and action, but sometimes one had to get their hands dirty. He prayed the threat would soon end. If only everyone aboard knew of the true danger just days away, but they did not and never could.

A knock came at the door. "First Vicar?" It was the young technician from before.

"Come in," Adrian said. He straightened himself in the chair.

The young man came in slowly and closed the door. He had an odd sense of determination. Adrian wondered what on earth for. "Well, I heard what you said. And I just want to say, we're with you, sir." He turned and pointed at the holoscreens in the broadcast room. "The people, sir. They're cheering your name, all over Olympus Deck. They want to help."

Adrian smiled. "And so they will. The OSD and peace-and-compliance officers will need all the help you can give."

"You can count on it." The technician beamed; it was clear he had never spoken so candidly with someone who commanded so much authority. "Serena is on her way back now."

Adrian nodded. "Send her in when she arrives and make sure any recording equipment is disabled as well."

The technician jumped toward the door to do what he was

told, all the while still smiling from talking with the First Vicar. Folks had always acted differently with Adrian since he was elevated to First Vicar. It was as if he now possessed some divine insight over them and their souls, so they were eager to do what they thought he wanted. That was of course untrue, but Adrian did indeed have authority over their physical selves, so he didn't try to stop their belief.

The distinctive hissing of the outer doors to the broadcast station pulled him out of his thoughts. He watched Serena Owens step into the station and look directly toward him. The room he had made the announcement from was where she usually worked. Adrian knew Serena took great pride in the way she presented and composed herself, so he was shocked to see the state of disarray she was in now. Her long blonde hair was somewhat tangled and disheveled, and her clothes seemed to be the same ones from yesterday's broadcast, but her face carried the same grace it always did. She had probably been working since the explosion the night before. Nobody looked their best right now. Adrian stood as she entered the room.

"Adrian," she said in a hushed tone. "What is it? Did you find my daughter?"

For a split-second Adrian thought she was talking about her younger daughter, Rose. There had been a report that his officers had lost track of Rose right before the bombing, but he did not have the heart to tell Serena. He admired her pale blue eyes. Even with a clear lack of sleep, they were as sharp as ever. In her role as the voice of *November's Dawn* the two of them had become very close and he relied on her a great deal. But now, nothing was easy. Adrian shook his head slowly, taking a gamble on what she might know. "No, I'm sorry." He stepped closer to her. "I'll find her, Serena."

Serena took his hand and shuffled out of view from the

technicians. "You promised, Adrian. You promised you would find her and keep her safe."

"I know. And I will." Adrian stiffened. "A task that would be made much easier if I had any idea what she knows. They found the old engineer with a broken holomessage. You're sure you don't know what the message was?"

She looked at the ground and sniffed. "I don't. You don't know how much it hurts me to say I don't know. I feel like I don't know anything about her. After Dominic's accident, we just . . . Well, we just grew apart. I had to work more than ever, and he was always closer with her than I was anyway. I never knew how to connect with her, and she was more comfortable with Felix and the other engineers. After a while I stopped trying." She looked up and her eyes hardened again. "I'm sorry. I didn't mean to carry on."

Adrian gently touched her shoulder. "It's okay," he said quietly. "But that's why I asked you here. Things are happening on *November's Dawn*. Things I can't seem to explain or find the cause of. Serena, I know the pain you bear, and I've done what I can to see you taken care of since the accident, but we need to talk about your husband. We need to talk about Dom."

"Okay," Serena said. "But first I want Rose brought to Olympus. After the attack in the Garden, they won't hide in the shadows anymore. What if they target me because of my connections to Olympus? My daughter is not safe with a few officers in Aegean."

Adrian hesitated but nodded his agreement. Those pieces were already moving.

CHAPTER TWELVE

"You shouldn't have told Marcus anything, Josie. Now he thinks you know something valuable, and he's going to want it too," Miles said in a hushed voice. He sighed and put his head back. "It's just we hardly know what to do with what your dad told you. The more people who know, the more dangerous it all gets."

Josie paced back and forth across the small cabin and looked back at Miles on the cot with bandages wrapped around his chest and stomach, still resting from the explosion. She was just thankful he was finally awake and she had been able to sleep for a few hours. Her foot throbbed when she put her weight on it, but it hurt a whole lot less than when she sat for a while. "You don't get it, Miles. I didn't have a choice. You were unconscious; I couldn't walk. He was going to kick us out, or worse, turn us in, if I didn't give him something. I did the best I could."

Miles shook his head. "I know, I know. I'm sorry. I don't know what I would have done if the situation was flipped. I just don't trust him."

"And you think I trust him?" Josie asked. "I told him as

little as I could without seeming like I was lying. All he knows is that *November's Dawn* has more secrets than the OSD wants people to know. I'm sure he filled in the rest with his own schemes."

Miles stretched. "After the attack in the garden, they declared war on the OSD. Whatever he's planning frightens the lights out of me, but at least right now we're safe."

"Not for long. You didn't hear the First Vicar's announcement. He's authorized all means to find and destroy this group, these people." Josie waved her hand toward the rest of Bottom Bays.

"I didn't mean we should stay," Miles replied. "As soon as Doc Lee clears me, we should get out of here."

"Absolutely," Josie said. "Once I find out how to access Olympus Deck and the bridge."

"No. It's too dangerous to stay. And what if you get caught snooping around? Josie, I think Marcus would kill someone if he caught them stealing from him. We don't know anything about these people."

"You're right," she smiled. "But I know someone who does."

Miles looked at her for a moment before catching on. "Nope, no way. Joshua got us into this mess and whatever happened at the Garden of Tomorrow, he did it. He might be my brother but he's not the same brother I knew. What about your mom? She works in Olympus. She must know how to get there."

Josie shrugged. "She gets escorted by P&Cs to work. Besides, she would never help me. We don't exactly see eye to eye."

"What do you mean?" Miles looked determined.

Josie shook her head as memories bubbled up. In the years after her dad died, her mom had seemed to accept the status quo and the way the upper decks treated Aegean. And that was something Josie never understood. She remembered her parents trying to help everyone, no matter where they came from. She remembered feeling proud of that. Then the feeling was gone. Josie had decided it was because her mom was scared to do what was right. But after seeing how hard life could become, maybe her mom had no other choice to protect her family.

"Look, we can't leave until you can walk. That gives me time to figure things out. And we've talked about this. I have a chance at fixing all this and I'm taking it."

Miles sunk into the cot. His voice was low. "How do we know your dad is even right? I mean, who's to say we go back to the surface and things wouldn't be the same way they are now? With the same people in power who always have been?"

Josie frowned. She wanted to say in the end it would be okay, and they would be safe. But she didn't know that for sure. She really didn't know a lot about what she was supposed to be doing and wondered herself whether her dad was right to give her the message and the Heart of the Dawn.

"I don't know, Miles. But if I don't try, then what's the point? Olympus, the OSD, the companies, none of that will change if I don't try. Maybe there are other ways to create change, but I don't see them. At least nothing that wouldn't take years. And we don't have that kind of time. They've forgotten about everyone on Aegean. I think, it's time they heard our voices." She knew those words were for herself as much as Miles.

The thought of her dad being wrong was too much to bear. If he thought the surface was the only option, then he must have tried everything else. For her, it was the surface or life in prison, or worse.

Miles gave a weak smile. "I know things need to change. I'm just worried. All I wanted to do was keep you safe and look at us." He waved his hand all around the cabin then at himself. "Look at me? We're running for our lives, and I don't see an end to that. I would have died if it weren't for you. All of this is just so wrong."

Josie stared at him for a couple seconds. The familiar feeling of butterflies and nerves grew. What Miles described was all too familiar. She sat on the edge of Miles's cot and looked at the ground. "I think you're forgetting how brave you've been. You're the one who saved me from Reyes. You've been there for your mom when no one else was. You're the only one I can trust at a time I've never been more scared. I did what you would have done for me, that's all."

"Yeah, I guess." He looked away. A thin wet line glistened down his cheek.

Josie touched his leg, trying to be caring but it was just clumsy. Miles met her gaze, and they sat in the moment for a few more heartbeats. Her face flushed with a now familiar heat. "Okay, so it's settled. I'll be back in a little bit." She stood and headed for the door.

"Josie?" Miles called. She looked back. His mouth opened but closed just as fast. "Thank you, for saving me, I mean. I haven't had a chance to say it."

She smiled. "Always." The lever turned and she stepped out. The passageway was decrepit with pipes and wires covering everything.

A small toolbox was left on the ground ahead. Wrenches and other tools scattered around it. Near the bottom of the wall a steady burst of steam billowed from a small pipe. Someone gave up on trying to fix the leak. She took a deep breath and knelt next to the pipe. Felix's teaching guided her. As an engineering apprentice, she had seen this issue countless times and understood immediately why the last person gave up. It was a simple fix in the end but not an obvious one.

She removed a small access plate on the wall behind the pipe with a screwdriver. All the steam pipes had emergency shutoff controls spaced out throughout the ark. It never made much sense to Josie, but she supposed it was so just a small area could be shut off if needed. Whatever the case was, because of this, the electrical circuits that controlled the valves sometimes shorted and caused the steam to build up. Josie laughed to herself, knowing how much time the last person must have spent trying to patch the pipe when the valve was still closed.

She gently maneuvered her hands in the access panel. Felix had always pushed safety above all else, especially when working with a current. The circuit was black, a short had burnt out the fuses. The toolbox had a few extra. A familiar grinding sound signaled the shutoff valve opening as soon as the new fuses were in. After a few more moments, the steam faded away.

"Nice work, little fox," she whispered to herself.

"Tai worked for hours trying to figure that out. And here you come, fixing it in just minutes," Joshua's voice echoed from behind her. "Impressive work."

"Oh this? This was nothing," Josie said quickly with a flushed face. "Is there something you need? Or are you just here to be a pain."

"I was coming to see Miles. I also wanted to check on you."

"Well, I'm fine and Miles will be too. No thanks to you."

"No thanks to me? That's not how I remember it." Joshua turned and scratched at a paint speck on the wall.

"Is the fiery explosion slipping your mind?" Josie asked. "You nearly killed him."

Joshua's face hardened and he stared at her, but it was like he was looking right through her, like she was nothing. "You don't know what you're talking about."

"Don't I? It seems to me this group is a bunch of killers. That's it."

"We're killers?" Joshua scoffed and hit his palm against the wall. "You grew up in Aegean. Tell me, Josie, did it seem like life was good? Did it seem like things were how they should be? No. Everyone struggles. Nobody has enough. My mother is going to die because they do not value her life enough to authorize the treatment she needs. She deserves better. The OSD and Directors could care less if we all died. Meanwhile, only a couple hundred meters up the ark, there's a place that has everything. Enough for everyone on *November's Dawn* and more. Don't try to call me a killer when they've been killing us for years."

Josie stayed quiet, feeling somewhat guilty for going at him so hard, but she could not forget the screams from that night at the Garden of Tomorrow. No matter what justification Joshua gave her, she could not forgive that. There were better ways. "Your mom got some medicine, you know. I don't know how, but Miles got some for her. You might know if you ever went to see her."

Joshua's face scrunched up. "What? How? Nobody gets medicine like that. How would Miles?" His eyes darted toward the door to the cabin Miles was in.

"If you talked to your family, you might know." Josie never dropped her gaze from him.

He stopped before the hatch but did not turn back. "I'm doing the best I can, you know. That's all we can do, right? Try to make the world a better place?" He scoffed and glanced around. "Even if the world is nothing but metal and glass." He stepped into the cabin before Josie could say anything.

Josie leaned her head against the wall and thought about what Joshua had said. He was fighting for what *November's Dawn* had the potential to be, for the future she carried close to her chest in the Heart of the Dawn necklace. The thought crossed her mind to tell Joshua about her dad's message; she felt he would agree with her effort to return to the surface. But Miles's warnings crept back up. With every person she told, the danger to her and Miles grew. And even if she wanted to trust Joshua, something told her not to. Not yet. Once she figured out how to get to Olympus it would be different.

Folks would not go along with the upper deck's oppression anymore if they knew the truth. She could help create a new government where every voice was heard and there was no place for people like the OSD and Commandant Reyes. Then they would all be safe. Then Felix's death would be avenged. She sighed as the fatigue set in and tried to untangle the knots in her hair. It had been days since her last shower, and she could feel the dirt on her. She decided Doc Lee might be able to help or maybe give her some soap at least.

It took Josie the better part of an hour to find her way back to the makeshift infirmary. Not quite remembering where it was and wanting to avoid any unwanted attention made the trip much longer than it should have been, but she was thankful to have been granted some freedom in the Hades Fist headquarters. She knocked on the cold door of the infirmary.

"Enter," Lee's voice returned from the other side.

Josie took one last look behind her and then stepped into the room. The room was dark, not like when she had been in it before, and it did not seem like anyone was being treated.

"What's your injury?" Lee called from a small open hatch set off from the infirmary proper.

"I don't exactly have any injury."

"Then why are you here?" Lee's response was sharp, and she poked her head through the open hatch. "Oh! Josie dear! I'm sorry, I was expecting someone else. Or preparing for some ghastly injury."

Josie picked up some small scissors sitting on an empty cot and fiddled with them. "Do injuries on missions happen often? I don't know much about Hades Fist but from what I saw at the Garden of Tomorrow . . . Well, you must be busy."

Doc Lee eyed her for a moment then her shoulders sagged slightly. "No, it wasn't always like what you saw the other night. We used to have much more idealistic intentions. Hades Fist has always been about the collective good for all on *November's Dawn*, not just those on Olympus. That's why we were different from the OSD and Directors." She sighed and leaned her hands against a cabinet. "I'm not so sure anymore."

Josie ran her fingers through her hair, the knots still held fast. Her earlier interest in finding soap seemed very small and unimportant now. "Lee, I need your help."

"Of course, is it your foot? I can get a clean bandage on there."

Josie shook her head. "It's about everything going on. I think I have a way to save everyone. Only without the bombs and the chaos."

Lee put her finger up to her lips and came close. "Is this what you told Marcus?"

Josie sighed. "I told him some, but not all. I had to, or he was going to throw us out."

"I know, I know." Lee put her finger up again and beckoned Josie to follow her into the other room. She closed the hatch behind them. "I'm sorry for that, Josie, but we can't risk being overheard. The things happening now are unlike anything I can remember. The lower decks have always had to fight for more, but the tension is different now. I fear we are one step away from something terrible."

"What do you mean?" Josie asked. Lee's face was so close Josie could feel the warmth of her breath.

"I don't know what you told Marcus, but he flew into a rage

afterward." She laughed nervously. "The First Vicar's announcement didn't help either. Normally, he can be reasoned with but in recent months his temper has grown. If you can believe it, Marcus was once the idealistic one; now he thinks of only vengeance." Lee smiled sadly as if a fleeting memory faded before her. "This fury was something else entirely. I will say this, I believed in Dom Owens. He was one of the best men I've ever known, and I trust in his daughter."

"You knew my dad?"

Lee stepped back. "Yes, Dom was the one with the original idea for Hades Fist. We weren't called that then, mind you, but the idea was the same. Both your parents were part of it. You didn't know?"

Josie shook her head. She never knew. She pictured her parents where she was now, fighting the same fight. Her chest tightened so much she thought she would pass out. None of which Lee missed.

"Oh dear." She reached for Josie's hand. "I'm sorry. I thought your mom would have told you about it all."

A familiar dryness squeezed Josie's throat. She wiped her cheeks, the last thing she wanted was for Doc Lee to see her crying. She was tired of crying. She wanted to be strong.

Lee pulled her into a firm hug. "It's okay, Josie. It's okay to feel."

Josie sniffed and pulled back. Her mom never told her anything about this double life her parents lived. No doubt to protect her, but it still hurt. "It's just, for years I knew nothing and wanted so badly to know more about my dad."

Lee pushed a lock of Josie's hair back behind her ear and put her palms on her cheeks. "Take it from me, Josie, as someone who has dealt with her share of grief, it's never fair. And it never makes sense. The only thing you can do is keep going. I know your dad would be so proud of you. You remind me of him so much, and every day I wish that accident hadn't taken him. I was so thankful we didn't lose Marcus to it as well."

That sent a whole new tingle of dread through Josie. Her dad's words from the holomessage whispered to her. He had been followed. Someone had been after him. It was no accident. Lee apparently didn't know that either.

A curious and terrifying thought crossed her mind that sent a cold shiver through her body. Marcus had been with her dad. He had to know the truth of what happened.

Could he have even been involved? No. She pushed the thought from her head. She needed to take things one step at a time.

Lee shook her gently. "Josie? Josie, are you okay?"

"Yeah. Sorry." Josie looked down. "I was just thinking about my dad."

"I know," Lee said in a soothing voice. "Now tell me, what is it you need my help with?"

Soap and getting clean were the last things on her mind now. Josie went over her plan in her head one last time, fearing that Lee would ask her questions she could not answer. The goal was simple enough, get to the bridge and figure out what the Heart of the Dawn necklace was for, but the exact details were vague. She hoped Doc Lee would have some better thoughts.

"Well, I've been thinking," she said. Lee looked at her expectantly. "I need to get onto Olympus. Can you help me?"

"A tall order," Lee mused.

Josie scrunched her face. "Tai said something about one of the elevators being able to go to Olympus Deck, but only with the right access codes."

Lee smiled, the sort of smile that sent even more questions through Josie's mind. "You think I can help you get the codes. Maybe Hades Fist has them stashed away somewhere?"

"Well, yes. I mean, I've gone over it in my head. Why would Marcus possibly order an attack if he didn't have something else in mind? And it doesn't take a reactor scientist to know change only comes from Olympus Deck, no matter who's driving it."

"You have a sound head on your shoulders, Josie Owens. Just like your dad. He would get so worked up about his plans and ideas . . ." Lee stopped and looked down her nose at Josie. "But I'm sorry, there's nothing to do. Marcus will never give you his ticket out of Bottom Bays, nor does he trust me enough to share his plans anymore. I reckon he has a set of codes and maps too, only I can't think of a way you can get them. At least not a way that isn't much too dangerous."

Josie sat a little straighter to meet Doc Lee's stare. "You say I have a good head on my shoulders? You don't know the half of it. I'm not giving up. I'm doing this for my family, for Miles, for Felix. For every one of us on *November's Dawn*. This system has to end, and if you won't help me, I'll find people who will."

Lee sat still but for the slightest twitch in the corner of her mouth. "It's clear I have underestimated you," she said. "And if I have, I'll bet others have too, that could give us an edge. What about Miles? Your family? Have they accepted the danger this path brings as well?"

Josie had already thought of that. "Miles is with me. I know he is. And my family? Well, my mom made her choices, just as I will make mine."

Lee nodded. "If Marcus does have access codes, they will be in his cabin. Where he conducts his business from. But I don't have access to his cabin."

"Who does?"

"Joshua. He's one of the few Marcus trusts."

Josie cursed under her breath. "Is there anyone else that can get me in?"

"I'm afraid not," Lee said. "Joshua is young and ambitious and not without his shortcomings, but he has a good heart, and he will help. And I have already asked him to come here for another matter. That can wait though."

"Well then I guess this is our best bet." Josie slumped down in the chair.

"You'll have to leave as soon as you get the codes. If Marcus finds out while you're still here . . ." Lee shuddered. "Well, let's just say it will be much better if you're gone."

Josie could only imagine what Marcus was capable of. She had no doubt he was a man who would do whatever he thought necessary to protect what he wanted. And she was pretty sure that whatever Marcus wanted wasn't what she wanted too. Josie shivered and pulled her arms together. Her nerves grew by the minute.

"What if Marcus finds out you helped me?" Josie wasn't sure she wanted to hear the answer.

Lee chuckled. "Marcus and I have been in this together for a long time. He does things his way, and I do mine. Don't worry about me, Josie. I can handle myself."

Three knocks came at the door to the infirmary. Lee opened it. Josie ducked behind a partition and waited for what was to come.

"Doc, good to see you," Joshua's voice echoed. "I don't see a reason for this visit though. I'm not hurt."

"A blast like that can have all sorts of effects on the body, seen or unseen. And Marcus ordered it anyway."

"Can we make this quick, Doc? Marcus has me running all over the place."

"It'll take as long as it takes."

Josie figured that was her que. At least, it would be now or never. She stepped out from behind the partition. Joshua's shirt sleeve was pulled high as Doc Lee pressed a needle to his arm.

Joshua sighed. "I should have figured she'd be here."

"Hear her out, Joshua. And keep still or I might stick you in the wrong spot."

Josie stopped about a meter away. "Look, it's clear you don't want me here."

"You just don't understand—"

"Let her talk," Lee said.

Josie looked back and forth between them. They were clearly very comfortable with each other. "As I was saying," Josie said, annoyed now, "you don't want me here. I don't want to be here. Help me get what I need, and I'll be out of your hair."

"Won't this be good," Joshua muttered. Nevertheless, a stern look from Lee quieted him all the same.

"You talked about access codes to Olympus on the elevator. I need them."

He looked from Josie, to Lee, and back to Josie before frowning. "You can't be serious?" he said. "I mean, look at her. Whatever she has planned might fly in the lower decks. But on Olympus? They would spit her out in no time. Besides, I don't have the codes. What do you think I can do?"

Lee leaned in close. "Joshua, this is not a laughing matter. This young lady needs help. I expect you'll be giving it."

Joshua met her gaze. "You're wrong if you think I'm going to go against Marcus."

Josie let out her pent-up breath. There was never a good chance of getting Joshua to help, but the disappointment still stung.

"Oh, I think you will," Lee said with a knowing smile. "Or Marcus might find out about the supplies you and your friends have been lifting out of our stores. Quite a little operation you've made yourself."

He sat quietly for a moment. Then a sly smile crossed his lips. "Okay, fine. This could work. Good thing Marcus is gone right now." He briskly walked toward the door and looked back. "Well? You coming? Or is there some other ridiculous demand?"

Speechless, Josie looked at Lee.

"I've been saving that card for a while now. Make it worth it. Go," Lee said and smiled.

"Thank you," Josie whispered as she ran past the doctor.

Joshua caught up quickly and ran ahead, leading her to a large supply room. "Follow me and be quiet."

The moment she got the codes from him, she was going to Olympus. If Miles stayed here, he would be safe—at least safer than going up against the OSD. Josie knew he would be hurt by her leaving, but she could live with that. She couldn't live with him getting hurt again, or worse.

The crates in the supply room eventually gave way to a derelict passageway that looked like almost every other one in the lower decks. Only this one had almost no lights on.

"Where are we?" Josie asked. Her foot was throbbing again but she wouldn't let Joshua see her pain.

Joshua leaned on his knees and pointed down the passageway. "Marcus's cabin is down there. The crates make it harder to get to; he thinks it makes it safer," he said, as he slipped a communicator in his pocket.

Josie hadn't seen him holding it before but didn't have the interest to ask after the run. "Just get on with it."

Joshua bowed. "Of course, this way." This time he walked, which Josie was silently thankful for. The last couple days had been exhausting. It amazed her she was even still able to function at all. Joshua pulled out a flashlight as they went deeper and deeper in the passageway. The air was starting to turn colder as well.

"Are you sure this is the right way?" She tried to keep her voice steady, even if she could feel the apprehension building in her head.

"Feeling a bit of nerves?" Joshua asked. "We're going the right way," he said dryly and shined the flashlight onto a hatch off the passage. "Here we are." Punching in the access code, the hatch groaned and opened. "We only have a couple minutes now, hurry."

Josie followed him into the cabin. It was dark and cold. A solitary metal desk sat in the middle of the room, surrounded by a few chairs. Joshua walked over to the desk and turned on the holoscreen placed on top of it. It lit up the cabin and the figure in the corner.

"So, this is how my generosity is rewarded?" a deep and all too familiar voice boomed. "With thievery and lies."

The blood drained from Josie's face, and the emptiness in her stomach made her want to throw up. There was nothing for it now, she was trapped. Her eyes met Joshua's, and he returned an apologetic look.

"Sorry," he said. "I told you. Nobody goes against Marcus."

CHAPTER THIRTEEN_

Marcus sat with his hood up in the corner of the room. His bulky stature and shadowed face gave him a commanding presence. Josie did not have the heart to move; she was fighting hard to keep hold of herself, least of all to not to show Marcus how frightened she was.

Marcus looked back at Josie. The corners of his mouth turned up in a wicked smile. "You trust far too easily for someone with information as valuable as you have."

Josie turned her head to hide her embarrassment. Her breathing became shallow. Miles had begged her to be careful, to trust nobody. She had trusted his brother and been careless. An idiot who walked right into the trap.

"Ah," Marcus chuckled. "I see you do know your own failure." He stood and walked around the desk. Joshua anxiously waited for what Marcus would do next. "The only question I have left, is what to do with you, Josie Owens. I suppose I might turn you in to the P&Cs, buy myself a bit of goodwill with them. Especially after this newly authorized campaign against my people." His face darkened, and he slammed his fist onto the desk. "Damn First Vicar Frost!" he shouted. "His weapons complicate things."

"They won't be able to stop us. Not with what we have planned," Joshua chimed in.

Marcus glowered at him with the stare a man gave only when he knew he commanded the fate of the other.

Joshua stiffened, disengaging from the conversation.

Marcus returned to his thoughts. "No, I think not. Turning you in to Frost would only give him further justification to unleash that dog Reyes against us." He stroked his chin and looked back at Josie, then smiled, as if overcome with a most amusing idea. "Perhaps we might use you after all." He pulled out a small data cartridge and spun it around in his fingers. "I hear this is what you were after? The codes to access the glittering pinnacle of our great ark." He tossed the cartridge up in the air and caught it.

Josie's eyes never left it.

"I had plans for these, but I suppose plans change."

"What do you want?" Josie tried her hardest to keep her voice calm and leveled. This was clearly a negotiation and she wanted to seem strong and in control, not scared and small.

"So you are interested then?" Marcus's eyes gleamed. "Good, you can see reason. I think we might be able to help each other after all."

Josie bit her tongue to hold back the snide comment she had. This man had ordered the Garden of Tomorrow explosion, and no matter how just their cause might be, Josie could not come to terms with the death it had caused. But Marcus was in control now.

"You see." Marcus opened his arms wide. "Hades Fist has a problem. Much like the rest of *November's Dawn*, we are starving. There isn't enough medicine to keep disease at bay. We fight for a cause, yes, but like the common Aegean Deck laborers, we toil at our task with no clear vision for our future."

Josie fixed her attention on his words. Marcus had lowered his outward facing strength and spoke of the true trials they tackled. Joshua also seemed surprised by his candor in revealing their weaknesses to a stranger.

"But most of all, we need electricity, more power than we currently can siphon off *November's Dawn's* systems without attracting undue attention and giving away our location. If the OSD is serious about this new crusade, we need more power to survive in wretched Bottom Bays." He scoffed as he looked around the decrepit cabin, even if the bright lights from the holoscreens brought some life to its walls.

"I don't see how I can help—" Josie said.

"You trained to be an engineer, yes? I suspect you know more about our ark's systems than most under my command. The details are unimportant right now, you only need to know you are needed. And if you prove your worth." He spun the data cartridge in his fingers again. "You can go about your way."

Joshua walked close to Marcus and spoke in a low voice. "This isn't a good idea, sir. As soon as she has a chance, she'll run."

Marcus chuckled and put a hand up. "That's why you will be part of this mission. You will make sure she does what's needed. In any case, if she runs, she betrays the only friends she has left on this ark." He looked at Josie. "And I can tell you this, in the darkness below, *November's Dawn* does not provide for those who are alone."

Josie nodded. Marcus was being vague and that worried her, but everything was a cause for worry right now. If he needed her to fix something, she was reasonably sure she could do it. Something else was on her mind too. Doc Lee had said her dad was a founder of Hades Fist. There was no way she was missing her chance to find out more.

"Did you really know my dad?"

A strange look overcame Marcus. His eyes glinted with a hint of a memory. "Aye, I knew Dom. But no matter, we are here, and he is not. Help my people, prove your worth, and I'll give you the access codes."

"Fine," Josie said. "So what do I need to do?"

Marcus clapped and walked to the cabin door, the hitch in his stride even more apparent now. "We rejoin the others. We must prepare."

"Come on," Joshua said with some annoyance before following Marcus.

Josie let out the most relieved breath she'd ever had. Her head was pounding from the whole exchange and the riveting fear she had been feeling had not completely worn off. Marcus had been reasonable to some extent. Yet she played a dangerous game, and she knew it. But there was no other way—at least none she could see. Joshua was busy typing into the communicator while they snaked their way back through the maze of crates that shrouded Marcus's cabin from the rest of Hades Fist's hideout. She realized that must have been how Joshua warned Marcus when they were running.

"I still know about your little side business with stolen supplies," Josie whispered to him. Marcus was some steps ahead of them and he had put his hood back up so she was reasonably sure he could not hear. Knowing Joshua's secret gave her some hope and a sense of security and maybe even some leverage.

"And I appreciated you not revealing it," Joshua said, although his voice was not at all appreciative.

Josie smiled to herself. "Just remember, I know. I can keep

secrets. But also, sometimes they just slip out of me. Probably because I'm just a silly girl."

"Have you sent the message?" Marcus called back.

Joshua sprang forward a step. "Yes, they are gathering now."

"A message?" Josie asked.

"Yeah," Joshua said snidely. "Telling everyone to gather. This is what you want, right? A chance to be the hero."

Josie blanched. "What I want? I want to help everyone, all of us. Bottom Bays, Aegean. Hell, even Delos and Olympus. Sorry, I guess I don't think the right way is killing the few people we have left."

Marcus stopped, apparently having been listening. "You're idealistic. As I once was. But when you've lived as long as I, seen the things I have, well, at some point the idealism fades and all that's left is broken promises and a quest for vengeance. The deaths at the garden were a necessary sacrifice."

"You're wrong," Josie shot back.

"Joshua! Marcus!" Tai ran around a particularly tall column of crates. "Oh! I got your message. Everyone is in the infirmary. When are we going?"

"Soon," Marcus said.

Nobody spoke the rest of the way. Far ahead a few stragglers ran toward the infirmary. Josie was curious to see how many people would be there, and how strong Hades Fist actually was, but not curious enough to ask anyone about it. She thought about Miles and told herself over and over that he was safe, if only she could just see him to be sure.

Doctor Lee stood outside the infirmary. Leaned up against the cold metal walls with her foot back against them and her arms crossed. Josie's stomach turned as she wondered if Marcus would blame Lee for helping her. They clearly had a complex history and relationship. Lee's eyes darted to Josie when she saw her, a fleeting glimpse of relief that came as fast as it went, but she did not acknowledge Josie. Instead, she locked eyes with Marcus. "This is it, you know. The garden was one thing, but if we go through with this, there won't be any going back."

Marcus pulled back his hood. "There was never any going back, Amalia. You knew that once." He walked past her and pushed through the doors.

Josie came in last. Lee gave her hand a quick squeeze as she passed, clearly feeling responsible for her present situation. Josie did not see it that way though. She had been careless and got caught. Now she had resigned herself to helping Marcus, or everything she wanted would be gone. Aegean Deck would continue to suffer and starve, and she would never get justice for her dad and Felix, their truth dying with her failure.

Marcus moved to the center of the room. There were about twenty gathered, mostly younger faces. Some wore factory jumpsuits that were common on Aegean Deck, but there were a few dressed in pieces of upper deck quality. It seemed that Hades Fist had at least some support outside of Aegean. All their clothes were battered and restitched in many places. Hard times had made them lean. Even though they came from different backgrounds, each one had a similar focus in their eyes as they prepared to listen to Marcus. They were hungry for change, and they would fight for it.

"Friends, the moment we have all been waiting for has come, and by some stroke of the universe's great irony, it comes during First Vicar Frost's week of celebration. He would have you believe this celebration is a testament to our strength, to the world *November's Dawn* provides. Oh, the world is good for those on Olympus, but what about us? We toil and suffer under the OSD the same as we always have. That will change, my friends. The Garden of Tomorrow was only the start. We will show every person aboard this ark that the OSD cannot provide for them any longer. Their rule has ended. Another opportunity has presented itself." Marcus extended his hand toward Josie. "The newcomer in our midst has volunteered to be a part of our next mission, a mission to strip some of the very power that gives Frost his iron grip upon our throats and take it for ourselves."

A cheer went up from those gathered.

They were hungry. They were ready.

"Yes," Marcus continued. "This is a moment to reflect on our success, but do not become complacent my friends. After tonight, we will be waking up in a new world. Joshua's team has already volunteered for service. Tell me, who among you wish to strike a blow to those who would destroy you?"

"Me!" Tai stood from a cot and raised her fist. Another cheer followed.

"Me too," Lee said.

That surprised Josie, and she looked at the person beside her. "Doc Lee?"

Lee smiled. "This mission could be dangerous, I can help."

Marcus stopped. An agitated look crossed his face, but he masked it quickly with a smile. "I am pleased you've decided to recommit yourself to the cause." He looked around the room again. "Is there no one else?" Nobody said anything. Josie could not help but feel like she did not know everything going on.

"I will go," Miles said clearly from the door of the infirmary.

Josie spun around, hearing Miles's voice brought an immediate sense of relief and happiness, even if she had just seen him only hours ago, especially since he stood tall in the doorway.

"Then we have our crew. You will leave at once." Marcus clapped his hands. "Joshua will have more details for you. Do not fail us, my friends." His gaze fell on Josie. "You know as well as I what we all have to lose from failure."

CHAPTER FOURTEEN_

THE OTHER MEMBERS of Hades Fist left the infirmary after Marcus's speech. Josie thought about what he said. She agreed with the idea of it. The lower decks had suffered long enough. It was time to take back some power from the OSD. But she couldn't go along with hurting innocent people. The last thing she was going to do was trust Marcus or Joshua. She had made that mistake once and would not make it again.

Still, it was remarkable how much respect Marcus Abbott commanded. The only other person Josie had ever seen with that much influence was First Vicar Frost. Both were dangerous, both had silver tongues. The irony of their similarities was not lost on her, nor was the unease it brought. If anything, it made her wonder if Marcus's vision for the future was actually like how things were now, only with him at the top.

It seemed if the same kinds of people were always in charge, then the same oppression was bound to happen. That's why she believed in her mission. If the old sources of power and constraints of *November's Dawn* itself were gone, new leaders and voices could rise. She just prayed the surface would offer that chance and they would not repeat the mistakes the leaders of the old world had made. They had already destroyed the world once.

Joshua strummed his fingers on a table as the room emptied. Another man Josie did not recognize stayed behind as well, about the same age as Joshua. He stood behind Joshua with his arms crossed.

"So what's the job?" Tai asked.

"Marcus needs us to go to one of the legs of *November's Dawn*," Joshua said. "Specifically one of the turbines that each leg powers. We need to reroute the power to Bottom Bays. That's where you come in." He looked at Josie.

"Won't that mess with the legs? What if we bust it trying to steal power?" Tai asked.

Josie shook her head. "It won't happen. The other legs are built to assume the work if one broke."

"Josie was the best of the new engineers. Mags said so herself. She'll get it done," Miles said.

Josie hid her face from Miles. She was grateful for his confidence, but part of her wished he had not said anything. It just added to the pressure she already felt. Everyone counted on her, and she could not escape the thought of what would happen if she failed. She tried to focus on the job in front of her and take it one step at a time, but those doubts never left the shadows of her mind.

"I hope so, for all our sakes," Joshua said. "We go as soon as the last shift is over, most of the workers and P&Cs will be gone." He pointed at Miles. "Come with me. We have to get the weapons and tools ready. Matias, you stay here. No one leaves."

Miles shrugged and followed his brother outside. "I'll be back soon," he whispered as he passed.

Josie threw herself on the nearest cot when he was gone and started fidgeting with her still knotted hair.

"I'll be in my cabin getting ready if you need anything, girls," Doc Lee said.

Josie nodded from the cot. The other man, Matias, sat at the table. He pulled out a pair of shimmering dice and a small cup. She could hear the dice slide across the table again and again.

Tai slid onto the cot beside Josie. "I heard you were the one who fixed the pressure leak in the passageway?" Tai's brown hair was pulled back tight, and her warm almond eyes accentuated her toned face.

Josie opened an eye and scooted up on her elbows. "Yeah, that was me," she said and kept her eyes low.

"Oh no! I'm not upset, Josie. I think it's cool," Tai said enthusiastically. "I mean, I try to fix things, but I've never been much good. It seems you have the knack for it."

"You really think so?"

"To get Marcus to let you in on this mission? You bet. Maybe you can show me some stuff sometime?"

Josie sat up even straighter now, a smile crept across her face. "I'd love to."

Tai beamed then reached into a pocket and pulled out a handmade, wide-tooth comb. "Here, I noticed you pulling your fingers through your hair. I thought this would help."

"Thanks," Josie said, face reddening and very thankful for the comb.

Tai watched her untangle a particularly stubborn knot. "So," she said when Josie was mostly done, "that boy, Joshua's brother, tell me."

"Tell you what?" Josie's excitement started to fade at the turn in conversation. It was obvious Tai wanted more, but Josie didn't know what to say. She had always been terribly awkward around other girls her own age. And Tai was older, Joshua's age at least, that made Josie even more unsure of herself.

Tai was relentless. "Oh, come on. You know there's something. It's as clear on your face as when the Galley Markets light up for the day."

"Well, I don't really know." Josie relented and turned away. Her face got hot again.

"I think you do. I know Miles does too."

Josie turned back to her. "Wait, what do you mean? Miles doesn't like me like that. He's helping me do the right thing. That's all."

"That's all," Tai mimicked Josie, but not in a spiteful way. "Take it from me, Josie, as someone who's had a crush or two. It's always easier to spot it with other people than with yourself. Miles cares about you, a lot."

Josie's heart was in her throat, and she felt like she was positively burning up now. She pulled at a knot of hair. "I'm telling you he doesn't. You should see some of the girls from my class. They're beautiful. I don't compare to them."

"You hate the things that make you different, I get it. And I'll bet you hate those other girls more for it."

"Well, yeah," Josie said, fully embarrassed now. She hated admitting it. Her differences were something she always lorded over the other girls, like she was somehow better than them, even if no one seemed to want to talk to her. But Tai was right, part of her wanted what they had.

Tai put her hand on Josie's knee. "There's nothing wrong with being different. It took me a long time to realize it too. Someone once told me the cage that holds you back was built by your own two hands, designed by your own demons. Your hair makes you stand out, your freckles sure. But that doesn't matter in the end. And Miles? Well, I think he sees that, or else a boy his age wouldn't be here chasing you around. Trust me, there's something there."

"You really think so?" Josie was allowing herself to hope

and it was dangerous. But the daydream was too sweet to dismiss.

"Yes," Tai said directly.

When Odette told a particularly cruel joke about how Josie's dad had abandoned her family, the whole class had laughed—except for Miles.

"It doesn't matter. I've never done this, and I wouldn't know what to do. Or what to say." Josie looked around the room. The two other men were still busy playing dice. "And look at what we're doing? It wouldn't be worth it."

"Wouldn't be worth it?" Tai asked. "It's never been more worth it. I mean, that's what we're doing, right? Fighting for those we care about." Tai's thin lips turned up in a sweet smile, and she winked.

"You sure seem to have a lot of wisdom, Tai," Josie said. "At least way more than most people."

Tai shrugged. "Maybe. But I think most people can see it. It's just they're too scared to say it out loud. Besides, it's not like I haven't felt like you do now." She smiled and glanced toward the door but looked as if she had just remembered a sad memory.

Josie watched her for a minute more that slowly slipped into another daydream of what it would be like if Tai was her friend in class or if she had been able to remain friends with Nila like she was so long ago. They'd laugh and pass notes. Josie would even show some of the things she'd fixed. No way Odette and the others from Olympus Deck would mess with her then. But her classmates' laughing faces danced around her all the same—they always did—and that daydream came crashing down too.

"I'm sorry," she said, pulling her knees to her chest. "I just . . . Why're you being so nice to me?" Josie knew she was being overly suspicious. Tai seemed genuine, and Josie liked her a lot.

But she had fallen for it before, and she could not help but feel someone had put Tai up to it.

Tai cast her eyes down and stayed silent. After a couple moments, she looked back up. The corner of her eyes glistened.

"Oh, Tai! I didn't mean anything by it. It's only—"

Tai smiled and sniffed. "No," she said. "No, it's nothing you said. It's just . . . I had a sister once. A little sister. Her name was Aika."

"I have a little sister too. Rose." Josie wasn't sure what else to say.

"Then you know what it's like. How you love them."

Josie nodded. Even if Rose annoyed her sometimes or got into her stuff, she would always do anything to protect her.

"When Aika was little, she got sick. My parents tried to get her the help she needed. But Aika wasn't deemed important enough to save. Can you imagine?" Tai's voice turned hard and cold. "Anyway, that's why I'm here. I never got to be a big sister for Aika. I never got to talk with her about boys or do her hair and dream about what the world was like before the flood. When I saw the way you and Miles looked at each other just then, I guess I wanted to be part of that."

"Tai, I'm so sorry," Josie said. She couldn't imagine losing Rose. She would never forgive herself. Tai must have felt the same way, but she was still fighting for what she believed in. What scared Josie the most was the thought that Tai's nightmare would have probably happened to her family as well if not for her mom getting that job on Olympus Deck all those years ago. Would they have starved too? Would Rose have been the next victim of some sickness? She had always held it against her mom for taking that job, like it was a betrayal. Now she wasn't so sure.

Tai wiped the corner of her eye. "It's okay, Josie. It's me

who should be sorry, putting myself where I don't belong like that." She laughed nervously. "You don't even know me."

Josie frowned for a minute, then put her open hand out to Tai, whose brow scrunched up before she shook it hesitantly. "Hi," Josie said. "I'm Josie. Josie Owens." She wanted Tai to know she was not alone.

Tai's eyes twinkled. She took Josie's hand wholeheartedly and laughed. "Hi, Josie. I'm Tai."

Josie giggled and looked down. "Sorry, I don't know where to go from here. I don't exactly have a lot of friends." Josie looked down. Tai was older than her and probably thought she was being dumb even if she was humoring her.

"It's okay, Josie. You don't have to worry anymore. You're with a friend."

Josie felt giddy and oddly hopeful. It was followed by relief that Tai was being genuine. If it was not for the grim reality of the situation, Josie would have been happy with how things went. She had made a friend.

"Where is your sister Rose now?"

Josie smiled, but it was bittersweet. "I had to leave her with a friend when I started running from the OSD. I think she's safe, but I just don't know. I want her to be safe more than anything. And I hope I did the right thing by leaving her behind."

Tai moved over to Josie's cot and wrapped an arm around her. "You did." She swept her hand across the infirmary. "This life isn't for a little girl. She's going to be okay. You know how I know?"

"How?"

"Because she's got a big sister like you who wouldn't let a thing happen to her. I'll bet she knows that too."

Josie closed her eyes and remembered the day she'd left Rose. It felt like ages ago, even if it really was only a couple days. Rose had been clutching her small stuffed bunny, her blue eyes wide, so sweet and full of innocence. Blissfully unaware of the reality of life on *November's Dawn*, but that would come in time. For now, Josie wanted Rose to keep holding onto her little bunny for as long as she could.

"Well," Tai said, standing up from the cot. "It won't be long now. I know the nerves are tough, nothing really helps that, but I have a good feeling about you, Josie Owens."

"Thank you, Tai. Really," Josie said as she watched Tai walk to the center of the room and sit on the floor and stretch her legs out.

Tai laughed. "What? I like to be loose before a mission."

Josie could not help but laugh as Tai sprawled out in another stretch.

The doors to the infirmary opened. Joshua and Miles stepped through, each with a large backpack. Joshua carried a brown bundle, but Josie could not tell what was in it.

Doctor Lee poked her head back into the room. "Are we ready?"

"Aye," Joshua answered. Matias came up to him and took the brown bundle. He pulled a jet-black baton from it which crackled with electricity.

Josie jumped up to Miles. "Here, let me help." She slipped a hand through the strap. Her leg buckled slightly under the new weight. Miles slid his arm through hers.

"Are you okay?" he asked. He started pulling the bag back onto his shoulder.

"I'm okay. I can help." Josie regained her balance. Her foot hurt but she was determined to help. "What's in these?"

"Tools, wrenches, cutters, a few other things. We're taking power. You need tools for that," Joshua said from across the room. He bent down and retied his boots. "Okay, everyone, listen up. Marcus wants power from one of the leg turbines.

We've done some snooping around and leg 193 is going to be our best bet. It's in Aegean and far enough away from any cabins or industrial bays that we shouldn't attract much attention."

"What about P&Cs?" Josie asked.

"Hopefully, they know what's best for them. If not . . ." Joshua waved one of the security batons back and forth through the air as electricity hummed around it, making his meaning clear.

Josie scoffed but said nothing. The plan was clearly hinged on the theory there would only be a few P&Cs, since there were only six of them going. If there were more than a couple P&Cs, they would be in a world of trouble. But she had agreed to this mission and backing out now would mean the OSD had won. That Felix had died for nothing. She needed the elevator codes. Too much depended on this now.

"You won't have much time to reroute the power. Are you sure you can do it?" Joshua asked.

"I don't need much time," Josie lied. In truth she was not sure how long it would take. Felix had taken her along to work on some smaller turbines and generators a few times, but she was by no means an expert.

"You're sure about that?" Miles whispered, apparently having noticed Josie's furrowed brow.

"Yeah," Josie whispered back, trying to sound confident. "How different can it be from the generators folks use in the Galley Markets?"

CHAPTER FIFTEEN_

A subtle knock came at the door. "First Vicar, are you ready? It's time."

Adrian recognized George's voice, the peace-and-compliance officer who accompanied him everywhere.

He finished reading the last line and folded up the paper in his hand then slipped it into his breast pocket. He took one last deep breath of the purified air coming from a small machine on his desk and closed his eyes, letting his mind tantalize him with fleeing thoughts of peace and rest. Rest that would not come until his work was completed.

"First Vicar? The celebration will begin soon," George called and knocked again.

"Yes, yes. I will be right there." Adrian stood and flattened his vestments. It was time. His announcement of their fight against Hades Fist had shocked many on *November's Dawn*. Now it was time to placate their fears and worries and return their attention and faith to the celebration of the Turning and the OSD. They needed to be reminded of the protection and prosperity *November's Dawn* provides and how quickly it could all disappear if dissident groups like Hades Fist gained a foothold. He had written a sermon he hoped would do precisely that. Cornelius Graham's portrait stared down upon him as he walked to the door. It was as if he could feel his mentor's gaze burning into him, a constant reminder of his duty and what would happen if he failed. There could be no false step now.

Adrian waved his hand at George and the other officer who flanked his door as he stepped through. "Is everything ready?"

"Yes, First Vicar. The bulkhead water breach in the Garden of Tomorrow has been sealed and all bodies removed," George responded.

Adrian raised an eyebrow as he peered at the officer. "And?"

George stiffened. "And the fetterball sector has been left where it fell, First Vicar. To demonstrate the deadly seriousness of this peril. Just like you ordered."

"Good," Adrian said. He walked down the hallway for a moment before stopping. "I'm not a bad man, you know, George."

The officer gasped and his face turned scarlet. "First Vicar, apologies. I meant nothing of the sort. It's just, with everything happening, folks are on edge. Not only in the lower decks either. There're whispers on Olympus."

"Whispers?"

George gulped. Adrian was clearly making the man nervous. "Yes, First Vicar. Whispers."

Adrian turned and kept walking. Perhaps the people needed more than just a sermon to remember their loyalty to the OSD. He sighed. The news was troubling. Adrian wanted to question the officer more, but he doubted he would have any more information, nor did he believe it was the duty of a stationed P&C officer to deliver such intelligence. That should have come from his commandant.

"Where is Commandant Reyes?" Adrian said.

George sped up to not shout. "He has been leading the effort against the terrorist groups, First Vicar. Shall I request for him?"

Adrian nodded. "I want an update on his efforts." The use of holorifles still troubled him. It was an unprecedented authorization of force against the citizens of *November's Dawn* and that reality was not lost on him. Oversight kept order and even though he trusted Reyes, the commandant's inclination toward force first and questions later was something Adrian could not lose his grip on. As he made his way to the elevator and Delos Deck, the holoscreens in the hallways flickered with the newest broadcast of Jack Burlesque and Donna Albert. Adrian had never been much of a fan of Jack. The deacon's holoscreen personality had always seemed unnecessarily grandiose and vain, but at least he was a staunch believer of the OSD. In the end that was what truly mattered.

"This is a bold and calculated move by the First Vicar," Jack monologued. "By announcing this campaign against the terrorists publicly, he has signaled nobody is above the law that keeps *November's Dawn* moving. But the question has to be asked. What will happen if he fails?"

"And during the celebration of the Great Turning, no less," Donna added.

"Exactly," Jack said and slapped his fist on the desk. "This is the biggest moment in at least the last decade. And now its success isn't just tied to *November's Dawn* navigating through some of the most dangerous parts of the flooded world, but also how well the OSD can keep peace and order aboard the ark after the attack on the Garden of Tomorrow."

"After all, that's the agreement, right? We give our faith and support to the OSD and in return order is preserved? Clearly Olympus Deck would have a hard time keeping *November's*

Dawn running if the lower decks suddenly decided to stop working the factories. And the lower decks in turn would have no idea how to run the ark's complex systems," Donna said.

Adrian sighed. He did not necessarily fault Donna and Jack for their banter, and he normally played some part in the discourse. But now they were dangerously close to rocking the foundations their society was built on. That was something Adrian would not oblige.

Jack chuckled. "Well, I wouldn't say it's that simple. We all owe our loyalty to the OSD as they were entrusted as the caretakers of *November's Dawn*. But I suppose you could call it a sort of agreement, yes. First Vicar Frost has shown himself to be temperate, and the people love him for it. But this business with Hades Fist is nasty. Even on Olympus, some citizens have been afraid to leave their apartments. We have reports the terrorist movement could be growing in the lower decks. First Vicar Frost and the Directors must be under tremendous pressure right now to show this sort of disunity will not be tolerated." He turned and looked directly into the camera. "This is a critical moment for First Vicar Frost's continued leadership. And I for one wouldn't object to harsher measures being taken against these terrorists."

Donna nodded intently. "What can you tell us about these terrorists? Hades Fist, what do they stand for?"

"Not much. Up till now they seem to have been a pretty quiet and shadowy group. It's clear they want to dismantle the systems we have in place that keep us all safe, and they've shown they're willing to go to great lengths to do that. What do they stand for? Anarchy. Chaos. Lawlessness. If you know or hear anything about this group, it is your duty to alert your nearest peace-and-compliance officer immediately."

Adrian tuned the rest of the broadcast out. It was shortly replaced by a company ad for canned fish from Director

Clarke's cannery, featuring a talking lobster with a small monocle promoting a bright new packaging for the same old fish the cannery processed. The idea of it was absurd, but the masses consumed the short ads with a voracious appetite.

They turned the last corner to the elevator that would take them directly to Delos Deck. From his suite he had an elevator bay that could reach any part of the ark. It was one of the benefits of being First Vicar. Commandant Reyes stood at attention in front of the gilded metal gates of the elevator. Four peace-and-compliance officers flanked him, each one carrying a holorifle. The commandant had seemingly wasted no time in arming his force with the weapons.

Commandant Reyes saluted as Adrian neared. "First Vicar," he said in a rigid tone. His lips carried a slight smile. He seemed almost happy. A most unusual look for someone who never even let his shoulders slouch.

"Commandant," Adrian replied. "Report?" He wondered what the commandant was so happy about.

"We've detained several people from Aegean with connections to Hades Fist. I believe they have information regarding the Garden of Tomorrow bombing."

Adrian raised an eyebrow. "And have they provided any information?"

"Some, but they stick to their false beliefs, First Vicar. They speak openly about the tyranny of the OSD. They cannot be allowed to spread such lies."

"No," Adrian said, half to himself. "They cannot."

Commandant Reyes stepped forward and looked right at Adrian. "They call for your removal, First Vicar," he said in a hushed tone. "I've done what I can, but . . ."

Adrian sighed. "But *what*, Commandant?"

"These terrorists must be made an example of." Reyes stiffened as his words faded. The corners of his mouth turned up ever so slightly as he looked expectantly at Adrian.

Now it was Adrian's turn to step closer. "And you would have me do what? Are they a part of Hades Fist?"

"I cannot say with absolute certainty, First Vicar. But they align themselves with the ideals of the movement. The intent and action are one and the same." He turned and locked eyes with Adrian. "You started us down this path with your public manifesto against these traitors. Do not falter now. Show everyone on *November's Dawn* what the penalty is. They're threatening our order. Our very way of life, First Vicar."

Adrian said nothing while he digested the commandant's words. Reyes was practically beaming, obviously ready and able to carry out any punishment for those deemed enemies of *November's Dawn*. The sinking emptiness in Adrian's stomach was tempered only by the duty he bore, a duty to the greater good and safety of *November's Dawn* and the survival of the human species. That was the great reality of his time. Order must be preserved, even if some freedoms had to be stripped away. This was a fight Hades Fist began, and he would finish it.

"Call off the sermon. And bring the prisoners to Aegean Deck, to the Arbiter's Arena. This ends now."

Commandant Reyes saluted. "Yes, First Vicar." He turned and flicked his hand at two of the other officers. "You heard him, go!"

They scrambled to follow his command.

"Reyes," Adrian said and grabbed the commandant's arm. "Have all the officers been outfitted with holorifles?"

"Not yet, First Vicar. Many in the lower decks and factories have not been. But soon."

Adrian nodded. "See to it they are. And bolster our presence in Aegean. I fear what happens next could turn dangerous."

"Not to worry, First Vicar," Reyes said and eyed one of the holorifles. "They would be a damn fool to go up against an officer armed with these."

"Yes, that is what I'm worried about," Adrian said as he stepped into the elevator.

Commandant Reyes punched in the necessary access codes and the machine rumbled to life. The sermon Adrian had prepared crinkled in his pocket as he ran his fingers through his hair. He had hoped to rekindle faith in their system of union between the upper and lower decks, the companies and the workforce, with the OSD acting as the connection between them all, but it seemed events in the lower decks were quickly moving past that.

Reyes stood in the corner with his hands locked stiffly behind his back—a soldier's stance. Sometimes Adrian admired the man's unwavering ability to do what must be done. This was one of those times. Never before in his years of leading *November's Dawn* had Adrian felt so powerless. All he could do now was take each moment as it came. If Reyes was right, and these prisoners were helping Hades Fist, directly or indirectly, there was no other option. The Directors and other powerful voices from Olympus Deck would not allow leniency. If this fighting was allowed to disrupt the efforts to repair *November's Dawn's* navigational computers, it would all be for nothing. He prayed that some might understand in time.

An automated voice emanated through the elevator's speakers. "A message for First Vicar Adrian Frost. Director Clarke will be joining you at the Arbiter's Arena."

Adrian sighed. The last thing he needed right now was Director Clarke's interference or so-called counsel. Often, he kept the peace between the companies in petty rows and squabbles. That was something he had no interest in doing now. But Clarke held a great deal of influence, especially among the other Directors, and had been at the Garden of Tomorrow when the bomb went off. It was not unreasonable to think he held a personal interest in tracking down the perpetrators of the crime. Perhaps it was good he would be present. Then Adrian could solidify support in his campaign against Hades Fist.

The elevator slowed. Adrian could feel it in his stomach, so he clenched his fist and tried to focus on the task at hand. Before long, the musical chiming signaled their arrival, and a gust of cool air greeted them. Adrian fought off a shiver. The air was always colder towards the back half of *November's Dawn,* even more so as they got closer to the outer bulkhead of the ark.

"This way, First Vicar. We are just off the Arbiter's Arena," Reyes said and gestured out of the elevator.

Several more officers stood at attention as they walked past, into a narrow passageway with a number of windows on either side, revealing rooms either filled with bunks, storage lockers, or various holoscreens and surveillance equipment. It was one of the many security checkpoints spread throughout the ark.

"Where are the prisoners?" Adrian asked.

"They're being brought here as we speak."

"Adrian!" a woman shouted from the far end of the passageway. "Adrian!"

Adrian froze. He knew that voice. For a split second he thought Serena Owens was one of the prisoners. That was ridiculous. He would never allow that to happen. Serena stormed down the passageway toward him. He turned his head and cast a hard look at Commandant Reyes. He tilted his head, deferring to Adrian's command, but a streak of annoyance flashed across his face. A hand signal ordered the officers who walked with them to stand down, giving Adrian some privacy as Serena walked closer.

"Serena," he said in a low voice. "What are you doing here?"

"Is it true?" she said. "There are rumors you've taken prisoners."

Adrian stiffened as they locked eyes. "It is."

Serena's expression softened. She stepped a little closer to him. Close enough only he could hear but still far enough away that those watching would not deem it inappropriate. "Have you questioned them? Do they know anything about Josie? Rose still has not been brought to Olympus either, Adrian. You said you would keep her safe."

"And I will," Adrian whispered hard through his teeth. "Rose will be safe. I promise it. As for your more wayward daughter. I'm sorry, I don't have any news. But believe me, I want to find her more than anyone." Adrian folded his hands together and took a breath. He knew Serena was scared, but there was so much going on and he did not have time for it now. And her daughter was yet another thorn in his side. It was not clear to him yet how she fit into everything, but the last thing he needed was for Josie Owens to fuel the fires of Hades Fist with whatever she had learned from the old engineer and the smashed up holomessage. Dominic Owens had been well respected and well known, that could give his daughter some measure of influence amongst the lower decks and made finding her even more important. Adrian reached out and took Serena's hand.

"Look," he said. "Go back to Olympus Deck. Wait for me. When I know more, I'll come."

Serena lowered her gaze to the ground. "Please, Adrian. Find her. No matter what she might have gotten into, she's just a child." She slipped her hand away from his and turned.

Adrian continued toward the Arbiter's Arena, so named for its use as a place of judgement for those who would erode the stability of *November's Dawn*. It would earn its namesake today. Adrian heard the low rumble of the citizens gathered through the metal doors that still separated the security checkpoint from the Arena. "How many are out there?"

"Several hundred, with more coming," Reyes said.

"Then I'm ready."

The door hissed as the mechanism to open it engaged. Adrian entered a large circular chamber. Bright floodlights ringed the upper supports that wrapped around the room. They were all focused on a single location, a raised platform jutting from the outer bulkhead of *November's Dawn*. Two figures, hooded and bound, were motionless on their knees on the platform. A ring of P&C officers stood below the platform, at the ready and positioned with large security shields. But what truly gave the Arbiter's Arena its infamous reputation was a series of five large hatches that lined the outer bulkhead behind the raised platform. Each one was about two meters wide and made of thick metal, strong enough to withstand rapid shifts in pressure, for these hatches opened into the chambers used to jettison those on *November's Dawn* convicted of committing the most grievous of crimes into the black abyss of the ocean. It was the ultimate punishment, and one that happened only in the most extreme of circumstances. In all the years Adrian had led the OSD, he had never used it, and only once did Cornelius Graham sentence a man to the abyss for trying to defraud the companies. The people quieted as Adrian approached the middle of the platform.

Director Clarke stood off to the side. "First Vicar, you have my support," he said and nodded slightly.

Adrian returned the gesture and focused back on the crowd. All of them followed his every move as their trepidation grew. Under the bright lights and unblinking eyes of *November's Dawn* the time had come. He turned and raised his hand, signaling to the officers to remove the hoods of the two prisoners.

A young man and woman, both blinking and squinting as the floodlights barraged their senses. He figured they could not be past their twentieth year. This was not what he had been expecting. These so-called prisoners were kids. It was hardly believable they had actionable information about Hades Fist.

Adrian sighed and he glanced over at Commandant Reyes who stood at attention next to Director Clarke. Part of him thought Reyes withheld that information purposefully but dismissed the idea of Reyes directly undermining him like that. Most of the crowd seemed to be from Aegean and they were growing more and more restless by the moment. They knew something was wrong; they only waited now to see what it was. Adrian had called for this judgement. Going back would only see him lose support from the upper decks and the Directors. Order was the only way.

He opened his arms up to the crowd. "Citizens of *November's Dawn!*" A few scattered cheers went up. "It is with a heavy heart that we find ourselves here. Today, a day of celebration, of hope for the future, has been taken from you again, replaced by the fear and instability that Hades Fist would rule our lives with. To threaten our order is to threaten the very foundations of our society. This we cannot abide."

He turned to the prisoners, their faces a painful mixture of confusion and fear. Whatever innocence they might have had was gone, stripped away the moment they aided the enemy. The heat of the bombing in the Garden of Tomorrow washed over his face again. Were those that died not innocents? Yet Hades Fist had orchestrated their deaths all the same. No, there were no innocents anymore. Too much was at stake. "Confess your crimes before the Order of Scientific Discovery and your fellow citizens, that we might find mercy in our souls."

One of the prisoners, the young man in the uniform of a mill worker and with a tangled bunch of brown hair, mumbled something.

Adrian stepped closer. "Yes, my child?"

His eyes hardened. "I have nothing to confess," he sneered and spat at Adrian's feet.

Rage flashed through Adrian's mind, but his better sense returned just in time. All of *November's Dawn* watched. He stole a glance at Clarke and Reyes. Both had unflinching expressions.

"Do it," Adrian ordered the officer standing behind the young man. Another officer stepped forward and together they pulled the would-be terrorist toward the first metal hatch.

"You won't get away with this!" the young man screamed.

"We shall see," Adrian whispered and turned back to the crowd.

Their roar grew steadily now. The ring of officers shifted against the new movement. Their large shields jolted as they pressed against the throng of people. The two officers shoved the prisoner into the hatch. It closed with a resounding thud, muffling the young man's screams. They turned and waited for Adrian's authorization, a final validation before sending the young man into the deeps. Adrian nodded and the sound of the crushing weight of water against the rapidly expelled air echoed from the chamber. Through a small viewport, the first thing Adrian saw was a rush of bubbles. Then a dark silhouette. Then nothing.

"This is the future that awaits you! Confess and be redeemed!" Adrian said to the remaining prisoner, but loud enough for all to hear.

"Mable, please! My baby, please! Confess. Let them find mercy!" a woman wailed from the front of the crowd. She pushed against the ring of shields. One of the officers lost his footing, opening the slightest of cracks. The woman slipped through it and collapsed onto the ground in front of the platform. Two officers immediately moved toward her.

"Wait!" Adrian ordered and put his hand up. The officers stopped on either side of the woman. She whimpered as they gripped her shoulders. Adrian looked at her and then back at the second prisoner. "Your mother?"

The young woman lifted her head; tears lined her eyes and cascaded down her flushed cheeks. She nodded, her eyes never leaving her mother. Adrian stood by as the unspoken connection between mother and daughter burned bright. It was electric, as if he could feel those last desperate feelings, those unspoken words, the fleeting finality of it all. But it did not have to be the end. All the young woman had to do was confess. There would still be punishment, but she would live. Every second built up Adrian's hope she would confess. That no more would have to die. The crowd stood silent, quiet enough to hear the rustling of their sleeves. Their anticipation was at a turning point.

"Mable, please. Please confess," her mother begged.

"Confess, my child. Go home to your mother. You need not bear the punishment for the actions of Hades Fist," Adrian said.

The young woman looked at him. A teenager dancing on the edge of a knife, her entire life spent leading up to this singular moment. In a twisted sort of way, Adrian almost admired her. For she held in her hands the very power over her life and death. No burdens or faithless responsibilities, only choice, and what may come after.

"I'm sorry," the young woman said.

"What?" Adrian said.

She looked back at her mother now as her lips trembled. "I'm sorry, Mom, for everything." Her shoulders stiffened, and her eyes flicked up to Adrian. "I've lived under the chains of Olympus Deck my whole life, but not anymore. You don't own me, and we will resist you. I have nothing to confess." As her words faded, her brow softened in a sense of peace.

Adrian closed his eyes. He saw Serena and Josie in this girl and her mother and the bond they shared. Much like Serena, this woman would clearly do anything to save her daughter. Adrian wanted nothing more than to make the whole thing go away and tell the girl to go home and stay out of trouble. But the die had been cast and the decision made. A senseless choice, but one he did not have the power to sway anymore. His duty to *November's Dawn* demanded he press on, even if it tormented him.

"Do it," Adrian commanded as the young woman was pulled into the next hatch. Yet there were no cries or futile pleas for mercy this time. Not even anger. He could have understood anger, but this was different. It confused and frightened him. The young woman closed her eyes and lifted her head high as the hatch closed, unleashing the tempest of water and pressure within. All he could see was Josie's face disappearing into the endless dark.

Her mother wailed as the crowd erupted into chaos. The executions had enraged those from the lower decks. A few roars of approval echoed amongst them, but they were drowned out. Then the unrest boiled over. It rippled out across the crowd as people now saw their neighbors and friends from different decks as enemies. The people shifted violently. Their bodies were packed together into one unstoppable force. Their fervor was on the verge of spilling into an outright riot that would consume the officers and officials from Olympus Deck.

Above the chaos, Adrian shot a look toward Commandant Reyes and Director Clarke. "Contain this," he growled.

Reyes nodded and began shouting orders to the P&C officers. A line of them ran to the edge of the platform, each one carrying a holorifle trained squarely on the crowd.

A sense of dread hit Adrian when he saw the holorifles at the ready. This was not what he had intended. These people may be disturbing the peace, but they were not terrorists to be equally condemned. "Reyes!" he roared. "Without killing!"

Commandant Reyes hesitated a moment, as if weighing the thought of still giving the order and opening fire on the crowd. Several unbearable moments later, he ordered the officers to stand down, then jumped down from the platform and locked rank with his officers as they tried to turn the tide. In a unified movement, officers began pushing into the crowd, dispersing quarrels as they dug deeper into the mass of people.

Director Clarke shuffled closer to Adrian. "What are you doing? You must finish this, First Vicar. Use the holorifles. They cannot be allowed to endanger us all," he hissed. "How many did they murder at the Garden of Tomorrow? And now that girl, Josie. She's drawing them to their cause. How many more will they kill?"

Adrian could hardly distinguish Director Clarke's words from the growing disruption of the fractured crowd. All he could see was the young woman's face the moment the hatch closed, so confident in her belief that she was willing to die for it. He had never seen anything like it.

"First Vicar!" Director Clarke's bony fingers dug into Adrian's arm, snapping him back to reality. "Finish it, Adrian. Give the order."

Another moment passed. Adrian turned to look at the crowd. They had fully devolved into brawling with each other now, but it seemed the officers were slowly putting down the fighting. "These people did not bomb the Garden. It is time you leave, Director. I will not open fire on my own people. Not for a crime they did not commit."

"What are you doing?" Director Clarke said. "They will kill us both if they have the chance! They must be put down first."

Adrian spun around and slammed his open palm into Clarke's chest with enough force to make the man recoil back a step. The older man's eyes went wide, the shock of it scrawled across his face.

"Your warmongering has no place here. I will take no more life today," Adrian said.

Director Clarke's personal guards stepped up but backed down when Adrian's own officers readied their weapons.

"Don't forget, I am *November's Dawn*," Adrian said as he stared Director Clarke dead in the face.

"For now." Clarke sneered and turned away. He scurried with his guards across the platform toward the security checkpoint.

CHAPTER SIXTEEN

JOSIE DUCKED behind a row of empty crates that were waiting to be filled with processed fish from the cannery, one of the great factories that supplied food to *November's Dawn*. The passageway was lined on both sides with them and offered some protection from prying eyes, but her concerns still grew.

"I thought the idea was to stay away from the factories?" Josie whispered to Joshua, who slid up next to her.

"I said leg 193 was far away from the industrial bays, not that we wouldn't have to go through them to get there," Joshua said as he peered over the boxes. "Come on!"

The rest of the group crouched low as they shuffled down the wide passageway toward where Josie and Joshua hid. A deep red light illuminated their way, giving the passageway an ominous feel. The cannery was controlled by one of the companies and the Directors rarely wanted folks not directly working for them coming to their industrial bays and factories. Ahead was a complex web of conveyor belts, hissing pipes, machines, and a great metal maw, lined with hydraulic powered teeth that consumed everything given. Coupled with the red lights and endless groans and screams from the machines, the cannery seemed to be a terribly dangerous place, where the safety of those working there was of little concern.

Now she saw how much better the engineers had it. Because the engineers worked for the entire ark, they technically reported to the OSD and not one of the companies. For the most part, the OSD allowed the engineers to carry out their duties as they saw fit. But the greed of the Directors and companies gave almost no protection to their workers.

"Look, most of the workers are gone right now from shift change, probably headed to Frost's celebrations as well," Joshua said. "And the easiest way to leg 193 is through the maintenance shafts that run behind the cannery." He pointed across the chamber, through the maze of metal catwalks, crushing compactors, and moving belts that powered the cannery. "That's our way in."

"Then let's go, there's no sense waiting in this heat any longer." Miles stood and readjusted the weight of the backpack he carried, leaving a strip of moisture where the strap had been.

Miles reached out and helped Josie. Matias had taken the backpack she had been carrying and even if she fought it at first, the relief of easing that burden on her injured foot was great. A burden Matias hardly seemed to notice when he strapped on the pack.

"We have to stick together now," Miles whispered in her ear. "No matter what."

Josie nodded, but his tone concerned her.

"How are you feeling, Miles?" Doctor Lee asked.

Miles instinctively reached up and rubbed the back of his neck. "Sore, but better. Thanks to you, Doc."

"Of course," Lee said. "Normally I would not have cleared you for at least a week but . . ." Her eyes darted around the passageway. "We are in anything but normal times it seems." Lee reached for Josie's shoulder and leaned in close. "Josie, I'm sorry about what happened. I underestimated Joshua's loyalty to Marcus. Are you okay?"

"What happened?" Miles asked, raising his voice. The group was coming close to the cannery's main chamber now and the noise grew steadily, as did the oppressive heat.

"It's nothing," Josie countered. "I let my guard down and Marcus tricked me. It's why we're here now."

Miles's face scrunched up, sending beads of sweat tumbling down. "Didn't I tell you not to trust—"

"I know," Josie said and walked faster. "And look at us now, just another thing I did wrong."

"I didn't mean . . ." Miles started.

Josie was already several steps ahead but heard Tai come up to Miles.

"Let me give you a piece of advice," Tai said as she got closer to Miles. She pointed up toward Josie. "Don't do that." She smiled briefly and fell back behind him.

"Tell me about it," Miles said under his breath.

The chamber opened, and Josie's eyes went wide as she saw the true size of the cannery machines and all the auxiliary structures and tech that went with it. The great maw opened, and a new blast of hot, heavy air fell on them. Even if the workers were gone for now, the machines never slept. They grumbled and consumed ever on, and in return gave much of the food *November's Dawn* survived on.

"Let's go," Joshua said and waved his hand toward stairs leading high up to a catwalk.

Heights had never bothered Josie much. She had been on the metal platforms in the Observatory and had been alright with it. But this was different; it was strange and unsettled her stomach. With every step, the metal grates under her creaked and groaned under the weight of the group. Every second was split by a new whistle or scream from the cannery's machines.

The deep red light that bathed everything in its sinister glow only made the whole ordeal more chilling. Only it was a chill she could not feel as every step higher and closer to the cannery led them deeper into the source of the menacing heat.

"I knew a boy who worked here," Tai said from the steps behind Josie. "Got his hand stuck under a press and lost a couple fingers. Now I see this place, it's a wonder that's all he lost."

Josie looked back. "That's horrible. I'm sorry. Is he okay?"

Tai shrugged. "Company let him go after that, on account of not meeting the productivity requirement. Come to think of it, I don't know what he's doing anymore, but that's life for most people. You know that."

"Yeah, and that needs to change. Someone should have helped him."

"Hey, you lot! What're you doing here? This is a restricted area!" a voice shouted over the roaring cannery.

Everyone on the catwalk spun around at once. Two P&C officers stood at the entrance of the chamber. The officers looked small from how high up they were now, but Josie could see one pointed his security baton up at them.

"Run!" Joshua barked.

The catwalk thundered and shook as they all began to sprint. The officer screamed at them to stop, but his voice was drowned out by the machinery.

"Do you know where we're going?" Doc Lee called up ahead.

Joshua didn't answer, instead throwing up a finger high up in front of him. Josie tracked where he pointed. A couple levels above them in between several massive pipes was a small hatch.

"I can lock them out once we're through," Joshua said.

Josie ran as fast as she could, but the pain in her foot slowed her considerably. The catwalk rattled violently under the stress. A warmth seeped across her injured foot. The blood soaked into her sock and spread fast across the bottom of her foot. Joshua turned and led them up another short set of stairs, and Josie had just enough time to look at the P&C officers chasing them. They were catching up, fast. They beat their batons on the railings of the catwalk as they chased, each time sending electrical sparks raining down on the cannery below.

"One more level. Let's go!" Joshua shouted back.

Josie twisted and drove her weight down into the metal grating, her foot slipped in her boot. The sudden shift buckled her leg and she fell to one knee, only catching herself on one of the railings. She couldn't tell how high they were, but clearly high enough that a fall would kill her.

"Come on, Josie," Miles said into her ear as he wrapped his arm under hers. As if she weighed nothing at all in that moment, he lifted her. His breathing was hard and fast, but the determined look in his eye had returned. The same look Josie had so often found herself drawn to.

The maintenance hatch was close now. Joshua ran down a walkway leading straight to it. Matias turned back and stood at the junction, shouting for them to hurry up. He pulled his own baton free as Josie and Miles passed.

"What're you doing?" Josie shouted when she saw he was not following.

"Get out of here!" he roared back.

"We can't stop," Miles said.

Josie resisted the urge to bury her face in Miles's shoulder as the catwalk shook more fiercely, its bolts beginning to give. The hatch was just ahead. Joshua was already punching something into the access pad next to it.

"I got it," Joshua said and stormed through the hatch; the others followed him into the safety of the maintenance shaft.

The catwalk screeched, releasing an ear-piercing sound as

the bolts securing it to the bulkhead sheared and it started slipping down the wall, just in front of the hatch.

"Hold on!" Miles said. He pulled Josie close and leaped over the ledge.

They both tumbled to the ground on the other side of the hatch, but they were safe.

"Matias, let's go!" Joshua shouted from the hatch opening.

Baton in hand and jaw clenched tight, Matias stood firmly on the unstable catwalk. He looked at the officers running toward him and then back toward Joshua, as if calculating the odds. He grunted angrily then turned and sprinted across the catwalk to the hatch.

"Come on," Tai said as she waved Matias forward, as if her determination would lend him speed.

Matias was halfway across the catwalk now, with the officers close behind him. Each blink brought him closer.

"Faster, Matias! Come on!" Joshua crouched low and wedged himself in the doorway. His arms extended as far as they could reach.

Matias was close enough for Josie to see his eyes glistening as he ran through what seemed a sea of fire, focused only on reaching the end. The catwalk shuddered and heaved, finally wrenching itself free from the bulkhead wall.

Josie closed her eyes and turned away, unable to watch anymore.

"Matias, no!" Joshua cried out; his voice shattered against the chaos.

Josie's stomach dropped. The pain in Joshua's voice was so real. It ripped through her. A final screech of sheering metal split the air as the catwalk slammed into a lower level. The worst must have happened.

Then a thud sounded next to Josie. She turned to see two bodies tangled together. Joshua and Matias.

At the other end of the catwalk one of the P&C officers fell into the depths of the machinery below. He had been faster than his partner and the catwalk had given way under his feet. The other one roared in anger and reached for something slung across his back. It was long and jet black, with glowing blue tubes down the side of it. Josie went rigid when she realized what it was. She had heard the stories. A holorifle.

"Joshua, close the door!" Josie screamed.

Joshua was still caught on the ground with Matias. The officer was bringing up the holorifle toward them now, separated only by the expanse made from the fallen catwalk. In seconds the weapon would be unleashed upon them. Josie reached up and slammed her palm against the hatch control panel. Arcing light and a torrent of power raced toward her from where the officer stood, stopped only by the resounding thud of the hatch slamming closed. The blast from the holorifle thundered against the metal hatch. Over and over, the officer fired. Josie had no idea how long the door would hold.

Josie rolled over onto her hands and knees and looked up at Joshua. She wanted to scream at him for not acting quicker. Adrenaline coursed through her.

Joshua looked down at Josie. The muscles in his jaw pulsed. "That was too close," he whispered, more to himself than anyone else.

Matias put a hand on his shoulder. "You saved me, Joshua. Thank you." After a moment he started down the passageway.

"The mission is over." Joshua's words were cold and flat. He offered nothing else as he stood and brushed rust off his shirt. Sweat still glistened across his forehead from the heat of the cannery as he followed Matias.

"What? No!" Josie shouted and followed him. "Joshua, please. We can't stop. We must finish the mission! We have to." She grabbed onto Joshua's arm.

He spun around with a wild look. "The mission?" he spat. "I thought Matias was dead just then. A half second later and he would have been. That might not mean much to you, but it does to me. No one is dying."

His words infuriated Josie. All she could think about was how Joshua showed zero concern when his brother Miles had almost died in the garden explosion. But she knew pointing that out would only enrage him. The close encounter with dying himself had clearly shaken him.

"I promise you." She looked around at Miles and Tai, Doc Lee, and Matias. "If we don't finish what we came here to do, you'll regret it." Josie stepped back, not realizing everyone was watching her.

"Joshua," Miles said. "Let's finish this. For Mom."

Joshua looked at them all, gathered there in the deep darkness of a forgotten passageway. Finally, his head dropped. "Fine, I won't stop you. But whatever happens now is on you." He turned and continued down the passageway.

Josie nodded and tried to swallow, but her throat was hot and dry and only made worse by shallow breaths.

"You okay?" Miles asked, gently touching her arm.

She nodded but as soon as her gaze met Miles's, she could not hold it anymore and had to turn away. A thousand different thoughts screamed in her head, each one clamoring to be heard, each one drowning out the rest. Her dad had entrusted the future to her, the weight of it smothered everything else. Why had Felix given her the holomessage? She was not ready for it. The responsibility was crushing, but what choice did she have now? They depended on her.

"I'm okay." She wiped her face with her sleeve. "Let's just go." She turned and followed Joshua deeper into the darkness.

CHAPTER SEVENTEEN_

Nobody said anything as Joshua led them through the maintenance shafts. In between the odd echo from their footsteps, a low, deep creaking, like metal being stressed over and over droned on. The rhythmic swaying of *November's Dawn's* stride along the ocean floor was more pronounced this close to the hull, and the impact of the legs shifting outside shook the whole passageway. Josie walked next to Tai and tried to let her mind wander instead of dwelling on what had just happened.

Joshua held up his hand, signaling them all to stop.

"What is it?" Miles said from where he was pressed up against the wall of the passageway.

Joshua pointed to the junction in the passageway just ahead. "Leg 193 and the turbine are just down there." He gestured for Matias to come closer and looked back at the rest of them. "Stay here. We'll check it out and be right back."

Nobody objected. Josie turned and slumped up against the wall. The coldness of the metal crept through her clothes. "It's so much colder here."

Doc Lee eyed Josie's foot and removed a roll of bandages

from her pocket. "That needs rebandaging." The streaks of silver in her hair glinted ever so faintly in the low light of the maintenance shaft.

Josie didn't object as she slid down the wall.

"It's easy to forget how far below the surface we are," Doc Lee said as she worked. "We're a mere handful of meters away from one of the harshest environments in the world. And it only gets worse from here. Soon we will be nearing the deepest part of the flooded world, the Obsidian Trench."

"Well isn't that a delightfully terrifying thought," Tai said in an offhanded way.

"And it should be, but we're here because we must be. So many have forgotten our history." Lee leaned back and continued, "After the great war, tectonic movement ripped the planet apart. The Obsidian Trench swallowed much of what was once South America. Now we've resigned ourselves to life under the waves, with celebrations to mark our acceptance of a throttled existence. But for all their tyranny, the OSD is right about one thing."

Miles perked up. "What's that?"

"*November's Dawn* does offer us all a chance, and it's our responsibility to make it a better life for us all. Frost just thinks his way is the only way. That an iron fist is needed for order. But there are other ways."

"What do you think the surface is like?" Josie asked. All she could think of were her dad's words. That *November's Dawn* could return to the surface. Then they would never have to fear the crushing dark again, and they could start over. But now she thought about something else as well. There was a chance the surface was more dangerous above than below. There could be threats they had no idea about. What if the waves were too strong or the air itself was poisonous? There were records of dangerous things in the old databases.

"Honestly, I'm not sure, Josie. Years ago, Olympus Deck would take scans of the surface to measure the storms and release the results to the rest of the ark. For a time, the storms seemed to be losing their strength, but the scans stopped. They said it was due to mechanical failures. Now I suspect it was because they don't want folks wondering what life would be like up there, even if it is impossible."

"Do you think we will ever go back? To the surface, I mean. Maybe we'd be able to rebuild up there."

"Perhaps one day. It's a nice dream, Josie, but right now, we have to survive." Doc Lee tied the bandage and stood up. "There. All done."

"Thank you." A slight smile crept across Josie's lips. She wanted nothing more than to tell Lee about her dad's holomessage. That there was still hope for the future she spoke of. But they were in the middle of a dangerous mission. She resolved to tell her as soon as it was safe. "You really think we can change things?"

"I didn't for a long time." Lee chuckled again and her lips turned up into a coy smile. "But you've reminded me of it. For years, I fought for a better future, and so many times I wanted to give up. But I see the fire in your eyes. In all your eyes." She looked at both Miles and Tai as well. "I'm ready to pass the torch, I think."

"But not yet," Josie said.

Doc Lee's coy smile returned. "But not yet."

All four of them jumped from a loud crash echoing down the passageway. "Tai! Doc!" Joshua's voice followed the noise. "Let's go!"

Josie let out one final breath. This was it. This was why she was here. Josie reached for Miles, and he gave her hand a gentle squeeze.

Two P&C officers were slumped up against the wall

further down the passageway. Joshua and Matias stood near them. "Not dead, only knocked out," Joshua said when he caught Doc Lee's stern look.

"They won't be for long," Matias added. "Let's move."

A final hatch blocked their progress. Above it a holoscreen flickered, reading *Leg 193* in bright neon lettering. Joshua reached back into his backpack and pulled out a small tool with several prongs sticking out. Without a word, he jammed it into the access panel for the hatch. Sparks jumped out. The hatch unlocked and opened inward. He must have read the confusion and interest on Josie's face, because he said, "I know what you're thinking, but this won't get you into Olympus."

"Just go," Josie said, hiding her disappointment.

They entered a large room about the size of three Aegean Deck cabins laid out. Control boards and holoscreens dominated the far end of the room. In the center sat the huge turbine, powered by the perpetual movement of leg 193. As Josie neared it, her fingers ran across its faded yellow metal casing. It hummed underneath her palm.

"Oh wow!" Tai exclaimed. She was at the far side of the room, near the holoscreens. Her face pressed against a small oval view port just above where leg 193 attached to the hull. "I've never seen anything like it."

Josie and Miles followed her. Lights on the outside of the hull lit up leg 193. Josie knew it would be large, but the sheer size of the great metal leg still took her breath away. It had to be at least a hundred meters long. The diameter of it was big enough she was sure all her classmates could wrap their arms around it in a chain and still not meet on the other side. The first section of the leg jutted straight out of the hull before a joint led to another piece forming the remainder of the leg that reached the ocean floor. But it was the movement of the giant leg that truly captivated her. It was slow and deliberate, and now when she closed her eyes, she could match the sway of *November's Dawn* to where the leg was shifting from.

"Look there." Miles pointed up toward a shimmering school of fish swarming near one of the exhaust vents on the leg.

"They follow *November's Dawn* into the depths by the heat and the lights," Doc Lee said.

Joshua tapped the turbine with his baton. "You're up, Josie. I hope you know what you're doing."

Josie nodded and approached the turbine and control panels.

"How can I help?" Miles asked as he set the backpack of tools down next to the humming turbine.

"I don't know yet," Josie whispered. A multitude of pipes, wires, and tubes ran up and across the walls. She wasn't sure she was up to the task anymore.

Miles looked over at Joshua and Matias, who had moved to flank either side of the hatch. "You got this. Just think."

"Okay, okay. I'm just redirecting power, that's all. The control boards. I should start there." Josie tapped her finger on one of the holoscreens. Status reports and notices flashed across it. She tapped through another screen, where the system schematics for the leg and turbine appeared as a series of diagrams and models. The models showed power generation in the turbine being directed through a network of transmission lines under the floor. A warning popped up, stating that unauthorized access of classified information was a severely punishable offense.

"Have you found anything?" Miles asked. He leaned over her to see the holoscreen.

"Not yet," Josie said. She brushed a loose strand of hair out of her eyes and typed in a command to access transmission controls. The control board responded with a shrill tone and red error message. "Okay, that didn't work."

"What's going on?" Joshua asked.

"Nothing," Josie answered. "Just getting a feel for it." She tried another command. This time a message appeared. "Got it! The transmission direction can only be altered when the turbine is disconnected from the leg," she read aloud from the message.

"Okay. How do we do that?" Miles asked as he looked back at the turbine.

"Joshua!" Matias called from the passageway. "We've got a problem."

Joshua looked over. "What?"

Matias stepped back into the room holding a small communicator. "I found it on the guard. He sent an alert."

"Damn!" Joshua slammed his fist against the wall. "Josie! We're out of time. Let's go!"

Josie typed a string of commands into the holoscreen that was met by a loud screeching sound coming from outside the hull. "Not yet," she said, this time more determined.

Joshua's eyes flashed with anger. Miles stepped a little closer to Josie to act as a barrier between her and his brother. Joshua looked at Miles. "Fine. But this is your call, little brother."

Miles nodded and moved closer. "But, Josie, won't they know what we did? Won't they just fix it as soon as we leave?"

Josie stopped. She was worried about that too. "I don't think so. I should be able to hide what I've done in the system. And it won't be enough power to trigger the failsafe. They might know we were in the room, but we could just be a bunch of deserters from the factories hiding out. I doubt they even think we're smart enough to tamper with one of the legs."

There was another reason she could not give up. She needed the access codes for Olympus Deck from Marcus, and she was sure he would never give them to her if they failed.

"Yeah, I guess," Miles said with a frown. "What do we need to do?"

"See that lever over there?" Josie pointed across the room where a hole in the floor exposed a metal pipe. Miles nodded. "That's the coupling between the leg and the turbine. On my mark you need to turn it."

Miles got on his knees and gripped the lever on the pipe. "Ready!"

"On my mark!" Josie said. "Three. Two. One!" She entered the last string of commands just as Miles started to pull on the lever. It didn't budge. "Miles, now!"

Warning messages flashed across the screen, and the screeching sound echoed through the room again, louder this time. Miles leaned into the lever. It still did not move. After several seconds the lever snapped free from the coupling. Miles flew forward from the momentum, his head slamming against the open floor panel.

"Miles, are you okay?"

"I'm okay," Miles said in a groggy voice. His head swayed gently back and forth.

Doc Lee and Tai rushed over to help him up. Blood ran down his cheek from a new cut. Miles held up the snapped lever and looked at Josie, his eyes empty. He tried to stand but lost his balance. Joshua steadied him.

Shouting echoed in from the passageway as did the sounds of boots against the ground. "They're coming," Matias said.

Josie ran to the bag of tools and grabbed a large wrench and fastened it around the coupling. She pushed with all her strength. The holoscreens screamed their warnings as the screeching grew louder.

Doc Lee grabbed the wrench. "I got this, go!"

Joshua slipped his hand under Miles and pulled him up. "Josie, we're done! We have to leave now!"

Miles ducked under his brother's arm and leaned against the control board. "I'm staying."

Josie stopped and looked at him. She took his face in her hands and pulled him close. "You've done enough, Miles. You got me this far. Let me finish it." She wiped a smear of blood off his face with her sleeve. "Joshua, get him out of here."

Miles nodded slowly as his eyelids fluttered.

"Go, we'll be right behind you." Josie ran back to the control board. Alerts blared but she was focused on the mission. She was an engineer. She fixed things. Everything depended on her now. If this failed, they would never return to the surface. There would be no justice for her dad and Felix and every single person who suffered because of the upper deck's cruelty. She had come too far to turn back now.

"Tai, let's go," Joshua called and worked across the room with Miles.

Tai looked back at Josie before following them out into the passageway beyond.

"Ready?" Josie said to Doc Lee.

"Yes, do it!" Lee shouted back as she pushed all her weight down on the wrench, trying to break the connection of the coupling. It gave way after several seconds. The screeching faded and the holoscreen status turned green.

"That's it!" Josie jumped up in excitement. She quickly keyed in the last string of commands needed to send the power to Bottom Bays. The turbine groaned in response. "No, no, no!" Josie slammed her fists on the control board.

"What is it?" Doc Lee asked as she ran over.

"The turbine," Josie said. "It's going to take too long to

restart. We're out of time." The sounds of boots against metal thundered from the passageway.

"Then I'll hold them off." Doc Lee pulled a small pistol from her jacket.

Josie eyed her. "Where did you get that?"

"I hardly think that matters now," Doc Lee said and laughed with newfound vigor. "How much time do you need?"

Josie glanced back at the control holoscreen. "Three minutes."

Doc Lee nodded and started walking towards the door. "Josie," she called back. "Be ready to run like hell." She pressed up against the wall to the side of the door.

Josie heard the voices of the P&C officers now. It was hard to tell how many there were, but it was definitely more than a couple. Across the room, Doc Lee stood still up against the wall. Their eyes met and she nodded before bringing the pistol up to her side.

Doc Lee glanced down the passageway. "They're here. I see at least six. They have holorifles." She kicked over a table and pushed it up to the door, making a barricade.

Josie reached down and pulled a large wrench close to her on the desk. Her palm slipped down the cool metal. The wrench would do nothing against the holorifles, but it felt right to hold it, like it gave her a chance. This could not be the end. She barely had time to think but repeated those words over and over in her head. Josie waited for it to begin and ducked down.

Doc Lee closed her eyes and pulled the hammer back on the pistol. She took one final breath and then aimed down the passageway. The P&C officers had not seen her yet. Her hand trembled. She exhaled and squeezed the trigger. Fire erupted in front of her as the blast pierced her ears. One of the officers fell to his knee as the bullet sliced through his thigh. She fired twice in quick succession. The bullets ricocheted down the passageway. The other officers shouted over the one who was wounded and readied their holorifles.

The passageway lit up from the flashing, bouncing blue energy the holorifles discharged. Doc Lee reached around the edge and fired again.

"Thirty seconds!" Josie shouted over the storm of energy and bullets.

Another holorifle blast whipped past the door. Lee shifted out of the way just in time. The energy smashed into the passageway, leaving behind a small glowing red orb of fire and melted metal. A few of Doc Lee's strands of gray hair smoldered. She grunted and fired back. A second P&C officer howled and collapsed.

"Come on. Come on. Come on," Josie whispered to herself. Ten seconds left. They were so close. One command away from it working. They only had one chance before the officers had them cut off and trapped in the turbine room.

"It's done," Josie said to herself. Slamming her finger down on the button prompted a low rumble from the turbine and outside leg. Green statuses flashed across the holoscreen. It worked. "Lee, let's go!"

Josie grabbed Doc Lee's free hand as she got close. She spun around, a wild look in her eye. "It worked?"

"Yes! More power is being siphoned to Bottom Bays now. It's not enough to trigger a warning being sent to the bridge."

A new barrage of holorifle fire raged across the doorway in front of them. The officers inched up the passageway toward them.

"Josie, on the count of three, run."

Josie nodded. The officers were firing blindly down the passageway they needed to run across. She gulped but was met with a wave of nausea and unease. She pulled her hair back behind her ears.

"One, two." Doc Lee reached out and fired three times. She tried a fourth but was met with a bone chilling click as the hammer connected with an empty chamber. "Three!"

Together they sprang across the threshold. Lee's last bullets had given them a split-second moment. It was all they needed. Josie's foot slipped from her blood drenched sock when she landed, but she caught herself and tried to block out the pain. Doc Lee sprinted right behind her, remarkably fast for her age. The officers turned the corner behind them and shouted for them to stop.

"Don't stop. Keep going no matter what," Doc Lee urged.

Josie nodded and turned her head just as a blinding flash of light flared down the passageway. The brilliant blue energy painted the dull gray walls with a cascading dance of color. Blistering heat rippled across her body. It was a heat unlike anything she had ever experienced. It consumed and broke upon her body with such ferocity she was sure it would kill her. The sheer force of it was next. Like the air itself was sucked away. It slammed into her body and threw her against the passageway wall. Her vision blurred. It was like a cloud of dust had exploded down the passageway.

"Lee!" Josie shouted and reached out, but her hand came up empty.

Doc Lee should have been right next to her. They were running together.

"Doc! Where are you!" she yelled, this time the fear echoing in her voice. The dust particles started to settle, leaving a thick layer on everything. Lee was gone. Josie's blood turned cold as she realized what had happened.

The holorifle had struck Doc Lee, its energy instantly vaporizing her into a particle cloud of ash and dust. Josie screamed, cut off by the feeling of nausea storming up the back of her throat. She covered her mouth and tried to swallow it down. It was too late. She fell to her knees, trembling as her stomach emptied. The vomit spread across the layers of dust. Its putrid smell mixed with the stench of burned flesh. Three P&Cs sprinted toward her. Only now she didn't have the will to move anymore.

Lee was gone and she was next.

CHAPTER EIGHTEEN_

A STRANGELY FAMILIAR voice shouted at Josie. It made no sense. She was alone. Doc Lee was gone. She was next. Nothing seemed to matter as her body slipped under its own weight. Coupled with her vision fading and the particles of dust still settling in the air, it was like time had slowed considerably. Josie let herself fall to the ground, sending small plumes of dust into the supercharged air.

"Josie! Josie, are you okay?" the voice called again.

Strong hands gripped her, but she kept her eyes closed. It was safer to keep them shut. She welcomed the unknown. The clamor of fighting and bone breaking impacts echoed down the passageway. The ringing in her ears made tracking the source impossible. Hands wrapped around her chest and stomach, slowly at first and then with more sureness. Again, she kept her eyes closed, unwilling to face whoever was carrying her. Whether from a fear of who it might be or a fear of who it might not be, she could not decide. The strong hands pulled her over broad shoulders and held her tight as they ran down the passageway.

"Get back. Let's go!" another voice shouted.

Boots thundered underneath. They moved faster now, away from the noise and panic, toward peace and quiet. Was that safety? Josie was not sure she cared anymore. Guilt choked her breath. She tried to swallow it back down but got only the foul taste of bile instead.

She had been so sure of herself, so determined she could reroute the power, she had refused to see the danger. She'd made a choice. What happened was all her fault.

One moment, all she could feel was sadness and relentless guilt over Doc Lee's death, the next nothing, just blissful emptiness. After a while, their pace slowed until it eventually became a walk. Whoever carried her breathed hard. His hot breath felt like a wet cloth against the exposed skin of her torso.

"We're far enough. I'll go tell the others," the second voice said.

This time the voice echoed as if they were in a great room. The faintest babbling broke against the familiar sound of metal walls, like water moving in a tub half full, only magnified tenfold. Josie knew she must be losing it as the haze in her head started to clear. The storm of emotions inched back into the dark recesses of her mind as conscious thoughts reemerged. She cracked open one eye to see the back of Joshua's head and a dark room beyond. With great care, her savior reached up and lowered her down, gently sitting her against the side of something very large and quite round.

"You're safe now," Miles said. He put his palm on her cheek.

Just as he pulled his hand away, Josie reached for it. She glanced up, meeting the torrent of worry flooding through Miles's eyes. The relief was short lived, cutoff by a cold chill sweeping through her body. The sight of the gash down his cheek he had suffered while trying to help her reroute the power made her tremble all over again. Miles had been badly hurt, and she still had refused to leave before finishing the mission. "Miles, I—"

"It's okay, Josie, just breathe," Miles said as he stood. "Let me see if there's somewhere you can lie down. I'll be right back, I promise. Tai, stay with her please."

Tai padded out from the shadows created by a huge balcony encircling the chamber. She knelt next to Josie and put the back of her hand against her forehead.

"Hi," she said in her usual melodic voice. "Just focus on breathing right now. I think you might be in a bit of shock."

Josie sniffed and nodded. She managed to take shallow breaths while she tried to calm herself. Tingling rippled through her body, like every nerve was on fire and every muscle ached. The back of her throat clenched and went dry.

"I think I'm going to throw up," she said and doubled over.

"You're okay. Just let it happen. It's okay," Tai said as she held Josie's hair behind her.

"I'm afraid it's not shock you're experiencing, Miss Owens." The voice was deep and low. Josie didn't have to look up to recognize it.

"Then what, Marcus?" Tai asked. "Nothing else would make sense."

"What you see here is the terrible effects of being in close proximity to a holorifle blast."

"Doc Lee really is gone?" Tai asked.

Josie nodded and clenched her fists. "I-I made a mistake," she whispered just as Matias walked by carrying a rifle she recognized immediately and would likely never forget. "Are those?"

"Yes. Thanks to Miles's quick thinking to double back, we were able to recover a few holorifles." Marcus looked down at Josie. "And rescue you, of course. Shame it was only you."

"Maybe you shouldn't have," Josie said, half to herself.

"Josie, don't say that," Tai exclaimed. "Come on, Miles should have a place ready for you now."

Josie took Tai's outstretched hand with some reluctance. A couple other members of Hades Fist walked by. They kept their eyes low. She knew they were all thinking the same thing, even if nobody said it. She could see it on their faces, in the way they cast quick glances at her. No doubt Joshua had told them what happened. She had messed up, and Doc Lee paid the price for it.

"Oh, Miss Owens," Marcus called to them as they walked. "A deal is a deal." He tossed the gleaming silver data cartridge into the air. "Was it worth it?"

Josie caught it between her fingers as she glared at Marcus. As much as she disliked him, she bit her tongue. Lashing out would make no difference now. She rubbed her thumb across the data cartridge while she read the embossed lettering, *Olympus Deck Access*, her ticket to the front of *November's Dawn* and the bridge, to everything she wanted, to everything her dad had entrusted her with. Her eyes hardened as she wrapped her hand around it.

"Keep it." She let the cartridge slip through her fingers and tumble to the ground.

She didn't want anything to do with it anymore.

"Come on, this way," Tai said, guiding Josie to a passageway off the main chamber.

The faint babbling water caught Josie's attention again. "What is this place?"

Tai stopped and looked back at the large room. "This is one of the old fisheries. Hasn't been used in years apparently. We use it though, kind of like a safehouse."

Josie squinted into the low light of the colossal chamber. She could vaguely see giant metal pipes coming in from the outer hull of *November's Dawn* and snaking around until they opened into even larger tanks of water. A small drip coming from one of the pipes rhythmically splashed into one of the pools.

"A damn waste," Joshua said from behind them. "The fish sucked in and processed here could be used to feed Aegean Deck and Bottom Bays. All we would need is someone from Olympus to input the access commands and people to help run the place. But it's 'not profitable' according to the companies."

Josie swallowed hard. Joshua's voice sparked the storm of emotions all over again. "Joshua, I'm sorry. I messed everything up."

"Yeah," he said, his voice low. "I'm sorry too." His blank face betrayed nothing except sadness, as if he were just now realizing the reality of what they were doing. Without another word, he turned and walked away.

"He just needs time, Josie. We all do," Tai said.

Josie thought for a moment. She was so tired of everything and craved some sense of normalcy, even for a moment. "Will you tell me about the boy you mentioned? The one that made you feel so special?" She knew she was prodding, but she needed a distraction. It was like some part of her wanted to hear Tai talk about something other than Josie's failure as if it would prove she was still her friend. It was selfish and she knew it, but part of her didn't care.

A light chuckle followed. It was the sweetest thing Josie had ever heard. "Maybe another time; I just don't feel like it right now. She probably wouldn't like to be called a boy though," Tai said with a twinkle in her eye.

It took a moment for the embarrassment to wash over Josie. When it did, her mouth hung open at an awkward angle as she tried to put together an apology. "Tai, I'm so sorry." It was hard to imagine how alone Tai must feel or the struggles she had faced in her life.

"It's okay. Most folks would have assumed like you did. I think sometimes they just don't know what to think of it."

"I think it's beautiful," Josie said quickly.

She never wanted to be the reason Tai felt alone or uncomfortable again. She never wanted anyone to ever feel like that again.

"Thanks, Josie." She smiled, but a distant sadness hung around her.

"Tai, Josie, there you are," Miles said, his head popped out of a hatch off the passageway.

Josie's heart fluttered when she saw him, but she couldn't tell if it was from relief or worry. *What would he think?* Her lips trembled. He probably hated her. This was likely all just an act. They felt bad for her, and that was it.

"Oh, I think I hear someone calling my name," Tai said with an uncomfortable smile. She gave Josie's hand a squeeze as she walked away.

Miles opened his arms up to her. "Here, I found some blankets. Just rest a minute."

Josie walked into a room that looked like an old supply closet. A thick layer of dust covered empty shelves and an array of poles, nets, wire cages, and other fishing tools. They had not been touched in years. Miles had made up a corner and spread out a rough fleece blanket.

"It's not much," Miles said. He plunged his hands in his pockets.

"Thank you," Josie whispered. She could hardly bring herself to face him. Instead, she sat down on the blanket and pulled her knees in close.

"So," Miles said while swiping his finger across the dust on one of the shelves. "What's next?"

She looked up. "Next?"

"Yeah. Next. Where do we go from here?"

Josie could barely stand the thought of what she had caused. "I just screw things up."

Miles's eyes hardened. "No, don't you see? You did what you said you would. The power was rerouted. That's only because of you. It's just, well, it's just other stuff happened too."

"Thanks." Tears welled up in the corner of her eyes. She buried her face in the crook of her arm. "All I see is Doc Lee running down the passageway with me. And all I can hear is Joshua begging us to leave and saying it was over. But I wouldn't listen. I couldn't." She choked through each word. "Don't you see, Miles? I got her killed. If it wasn't for me, she would still be alive. I just *had* to believe I knew better than everyone else."

"Doc Lee died for something, Josie. For what she believed in." Miles stood and put his hands on his hips. "Look, you think Marcus is the answer? In the end, he's probably no better than Frost. But you have a third possibility. If we can bring *November's Dawn* up to the surface and people see the whole world out there, then we can be free. That chance is gone without you."

Miles reached down and held his hand out for her.

Josie blinked and wiped her eyes. She wanted to take his hand so badly, every part of her screamed to do it, but she kept circling back to one thought, one inescapable reality.

More people would get hurt if she kept going.

But how many more would be hurt if she stopped?

She jumped as someone started banging on the hatch. "Oi! Everybody come to the main room. Something's happened on Aegean!" Matias shouted through the thick metal.

Miles grabbed the hatch lever and opened it. He turned back. "If you give up now, Reyes and Frost and all the rest of them win. Then Doc Lee and Felix . . . Well, they really will have died for nothing."

Josie sucked in as if she had been punched in the stomach. It made her want to scream at him, but Miles was gone before she could manage to say anything—probably because deep down she knew he was right.

Josie slammed her fist on the ground next to her.

People ran back and forth down the passageway outside, their boots and occasional shouts echoing, but she could not bring herself to move. The last thing she wanted was to see Joshua's disappointment, or Tai's pity. They were all better off without her. They were safer. Marcus was their leader. He didn't need scrawny Josie Owens making more trouble than she was worth.

The blanket looked so welcoming. Even if it was rough against her skin, she could hardly keep her eyes open anymore. It had been so long since she slept for more than a couple of moments. Maybe sleep would take her and give her peace. Perhaps then Doc Lee's and Felix's faces would not dance in front of her every time she blinked, each time breathing their final moments over and over. They silently watched her as she reached out to them, giving her a chance to stop it, giving her a chance to make it right and save them. She screamed at them to take her hand. Yet each time their eyes turned to dust and their bodies faded. She reached farther and screamed louder, but it never made a difference.

She couldn't save them.

They were dead, and she was here.

With every passing second, her body fell deeper into the blanket and her eyes became too heavy to manage until there was nothing left, just the bittersweet peace of nothing at all.

CHAPTER NINETEEN

A BRIGHT, warm light caressed Josie's face. It hugged her and spread through her whole body.

"Josie," a low voice said. Gentle hands brushed her cheek. "Wake up, little fox."

"Just a little longer, Dad, I promise," Josie squeaked. She reached her hands up out of the blanket and let out a big yawn. "It's just so cozy."

Her dad laughed. A sweet chuckle that always made her feel like she was the funniest person alive. Mom was the only one who could get Dad to laugh louder than she could, but that was fine by Josie. Her mom was funny sometimes.

"Little fox," her dad said slowly. "Come on, your mom is making your favorite breakfast. It's not every day you turn eleven. You'll soon be as old as me!"

She was so excited. She was so happy. Then it all faded away.

Josie blinked. Slowly at first but then with more purpose. A splitting headache welcomed her. The realization it had all been a dream crashed into her next. She quietly sobbed into her hand. The dream felt so real, she wanted it to be so badly. She had so many questions for her dad: about the Heart of the Dawn, how he had found out the truth about *November's Dawn*, if he thought she was doing the right thing. He always knew the right thing to do.

The room was colder now, so she pulled the blanket up. It was hard to tell how long she had been asleep. Based on how much her body still ached and her head hurt, it couldn't have been long. Still, she didn't hear any noises from the fishery anymore. She stood and wrapped the blanket around her. The passageway was dark, but low light emanated from the larger chamber. The now-familiar trickle and bubbling of water greeted her, but no people. Earlier, most of Hades Fist had been there. Now, she only saw the dark silhouette of a single figure, leaning up against the guard railing around one of the huge fishery ponds. A sigh of relief slipped from her when she saw it was Miles. She walked faster toward him.

"How are you feeling?" he asked, still turned away from her.

Josie stopped. "How did you know I was here?"

He pointed to the fishery pond but didn't turn. "It's so quiet down here. No people, no machines, nothing. I'd bet you could hear a pin drop if you listened hard enough."

"Where is everyone?" she said as she walked closer.

"Gone," he said. "A riot broke out on Aegean Deck. First Vicar Frost expelled two people out into the ocean, said they were conspiring with terrorists. They weren't much older than us." His voice was flat, emotionless, as if he were stating facts and nothing more.

Josie gasped. "That's awful."

Miles turned and nodded. "Aye. Marcus and the others went down there."

"But not you."

He eyed her for a moment before turning back to lean on the railing. "But not me."

Josie's heart fluttered for a moment, as if she needed to hear the words to confirm it. He had stayed with her. That was enough. "How long was I asleep?"

"Not long. An hour, maybe more."

Josie pressed her hands together. They both knew what was happening. But dancing around unspoken feelings was not what she wanted to do. It hurt too much. "Miles, I-I'm sorry for before."

All her feelings crept up from inside her. Their cold hands wrapped around her throat and made it hard to breathe. "I'm just so scared. I believed so much that if I did what my dad wanted it would all work out. But the truth is, he's gone and we're here. We're the ones who have to make decisions and then we have to live with them. And after what happened, I don't know if I can make the right decisions anymore."

"That's the thing, Josie. I don't think there's ever a right decision." He ran his fingers through his hair. "You can plan and prepare and think about it all you want. But when it comes down to it, in that one moment, we make a choice and then you have to live with what happens, just like you said. I think if in that moment you did what you believed with all your heart to be right, well, that's just it. That's all you can do."

Josie looked down at the ground and kicked at a loose screw. She wanted to believe what he was saying, perhaps if only to ease her own guilt, but she could not help how she felt. "I'm just so scared of letting everyone down."

Miles reached up and touched the outline of the Heart of the Dawn beneath her shirt. "Your dad wouldn't have given that to you if he didn't believe with all his heart you could make the right choice. For all of us." His lips were close to her ear. "I'm not giving up on you."

Josie closed her eyes and put her hand over his. "Thank you."

"Always," he whispered back.

Before Josie could say anything else a series of footsteps echoed from the passageway. A figure emerged out of the darkness, running with a slight limp and breathing hard. Black and swollen eyes glanced around the chamber. Then Josie's heart dropped.

"Mags!" Miles said and ran to catch her. He got there just as her strength failed and she fell toward him.

Josie followed right behind him. "Mags, are you okay? What happened?" Josie glanced back to where Mags had come from. Rose was not with her. She shuddered, as if a thousand needles rippled across her body. Her heart hammered uncontrollably.

Mags looked up with a hollow expression. "I'm so sorry, Josie. Little Rose. They took her. There was nothing I could do."

CHAPTER TWENTY_

JOSIE LOOKED Mags straight in the eyes. The engineer had just said what she feared hearing more than anything. The torrent of emotions spinning in her head was drowned out by one thought.

She had decided to hide Rose with Mags. Whatever came of that was on her.

"What do you mean they took Rose?" she said, far more angrily than she'd meant to.

Miles frowned. "Josie, give her a moment."

Mags put her hand on his shoulder and tried to pull herself up. "No," she said. "It's okay. There's no time."

"Mags, please. Just sit. In a moment you'll catch your breath," Miles said as he helped her against the railing.

"He's right, Mags. Just take a second." Josie had always thought of Mags as such a strong woman. Folks listened to her. They respected her. Seeing her beaten and bruised infuriated Josie. That was without even thinking about what might have happened to her sister. "What happened to Rose?"

Mags never brought her head up. "We were in my cabin

when they came. A couple of P&Cs demanding to see Rose. I don't know how they knew she was there." Her voice was faint. Josie latched onto every word. "I told them to sod off, but they came in anyway. When they found Rose hiding under a bunk, well, this happened." Her voice trailed off as she motioned to her face. It was a slight gesture, but the pain Josie saw behind it tore her to pieces. "They took her. Must be to Olympus I'd say. I'm so sorry."

Josie leaned against the railing. The three of them were quiet. Rose was gone, taken by P&C officers. Josie was supposed to keep her safe. She was always supposed to protect her little sister. That was what her dad had told her on the very first night they had brought Rose home. The memory of that night was like a warm embrace and took her far away from the chilled air of the abandoned fishery. Her dad knelt holding the smallest bundle Josie had ever seen. She could still see her dad's face. The way his eyes sparkled, and the corners of his mouth turned up as Rose's tiny finger latched around Josie's pinky.

"She's delicate, Josie. You have to be careful," he said softly.

"Delicate?" Josie mumbled back.

He laughed. "Like how you have to be gentle with the flowers you see in the garden? She's our very own Rose."

Josie's eyes sharpened. "She's not a flower."

"No, no." He laughed again and smiled. "But we'll keep her safe like she is. Can you do that, little fox?"

That was one of the last happy memories she had of him. She had been so proud that day all those years ago. Now there was only guilt that she was unable to keep her promise. But there was something else as well. It burned bright in her mind and refused to allow her own dark thoughts to extinguish it. She had to save Rose. She wrapped her mind around it. Her little sister needed her, and she needed Rose too. Josie knew in her heart she could never give up. Not like this.

"I'm going after Rose," Josie said, the words just kind of tumbling out.

She looked at Miles next. Would he come with her? He was still crouched next to Mags, but he smiled slightly. The sharp look returned to his eyes. Even on the verge of exhaustion, he was as handsome as ever. She wished he could just look into her mind and see all the words she could not say, if only to spare her feelings. They had been forced to run from the OSD together by things outside their control. Reacting to everything, controlling nothing.

This was different. She was going straight into the heart of danger, and he had a choice this time. He didn't need to risk his life for her again. She would go alone if she had to. One thing was clear above all else, it had to be his choice; she could not accept anything else.

"Miles, I—" she began.

He looked up. "I'm coming with you, Josie. We'll get her back, I promise."

The way the words rolled off his tongue, Josie had to bite her cheek to keep from smiling. It was as if all her worries and fears from a few seconds ago had vanished, and she was left with only the thought that whatever she had to face while trying to find Rose, Miles would be right there with her.

"Let's get Mags out of here and go," Miles said.

Mags waved her hand in the air. "Don't worry about me. I've been in worse scrapes." She looked at Josie. "Every second puts you farther away from finding young Rose. Go, lass. Both of you!"

"Thank you, Mags. For everything." Josie wanted to say more, but the words felt insincere. Mags put herself in danger to help Josie, and it seemed horribly wrong to leave her now, even if she insisted.

Mags clutched Josie's hand in hers. "Make us proud, Josie Owens. Never forget where you came from."

One thought stopped Josie in her tracks. The data cartridge. In her anger, she had thrown it away. The one thing which contained the codes to get into Olympus Deck, and she had thrown it away. She ran over to where she had thrown it. It didn't seem to be anywhere. "Miles, I'm such a fool. I've lost it." Her lip started to tremble.

"You haven't lost it," he said with a soft voice.

Josie spun around to see Miles smiling with the data cartridge in his hand. "I told you, I'm not giving up on you."

She wrapped her arms around him. His warm breath caressed the nape of her neck. "Thank you," she whispered, unsure of what else to say.

"Oi!" Mags shouted. "If you two lovebirds have had enough, the elevator's that way," she said and pointed toward a different passageway leading from the fishery.

"Come on, let's go," Miles said as he grabbed her hand, pulling her along as they ran.

The passageway opened to a narrow set of stairs. They took them two at a time and entered a small room with windows along one side overlooking the main chamber of the fishery. Scattered papers and an overturned cup sat on a lonely metal desk in the center. The most recent date on the papers was years ago. Metal filing cabinets took up most of the wall across from the window, a few were open, like their contents had been stripped out in a hurry.

"This looks like the foreman's office," Miles said as he peered into one of the empty drawers.

Josie nodded, but her attention was focused on something else. In the far corner was a gilded metal door. The bronze-colored face reflected the little light coming through the windows. It looked just like the elevator that had taken them down to Bottom Bays, which they had used to escape the Garden of Tomorrow and Joshua said could go all the way to Olympus Deck with the right access codes.

Josie tapped Miles on the shoulder and pointed. "I think that's it."

Miles walked to the door and gently wiped the dust off the keypad next to it. He punched one of the keys, prompting the door to jolt as the elevator came to life. Josie sighed in relief. The inside looked just like the other Olympus elevator, clearly decorative and certainly not intended for use by Aegean Deck folk. At least they knew this one could take them to Olympus if the codes she had fought so hard for actually worked.

The data cartridge glistened as Miles turned it over in his hand. The keypad allowed for manual entry of the code but below it there was a small indent in the interface that controlled the elevator that looked roughly the same size and shape as the data cartridge. Miles rubbed his thumb across the cartridge one last time then slowly brought it up to the indent. His hand stopped just before pushing it into the interface.

Miles stood perfectly still, the cartridge only a finger's width away. "Sorry," he said. "It's just, we're about to go to Olympus Deck. *The* Olympus Deck. I never imagined I'd see it."

Josie fell back on the balls of her feet. "I know what you mean. And that's what we're going to change."

Miles nodded and snapped the data cartridge in place. The interface lit up as the code transferred, turning on the holo-screen that controlled the elevator. There was a new set of destinations highlighted that Josie had never seen before. "Argon Square, Oceanus Apartments, People's Theater

District," Miles said and scrunched up his face. "They have a whole district just for theater?"

Josie shrugged. "Just keep reading. Where would they take Rose?"

Miles slid his finger down the list. "How about this one? The Offices of the OSD?"

"Maybe," Josie said with her hands on her hips. "But we can't just show up in the OSD's offices. We'd get arrested immediately. What if we go somewhere else, like here." She placed her finger back higher up on the list. "The Oceanus Apartments. Maybe from there we can find a way in?"

Miles clicked on the name. "Worth a shot. Maybe we can find clothes to fit in better."

Josie nodded and let her head fall back against the wall of the elevator. The lack of sleep over the last few days was starting to take its toll.

They were headed to Olympus Deck; she needed to be ready for anything. Four days ago, she would have been thrilled to have a chance to see Olympus Deck, even if she hated everything it stood for. Nobody ever got that chance. Except for a few people like her mom, but that was another story all together. One her mom never told her, no matter how many times Josie asked.

All Josie remembered was that one day, her mom was selected from a pool of folks across the ark to be the next voice of *November's Dawn*. And Josie had struggled with that ever since.

Josie wished she could see her mom now and tell her she was starting to see why her mom made the decisions she did. Her mom deserved to know that at least. Then an awful thought crossed her mind. She stopped and looked at Miles. His eyes were closed as he leaned against the wall.

"Miles," she said. "You don't think my mom had anything to do with what happened to Mags, do you?"

One of his eyes popped open, apparently more interested now. "Well," he said deliberately. "I never thought of it, but I guess it makes sense. She would have seen Rose was missing. Maybe she went to the authorities?"

"Maybe." Josie had to admit that was the most likely option. She might not agree with her mom, but she was not a monster. It was all the other possibilities that scared her. "It's just . . . What if the OSD is using Rose and my mom to try to get to me?"

Miles smiled softly. "We'll get her back. I know we will."

They spend the rest of the trip in silence. Each contemplating what they might find, but neither having any real idea of what that might be. The elevator ride was longer than any Josie had been in before, but she supposed that made sense. After all, she had never been on an elevator that could take her all the way to the bow of *November's Dawn* before. Several more minutes passed before an automated voice echoed through the speakers.

"Welcome to Oceanus Apartments. The OSD hopes you find your time agreeable. If you are not authorized to be aboard Olympus Deck, please report to the nearest peace-and-compliance officer for immediate detention and relocation. Remember, citizen, in the darkness below, *November's Dawn* will provide." A chime rang as the voice faded.

Josie rolled her eyes. "That can't have worked on anyone."

Miles shrugged. "I don't know. Some folks are pretty daft after all."

The elevator opened into a rather unspectacular room, small and gray like much of the ark and more fit for supply storage than anything else. A workbench wrapped around the room with tools spread across it. Other than that, it held nothing Josie found remotely interesting. Her eyes were drawn to the single door on the other side of the room. It was nothing like what Josie was expecting, and the crease in Miles's brow told her he was also curious about the lack of splendor.

"So this is how the other half lives?" Miles said.

Josie would have taken it as sarcasm except for the fact they both truly had no idea what to expect on Olympus Deck. "This must just be a storage room. I mean come on, you can't tell me our classmates from Olympus would live somewhere like this, do you?"

"And risk cobwebs falling on them? No, I guess you're right."

Josie glanced around the edges of the room. Cobwebs slung across every corner and those were only the ones she could see. She shuddered at the thought of something dropping into her own hair. "Come on, let's get out of here."

"Fine by me." He walked toward the door but stopped and looked at a pair of lockers in the corner. "Wait, look. Could be something to change into."

Josie looked down at her own dirty and battered jumpsuit. She had to admit they looked like they had run through the ringer and obviously didn't belong on Olympus Deck.

Miles was already opening the locker.

"Ah, here we go." He pulled out two new jumpsuits, both neatly folded and embellished by the gold piping that signified them as Olympus Deck engineers. He put them both on the workbench and began unbuttoning his shirt, revealing his toned figure and smooth dark skin.

Josie took one of the jumpsuits and ran her finger across it. Even the fabric felt softer and more luxurious than what they provided on Aegean Deck. She pulled the jumpsuit close and anxiously glanced at Miles then around the room, which now looked even smaller and less private.

He finished the last button and looked up. "Oh, sorry," he muttered, clearly embarrassed. "I'll go over here," he added and motioned to the far corner.

"Thanks," Josie murmured, sheepishly admitting her unease. She took her jumpsuit to the opposite corner and worked herself out of her old one. Thankfully, Miles didn't say anything while they changed, freeing Josie to focus on slipping into the new clothes as quickly as she could. Then she bundled her hair up underneath the matching engineer's cap.

"Are you ready?" Miles asked in a slightly muffled tone.

Josie turned. He stood with his face a hands-width away from the corner. "Yeah, I'm done."

Miles smiled as he appraised their new look. "Not bad at all. Now, let's find your sister."

Being in clean clothes immediately gave Josie an improved outlook on things, even if the dull pain in her foot never subsided. Now that she was out of her old clothes, she realized how much of an odor they held, which made her feel even more embarrassed that Miles had been with her like that. The only consolation, if it could be called that at all, was Miles's old clothes were equally soiled.

Miles cranked the lever that engaged the door's mechanism to open. As soon as the seal broke, a surge of cool air rushed into the room. It carried a strange sterile smell, nothing like the air Josie was used to on Aegean or in the Engineering Bay. Rays of bright light escaped around the edges of the door as it swung open. When her vision finally adjusted, they stepped out into the Oceanus Apartments and under a small overhang. Nothing could have prepared them for the sight that awaited them.

They stood on the edge of a great chamber, at least as large as the Galley Markets back on Aegean. But the differences between the two areas could not be more drastic. The clutter of generations of structures built upon one another was nowhere to be seen, replaced instead by large structures with sleek white walls and clear round windows, each one at least two levels high and some many levels higher. The buildings all sat neatly lined against grand paved avenues that snaked through the chamber, wide enough for many people to pass untroubled by others on the path.

A strange light illuminated everything and lent a peculiar glow to the white walls and decorations adorning each apartment. Josie's gaze tracked higher in the chamber, curious to find the source of the unfamiliar light and eager to study everything in the strange land of Olympus Deck.

She took two steps out from the shadow of the overhang. The light caressed her face and gently warmed her body. She gasped when the ceiling of the chamber finally came into focus. "Miles," she whispered.

Arrayed across the ceiling were thick networks of vast white clouds, emblazoned on a blue background like a canvas, slowly billowing from one side of the chamber to the other. The light pierced some of the clouds, its luminosity radiating through them, shining a pale orange and yellow. In the middle of the display, the source of the light gleamed strong and bright, a round beacon in a sea of blue. Josie had seen pictures of it before. She had heard the stories.

"What is it?" Miles asked with squinted eyes.

"The sun." Josie tried to keep her voice low but could not stop the smile from creeping across her lips. It was something she had never imagined seeing. A slight tickle of air glanced across her cheeks. But this was not the warm and thick air of any mechanical exhaust. It carried the same sterile smell from before and the coolness of it lifted away some of the heat coming from the ceiling.

She dared one last look at the ceiling, any more time spent in awe would certainly alert others they did not belong. But that was when she saw it, a slight wrinkle in the sky, in the corner between two clouds, almost like a flutter or a disruption from a sudden gust of wind. The two sides pulled apart from one another in an almost unnoticeable display of blue sparks. But to Josie, it was more conspicuous than her own red hair in a crowd.

"A holoprojection," she whispered to herself.

"What?" Miles asked as he came closer.

Josie risked pointing a finger toward the disruption. "They're using holotech. See? And the wind. This must have been what life on the surface was like once."

"Hmm," Miles said, shielding his eyes. "The light could be less bright."

"Really? That's what you have to say?" Josie retorted half-jokingly. Part of her still couldn't believe the secrets on Olympus that nobody in the lower decks knew of. "Come on, before someone asks what we're doing." She reached for Miles's arm but thought better of it. After all, there was no reason two engineers would walked around Olympus Deck holding hands.

They moved close to the edge of the path and kept their heads down as they passed the occasional person. Most were dressed in finely tailored clothes in every assortment of bright colors, all too busy maintaining their pretentious posturing to notice two lowly engineers that were likely performing routine maintenance.

The overall lack of P&C officers was strange. Maybe access was so restricted, the higher ups thought no one would dare commit crime on this deck—at least not the kind of crime P&C officers were in charge of monitoring. As they turned the corner between two particularly large apartments, the path opened into a plaza encircled by a few rows of trees and other greenery.

"I can't imagine what it's like to wake up every morning

and breathe in the trees instead of getting a mouthful of stale air," Miles said.

Josie nodded while she scanned the plaza looking for anything that could point their way deeper into Olympus Deck. "No wonder Odette always said she hated going to the lower decks, now we know why."

Her mind drifted to old memories. When she and Nila were closer. She pictured a young Nila running through these streets. Streets she herself would never be allowed to see. Josie hated that thought.

"Look there." She pointed to the center of the plaza where the glowing screens of an informational terminal broke through the light canopy of leaves.

The artificial breeze gently lifted the leaves as they got closer, revealing the immense legs of a great bronze statue of Cornelius Graham. At almost four meters high, the statue dominated the space and looked out over the Oceanus Apartments. The light from the holotech sun reflected off the statue and gave it an even greater sense of reverence and power that was only fitting.

"Josie," Miles whispered. In one swift move, he pressed them both against the statue.

Josie stood still between Miles and the statue while he leaned around the leg to get a better look. She knew better than to make a move now. "What is it?"

"Two people are coming this way."

"So let's just walk away? Nobody else has questioned us."

"Wait," Miles cautioned. His head was turned with his cheek so close to her she could feel the warmth coming from him.

She leaned her head back against the statue. It was no use arguing, and she trusted Miles's judgment.

"Shit," Miles whispered. A sidelong glance told Josie he hadn't meant to say it out loud.

"What is it?" She craned her head around the leg of the statue as well. The small hairs on the back of her neck stood up when she saw the two peoples' faces. "Is that?"

Miles nodded slowly. "Odette and Nila."

"Oh shit," Josie agreed.

The two girls giggled behind white lace gloves as they strolled through the plaza. Both dressed in blue blouses, short bright orange skirts, and matching bows. They were getting closer now.

"How do you want to play this?" Miles asked.

Josie ran through as many ideas as she could in her head. Each one sounded no better than the last. "Let's just walk away like we did before. I mean, come on, it's Odette and Nila. I hardly think they'll notice us."

Miles bobbed his head up and down, as if working out their chances, and took one last look around the statue. "Well, it's now or never." He nudged Josie around the other side of the statue, the side farther away from Odette and Nila.

Josie focused on walking as casually as she could, which led to her overanalyzing every step.

"What're you doing?" Miles whispered from right beside her.

"Sorry," Josie said. Her nerves were growing. The last few days had been dangerous, but this was terrifying. But the line of trees separating the plaza from the apartments was close. Ten steps, then nine, then eight. She glanced back and saw Odette and Nila still behind them but paid the two disguised engineers no heed. That brought a small sense of relief.

Josie turned her head back to the trees just as a gust of artificial wind swept into the plaza. Before she could react, the breeze rushed across her face, and sent her engineer's cap spinning into the air. Her hair tumbled down across her neck and shoulders. Josie nearly choked on her own saliva.

Miles looked at her out of the corner of his eye. "Just keep walking."

With only three more steps to the trees, Josie clenched her fists and did just that. Then she heard the words that turned her blood cold.

"Josie? Little Josie Owens, is that you?" Odette's voice rang across the plaza.

CHAPTER TWENTY-ONE_

Josie wanted to scream. They'd been caught completely out of their element on Olympus Deck. She had not turned to face Odette and Nila yet, but she knew their eyes were locked onto her.

"What do we do?" she whispered. "Miles, what do we do?"

Miles glanced around the plaza, finding it mostly empty besides a small group of people deep in conversation across the way. "Just stay calm. We can't make a scene, or we'll be caught for sure. Maybe we can reason with them."

"Reason?" Josie scoffed. "They tormented me for years. You think they care what happens to me?"

The look Miles gave her said everything. They were out of options. They had to try.

"Fine. But there's no way this ends well."

"It is you! I knew it was you," Odette shouted as they came closer.

Josie brushed a loose strand of hair behind her ear and kept her eyes down. For a moment a surge of hope nearly convinced her that Odette and Nila would be reasonable. Maybe even let them go. But she quickly squashed the thought. It had been years since she'd had any semblance of a friendship with them. Thankfully, Miles edged himself between her and Odette and Nila, forcing them to confront him first. Josie prayed he would be able to get rid of them.

"Hi, Odette," Miles said in a low voice. "And you, Nila. How are you?"

Nila blushed and put her arms behind her back. "Hi, Miles."

A throaty scoff from Odette shifted the focus back to Josie.

"Why are you here? And stop blocking Josie. Does she still have grease on her hands? Let me see. I'll bet she does." Odette snickered. Nobody else did.

Miles shifted his weight to one foot but otherwise didn't move. "That's a rotten thing to say, Odette."

Odette blanched, obviously not accustomed to someone standing up against her. Her eyes narrowed. "You're not supposed to be here. You know that, don't you?"

"Turn around, and we'll be gone before you know it."

Odette giggled and approached Miles and Josie. Close enough they could smell her perfume "I could, but we only just started talking. Don't be rude, Miles."

Josie strained to keep hold of her tongue, but every word made it harder. All she could see was Rose's face slipping farther away.

"What's the point of this?" Josie said as their eyes met. "If you've got something to say, do it now. Or else we're leaving."

Odette's cheeks flushed a crimson to match her own red lipstick. "You can't talk to me like that." Her voice dripped with rage. "See, Josie, I know something about what's going on. I've seen your face on the holoscreens." She whipped her attention to Miles. "And yours too, Miles Thomas. I couldn't believe it when her red hair blew out in the wind, and you were standing there right beside her. I thought, no, my eyes must be going all cross. But here you both are. And you know what, Josie? There's no one to protect you now. What's to stop me from shouting for some officers and watching them drag you back to Bottom Bays where you belong?"

Josie scowled. A list of insults she could hurl back zipped around her head, each one more hurtful than the last, but she hesitated. Fighting with Odette wouldn't help her find her sister.

They stared at each other for several more breathless moments. In a last-ditch effort, Josie softened her expression. "I'm looking for my sister. She's gone, and we're looking for her."

A blink betrayed a crack in Odette's anger, leaving room for an annoyed curiosity to take hold instead. "What?"

"It's true," Miles said firmly. "That's why we're here."

"Oh, can't we help them?" Nila sputtered with excitement. "It'll be like one of the programs we watch on the holoscreens."

"Help them?" Odette said. "No way. They're criminals. They should be expelled out of *November's Dawn* like those other criminals were."

Josie almost let her surprise show at hearing Nila stick up for them. Even if it didn't seem entirely genuine. She glanced around the plaza and assessed their next move. Nothing looked good. She had tried to reason with them, but Odette was about to call for guards. She was sure of it.

"Odette, stop," Nila said, the usual innocence gone from her voice. Odette's expression contorted into a bubbling mix of resurfacing anger and utter disbelief at being told off again. Nila pressed on. "Do you always have to be so cruel? Just stop for once. We always do what you want to do, and I'm tired of it. So not this time. We're going to help them, or I'll tell my daddy you're not being fair to me again."

Josie thought for sure Odette would counter with a sneering line that would back Nila down. It never came. In fact, Odette seemed to lose color at the mention of Nila's father getting involved. Instead, she only nodded and dropped her chin. Josie thought she heard her sniffle, but the wind made it hard to know for sure. Miles shrugged when Josie looked for his reaction, but she could see how tense he still was with his shoulders high and tight.

"Okay, tell us more," Nila said, completely unaware of Odette now. She put up her hand. "Wait, no, don't. Not here. Let's go back to my house first. Can't be too careful."

She stopped for a moment. "At least, that's what they'd do in the programs."

Odette groaned at the mention of bringing Josie and Miles into Nila's apartment, but a sharp look from Nila made her mouth close as fast as it had opened. Josie dared not question it. She was still trying to wrap her mind around the quick turn of events. These girls tormented her for so long and the idea that they wanted to help her now seemed just wrong and she was skeptical they could even be much help. It was far more likely Josie's time would be wasted. Time she could be using to look for Rose.

"I don't trust them," she whispered so only Miles could hear. She wouldn't make that mistake again.

"Agreed. But let's see where this goes. They know more about Olympus than we do."

"This way," Nila said in a cheery tone and led them down one of the wide lanes. Before long they stopped in front of a large, two-level building with the same white walls and round windows as every other building. Nila typed a code into the access panel. Odette huffed with exaggerated force when the door slid open and sighed several more times as they walked inside.

The room was dim with thick shadows cast in all the corners. It took a moment for Josie's eyes to adjust. She wasn't sure what to expect from the apartment, but this was about the farthest from what she'd imagined. A faint smell of wood rode on the now familiar sterile air and washed over a hallway styled in old Victorian décor. Dark walls outlined in ornate crown molding and paneling gave way to rows of bookshelves and grand cabinets, almost all made from deep brown wood. It was about as drastic a difference from the sleek white walls and minimalist design of the outside as possible.

Nila noticed Josie's interest and flourished her arms around the room. "My daddy loves old things. He says things were better when the world was ruled by kings and queens who bowed to no one." She stopped for a moment as if considering her words. "But I don't think so. I think people should have a say in what goes on."

"Look, Nila," Josie said. "You said you want to help me find my sister, right? We don't have time for anything else. We can't risk getting caught."

"Well, you should be caught. You're criminals," Odette scoffed. "I have to freshen up," she added and then escaped down the hallway.

"Same old Odette," Miles said in an offhand tone.

"Don't mind her," Nila said. "She gets like this when she feels threatened."

"Threatened?" Josie's interest piqued.

"Yeah, by you. Odette doesn't react the best when she thinks someone is going to show her up. She needs to feel the attention of people or else she gets upset. Most of the time I go along with it. It's just easier that way."

Josie bit her tongue. She had what seemed like a million questions for her, but now was not the time. "Nila, I can't believe I'm saying this, but thank you for not turning us in. But about my sister, can you really help?" She almost had to force the words out for how weird it was to have a normal conversation with Nila after so long.

"Oh yes. See we know someone. Well kind of know someone. Anyway, he knows everything that goes on around Olympus Deck. Always has. If your sister was brought up here, he's heard about it."

Josie was partly relieved by her answer and thankful Nila had a real lead, not just fanciful ideas about playing detective like from the holoscreen programs. It did little to ease her distrust though. She had to keep her guard up. Odette and her crew had taught her that, after years of training. "Great, where do we find this guy?"

Nila smiled with her head tilted. "We have to go to the Helios Club, of course." An expectant look crept across her face.

Josie and Miles both stood silent with unchanging expressions, neither having any idea what Nila was talking about. "What's the Helios Club?" Miles asked.

"You don't know?" Nila said with a raised eyebrow. "The Helios Club is the most exclusive establishment on Olympus Deck. Very chic. Only the brightest stars go there."

"And you can get us in?" Josie asked. It was hard to keep the blatant skepticism from tainting her voice.

"Getting into the finest places is something of a hobby of mine," Nila said and craned her neck over Josie toward the end of the hallway. "Odette," she called, "how do you feel about the Helios Club tonight?"

Odette poked her head around the corner. Half of her hair was dressed down. "Really?" She glanced at her loose locks. "Wait, with them?"

"Yes," Nila said flatly.

Odette came closer now. "But look at them. They'll never

get in," she countered and eyed Josie even more. "And look at her. Everyone knows her face."

Nila gently took Josie's hand in hers. "That's why we're going to fix her up," she said beaming.

"We are?"

"You are?" Josie echoed.

Nila nodded slowly. "If you want to get in, you have to look the part."

Josie glanced at Miles who had moved off to the side. "What about Miles?"

Nila and Odette turned their heads to Miles. "I can help," Odette said in a strangely pleasant tone. "I'll run home and get an outfit from my dad's wardrobe." Her eyes floated up and down Miles's slim but fit figure. The mention of going to the Helios Club seemed to snap her out of her earlier foul mood.

If Miles was uncomfortable, he made no show of it. "It's settled then."

"Okay, Miles, you wait here. Odette will get your clothes," Nila said. "Josie, you come with me upstairs."

Odette asked Miles questions about his favorite styles while Josie followed Nila up a wide staircase and through a large set of oak doors. Josie had to fight off the shock of seeing Nila's room. It was as large as her family's cabin back on Aegean Deck, and the great upholstered bed was flanked by two round windows letting in rays of light from the outside courtyard.

"This is all yours?" Josie said.

"Yep," Nila said. "It's not bad."

"I'll say." Josie couldn't imagine the life Nila led. Every part of it just turned out to be more extravagant than the last. And each part only made it clearer how much less those on Aegean lived with. She couldn't help but wonder why Nila had ever been friends with her when they had so many differences.

"What do you think about this one?" Nila asked from

across the room as she pulled out a calf-length deep-green dress with gold embroidered across the bosom.

It was one of the prettiest things Josie had ever seen, but she didn't know what to say. The gold embroidery caught the light from the window and sent it dancing across the ground in a kaleidoscope of color. Before she could answer, Nila held up the dress against her body and made a show of looking Josie up and down.

"Just what I thought," Nila said, half to herself.

Josie's body tensed. "What? What's wrong?" Her face got hot. For a half second, she was convinced Odette was about to burst into the room and spring the joke on her. They would laugh and ridicule her for thinking she could wear something so nice.

Nila looked up and noticed the frantic look on Josie's face. "Oh no, Josie, nothing's wrong. I only meant I knew this color would match you so well. I think we'll start with a shower and then your hair." She pointed at the bathroom door in the corner of the room.

Josie nodded and twirled the luxurious fabric between her fingers. For a moment, she was surprised Nila had her own bathroom in her room, but she reminded herself that this was Olympus Deck; everything was different here.

She slipped back into a thick robe after showering. She underestimated how much better she would feel after getting clean. Her situation seemed a little less dire now, though her uneasiness about trusting Odette and Nila was stuck firmly in her mind. Still, Josie couldn't help but feel like she was doing something wrong for being so suspicious of her.

She sat quietly in front of a vast vanity while Nila carefully worked out the knots in her hair. A couple of times, the force Nila used elicited a sharp wince, but as she worked Josie could see her hair straightening out. When all the knots were pulled free, Nila lathered something in her hair that made it smell fresh and look fuller, then wrapped her locks into thick cords and spun them together in decorative braids topped with a loose bun. It all worked together so well that for once, Josie liked how her hair looked. Next was the makeup, which Nila applied to match her own. Josie had never worn makeup. Not that she was against it, there just had never been any to wear. She wondered where Nila could even get makeup on *November's Dawn*. Maybe there was a stockpile of it somewhere? The smile on Nila's face said she was pleased with the outcome.

"Now, let's see you in that dress," Nila said as she turned away to give Josie privacy.

As the dress inched its way up Josie's body the familiar twinges of embarrassment returned. An engineer's jumpsuit was safe. If Odette and Nila were planning anything, what better way to do it than when Josie was already feeling naked and insecure.

"Maybe I don't need to wear this. I was fine with the jumpsuit," Josie said with the dress still half on.

Nila chuckled softly. "You're shy, that's all. Trust me, nobody wearing an engineer's jumpsuit is getting into the Helios Club."

Josie pulled the dress up in one final effort to fit into the tight cut. She sighed as the straps slipped into place. "I just don't get it. Why're you helping me?"

The look Nila gave was one of genuine surprise and distinct pleasure. "You look so pretty. We just had to get your hair under control and now, well look at you."

Josie gazed into the mirror on the wall. She hardly recognized the girl who looked back. The dress hugged her figure and she had to admit it was a good shade for her. She used a finger to push up a wrinkle that snaked its way across her forehead. Her mom had the same wrinkle. She was still more comfortable in a jumpsuit, but the allure of the dress was growing on her. Then she stopped. "You still haven't answered my question, Nila. Why are you doing all this?"

Nila's smile faded as she looked down. "I don't know," she conceded. "I never meant to be so mean to you before. I just let it happen, and I wish I didn't. I still sometimes remember how it was when we were kids."

"I can't just forgive you for everything you did, Nila. But if you help me find my sister. Well, I won't forget that you helped me." Josie reached out and squeezed Nila's hand.

"Come on," Nila said. "Odette and Miles should be ready by now."

Josie followed Nila back down the staircase to the dim hallway. Odette stood at the bottom step with her hair done back up, drumming her fingers on the railing as she waited for them. Josie gripped the banister a little tighter when Miles came into view.

He stood with his back against the wall, wearing a gray dress jacket with two rows of buttons going down the front and a short stiff collar fastened tightly around his neck. Matching pleated pants ended with calf boots. It was a traditional look for Olympus Deck and one Miles filled out exceptionally well. He hadn't noticed Josie yet and seeing him now made her imagine a life she'd never have.

Nila cleared her throat. "I just have to say it. You two look to have been born and bred on Olympus." She held a hand to her chest as she eyed Miles. "Good choice for Miles, Odette."

Odette beamed for the first time since Nila had told her off before. "I went with a subtler look, almost militaristic. I think it makes him look more refined. What do you think, Miles?"

He didn't answer. His attention was now focused solely on Josie as she took the last few stairs.

"Come on, let's give them a minute," Nila suggested.

Odette looked back and forth before finally understanding. "Gross," she muttered as she followed Nila out.

Without wasting a moment, Miles held out his hand for her to take. "Josie," he whispered with special emphasis on each letter. "I-You look . . ."

He was close now. Then they were touching. Josie consumed the heat of his body and breath as it cascaded down her bosom. His eyes never left hers. Like they were caught in timeless space where it was just them, where it would only ever be them, just like she wanted. Or did she? It didn't matter now that his body was against hers. Her lips begged to meet his. Fire crept through her. It was like her whole body ached for it. This was their moment. It was finally happening.

Then his pupils widened, and his whole expression shifted to a curious look she couldn't quite place. His lips pulled away as his chin dropped. As if he could not bear to look her in the eyes any longer.

A thousand thoughts flooded into Josie's mind and each one made her chest tighten. He had turned from her. Something tormented him. The tips of Josie's ears burned, but she fought it as best she could. She slipped a finger under his chin and lifted his gaze back to hers.

"What is it?" she asked, not sure if she truly wanted the answer.

Their faces were caught by a stray shaft of light from the window. Miles's eyes seemed to glisten a little brighter. "Nothing. You look perfect," he said in the same slow voice.

Josie felt like he was holding something back, but she wasn't sure how to broach it if he wasn't willing. A soft creak in the floorboard told her Nila and Odette were hiding just out of sight.

She turned to them, eager to move on and forget. "Ready?"

Nila smiled slyly as she turned the corner of the hallway. "I think the question is are you ready?"

Josie scoffed. "Let's go already." She walked toward the door but stopped shy from opening it. "Lead the way," she said to Odette and Nila.

CHAPTER TWENTY-TWO_

OUTSIDE THE HOLOTECH sky above was turning darker as it neared the end of its daytime cycle, replaced now with the faint twinkle of stars. As it did, lamps positioned along the avenues flickered on and bathed the Oceanus Apartments in a warm blue hue. They passed several others on the path, but nobody thought twice now that they were all dressed like Olympus teens. In fact, a few even cast leering glances toward Josie which made her wrap her arms around herself even more. All she needed was to get to this club and find Nila's mysterious contact, then she could get out of the dress and find Rose.

"Are we close?" Josie asked.

Nila pointed ahead. "Around that next corner."

When they turned the corner, they were greeted by a massive neon sign of the club's name hanging above one of the larger buildings set against the bulkhead of the Oceanus Apartments chamber. People waited to get in along the side of the club. Josie turned to go towards the end, but Nila beckoned her back.

"Just follow our lead," Nila said, giggling as the four of them walked right up to the officer positioned at the door.

Josie held her breath. Instinct told her to run. She tried to relax her body and walk like Odette and Nila, but she and Miles looked horribly stiff. The officer squinted at them with his arms crossed. Josie had to be ready for anything.

"Hello, Yuri," Nila said cheerfully. "Anything special planned for tonight?"

The officer dropped his arms almost immediately. "Miss Clarke! How wonderful to see you here again. And you brought friends."

He tipped his head to Odette then leaned in close to Nila. "Ask the barmen; they might have something for you," he said with a wink and pushed open the doors.

"What was that?" Josie whispered as they walked in. "You made it seem like we wouldn't get in."

Nila shrugged. "They let everyone in eventually. It's just some have to wait first." She grabbed Josie's hand and pulled her through the door.

The club opened into a large spacious floor with smaller rooms dotted around the edge. The entire place pulsed with energy. A band played electric instruments and synthetic harmonizers on a raised stage in the back. The lead woman's mane of purple and silver hair flew back and forth as she rocked her head. Flashing lights flickered across every surface and the band's music boomed throughout.

Everywhere Josie looked, there were people dressed in outlandish outfits full of feathers, shiny synthetic materials, and sometimes almost nothing at all. Everyone had one thing in common, they drank from tall cups full of a light blue liquid that seemed to have an inner glow.

Josie turned back to the group, but Odette had already gone off laughing with people Josie didn't recognize.

"So what do we do?" she asked Nila over the thundering music.

"You have fun!" Nila shouted back and then laughed. "Don't worry, I'm still going to help you. But he won't tell us anything if he thinks you don't belong here. So just relax for a bit, try to fit in. I'll go get us drinks."

Josie looked at Miles who was scanning the room with his jaw clenched.

"I don't like this," Josie said.

"I don't either. Let's go over there." He pointed to a secluded table off the main dance floor. "Less people."

Josie nodded and worked her way through the crowd. She tried to keep to herself, but the way people bounced around made it impossible. The room was chaotic and hot, and it was hard to focus on anything. Only the empty table offered any relief. Miles slid onto a seat next to Josie and picked at a button on his jacket.

"Can you believe all this?" Josie said in a low voice. Even if the club was loud beyond measure, she didn't want her words to be heard. "It's like these people don't care at all about the suffering of the lower decks."

Miles eyed her cautiously. "I don't think they do," he said leadingly, "but they'll see soon. With what your dad left you." He motioned toward her chest and the Heart of the Dawn concealed in her bosom. "That's the end goal, right? To end this divide once and for all?"

"I haven't forgotten." Josie looked off to the side. Whether because she could not face him or her own feelings, she couldn't tell. "I just can't worry about that right now. Not when they have Rose. That's all that matters."

Miles was about to respond, but his focus drifted to the corner above them. "Josie," he said solemnly. "Look."

They were underneath a row of holoscreens. She recognized Jack Burlesque and Donna Albert. Big, bold letters tracked below their styled faces. *Riots on Aegean. Who's to blame?*

Josie squinted to see the smaller square on the screen that was playing a loop of the riots. It looked like the Galley Markets. The haphazard metal shacks were easy enough to recognize. People pressed tightly together. Their faces ragged and bruised, and arms linked in unison. They shouted at someone out of the camera angle. The camera turned to follow. A group of P&C officers, two rows deep, stood with their riot shields in a formidable wall. Commandant Reyes stood in front of them. Unlike the rest, he didn't wear a helmet. His blonde hair contrasted against the black tactical gear of the officers. He pointed at the rioters and shouted something.

Jack Burlesque's voice droned over the video and made it impossible to hear what was going on.

"And here we see Commandant Reyes ordering the rioters to leave the area. This is after a deadly skirmish with the rioters broke out. Six Aegean Deck agitators were killed," Jack said, his showman's voice a sickening contrast to the message he delivered.

Donna covered her mouth. "It's terrible, Jack, to see such violence on our ark."

Jack nodded. "We're lucky to have a man like the commandant fighting on our side. The violence has disrupted all factory work on the lower decks and First Vicar Frost has instituted a curfew and cancelled any further celebrations planned in preparation for the Great Turning as this riot is showing no signs of slowing down."

"And all this during a week that was supposed to mark such hope for the future. That has to have ruffled a few feathers high on Olympus," Donna said.

"It makes you want to ask the hard questions, Donna." Jack turned and looked directly at the camera. "I for one want to know who's to blame for allowing such violence to escalate. I mean, the Garden of Tomorrow bombing should have been enough to see what was going on."

"Are you saying the First Vicar is to blame? Should he have done more to prevent this?" Donna interjected.

Jack seemed to wrestle with it for a moment, but then his expression softened. "It's not my job to assign blame. But I can tell you this. The girl who sparked all this, Josie Owens, has a lot to explain."

Donna smiled a wide toothy grin. "We'll be back, folks. Right after a message from our sponsor: Director Clarke's fresh, never foul, canned fish."

Josie looked from the screen and stared into the crowd of people dancing. They laughed and reveled without a care in the world, completely unaware of what was happening outside their deck. But the world was bigger than two people dancing. It was bigger than Josie and her sister too. In that moment, Joise almost felt a sense of duty toward the dancers.

Toward everyone aboard the ark.

"There you two are," Nila called. She hurried toward them carrying three tall cups of the same mysterious blue liquid Josie had seen others drinking. Nila pushed one at Josie.

Miles lifted it suspiciously and put the cup to his nose which wrinkled up in response. "What is this?"

"Floodrite," Nila said as she took a small sip then noticed how unsure Miles and Josie still looked. "It makes you . . . feel things," she added. "If you want to fit in here, you need to drink it."

Josie wrapped both her hands around the cup and gingerly put it to her lips. Staring down into it, she could see it did indeed glow from the inside. The liquid was thick, more viscous than water but less so than oil or grease.

Slowly she tilted it back and let the liquid come to her lips.

The floodrite was sweet with hints of a strange bitterness. It offered an immediate tingling sensation on her tongue and tumbled down her throat all at once when she swallowed.

Miles watched her intently. "So it's a drug?"

"Well, yeah," Nila scowled. "It's supposed to be used for sick people, I guess. But someone figured out it's way better like this."

Miles's nostrils flared, and he pushed the cup away as soon as Nila stopped talking. "What a waste. Excuse me." He stood up and stalked off.

Nila's smile faded. "What's up with him?"

Josie knew he was thinking of his mom and her sickness. "Nothing. He just needs some space. Nila, what about your contact? Where is he?"

Nila tapped her cup with her finger. "He's here. But I do the talking, got it?"

Josie nodded. She had played her part and done everything Nila asked. Now it was time to get what she had come for.

"Good," Nila said and pointed across the crowded dance floor to another secluded room. "He's in there. Stay close to me, I don't want you to get lost in here."

Josie dreaded the idea of wading through the crowd again. She took a deep breath as she stood. A rushing feeling flooded through her head and trickled down to her toes. "Whoa. Am I supposed to feel that?"

"You'll be okay. I told you, it makes you feel things," Nila offered.

Josie swallowed and followed Nila through the crowd. The music thundered in her ears and the edges of her vision began to blur. She reached out to steady herself but missed Nila as she vanished deeper into the crowd. Instead, Josie found the billowing cape of a stranger. He turned and flashed her a dirty look before ripping it from her hands.

Josie spun around, desperately looking for anything familiar. Her vision flashed in and out now. The air was so hot and close. Ahead was the exit. If she could get outside, maybe she could breathe again. Each wobbly step was a little victory. She focused on the door. That was her target as she pushed through the throng of revelers.

She was close now, almost there. Someone stepped in front of her, no more than ten paces away. It was Odette. She pointed right at Josie. Flanked on either side of Odette stood two P&C officers. Josie tried to turn but her head swam like a murky cloud. Above all, one overriding feeling took hold: escape.

Something caught her attention from the corner of her eye, something familiar, something safe.

Miles materialized out of the crowd, close but still out of ear shot. He was focused solely on her. He saw her stumble. A look of panic scrawled across his face. Josie could tell he didn't notice the officers coming for her. They would take him too if they saw him. She tried to yell to get his attention, to get him to stop.

It was too late for her. But not for him.

He didn't hear her.

She threw her arms up toward Odette and the two officers. He followed her direction. As if working out the odds, the look of panic faded from Miles's expression, replaced now by something far more primal: utter hopelessness. There was nothing he could do; she knew that.

But she wasn't giving up.

The flailing arm of a stranger pushed Josie back several steps as she fell into a group of people and collapsed to the ground. They roared their annoyance. The officers raced toward her now. Odette grinned right behind them.

Josie's eyes were so heavy. She blinked over and over. A

desperate last bid to keep them open before her vision faded out completely.

CHAPTER TWENTY-THREE_

THE MASSIVE TWIN spotlights on the front of *November's Dawn* blazed a clear path through the shimmering darkness of the ocean outside the glass-and-steel enclosed bridge that protruded out of the front of the ark.

Not that the navigation of the ark was left to the human eye. That was controlled by computers which automated most of the functions on *November's Dawn*. The same systems were now failing as the ark marched ever onward toward the Obsidian Trench, threatening to swallow them whole.

Adrian pressed his palm against the glass and let the cold creep through. From where he stood on the observation catwalk, *November's Dawn's* mighty legs flattened the rock formations it encountered and stepped over everything else. Columns of stone were pummeled into plumes of dust and debris, left to float in the endless currents. Nothing could match the sheer power of ark—nothing except the Obsidian Trench.

Adrian resolved that should the end come, he would stand in the same spot he was now to bear witness to his final failure.

He took one last breath before removing his hand from the impenetrable glass. Cold shivers slipped away as quickly as they had come. Dim light illuminated the walkway as he made his way back toward the central command deck.

"It's magnificent, isn't it?" a man called from behind him. "These towering columns of rock will continue to grow larger as we near the Obsidian Trench. The Pillars of Eternity, they're called. And *November's Dawn* will continue to rumble through them. Well, up until the trench, that is."

"Helmsman Ido," Adrian said over his shoulder. "I pray you have good news." It was a statement, not a question.

"The problem persists, First Vicar." A nervous giggle slipped Ido's lips as he moved close enough for a private conversation.

A silent glare from Adrian implored Ido to go on.

"We've tried everything to correct the navigational computers, but I fear we are no closer to resolving it than we were the moment we discovered it." Ido's hands were wrung so tightly together they were turning a faint shade of red, betraying his hesitation.

"I pray for all our sakes that is not all you have, Helmsman."

"We did find something." Ido cringed. "Apologies, First Vicar. One of the technicians found it. The source. It seems the navigation problem isn't just a malfunction. A virus has been burning through our systems. We didn't find it earlier because nobody thought to look for it, seeing as we're in an ark at the bottom of the ocean and not connected to anything in the outside world."

"How is it possible someone infected our system?"

"That's the thing, First Vicar. We dug through years of data. There hasn't been any new data uploaded to the mainframes for decades, not since the surface scans stopped—"

"What are you saying, Ido?" Adrian said with more venom than anticipated.

"The virus has been in our systems for years, but only recently has it been activated." Ido nervously looked around the walkway. "Someone knew this was going to happen. They wanted it to."

Adrian stared back at Ido for several seconds, but the helmsman's nerves had disappeared, leaving Adrian confident he had told him all he knew. "Is there any way to stop the virus?"

Ido shook his head slowly. "There are still things we might try, but we've never been up against something like this. I cannot tell you what will work with any certainty."

"Keep working, Helmsman. We are not giving up on *November's Dawn* just yet."

The hint of a smile crossed Ido's lips. He looked up and saluted. "Yes, First Vicar. We're not stopping now."

"Good man," Adrian said. "Oh and, Helmsman? Updates come directly to me. No one else is to know about this."

Adrian ran his fingers through his hair. He knew the helmsman was thinking the same thing he was. This was more likely than not going to be their end. They could always shut down the ark entirely, but that would only delay the inevitable. It would save them from an imminent death and give a few more helpless years to those onboard. No, he could not stomach the idea of giving up now. There was nothing he would not do to save his people. Graham had entrusted him with their future. That was his duty.

"First Vicar!" an officer shouted from the central bridge above him.

"What," Adrian roared.

"We have her, First Vicar. The girl from Aegean. Owens. She's been captured."

Some good news at last. Adrian almost smiled. "Bring her to my office."

The officer looked confused. "The commandant has her, First Vicar. He's taken her to the Pits, per your orders."

Adrian straightened and the hairs on the back of his neck stood up. He had made no such order. "Take me there at once."

CHAPTER TWENTY-FOUR_

THE DARK HOOD was heavy on Josie's eyelids. The officers had pulled it over her head when they captured her at the club.

Nila's blue drink dulled her senses, leaving her barely able to stand and helpless against her captors. Now its effects were wearing off, but they still left her feeling slow and mistrustful of her own thoughts.

Rough hands clasped both of her shoulders, silently directing her every move. Josie could see the faint outlines of figures through the hood, but it was only enough to know something was there, not enough for her to have any idea what was coming. The air was frigid, but unlike the chill that crept through most of *November's Dawn*, this was a damp cold. The dress Nila had given her offered no warmth against it.

It was not long before they reached a chamber. The floor was wet and stale air filled her nostrils. Thick leather bands strapped her arms and legs tight to the chair. The thought crossed her mind to ask where she was, or maybe to lash out and scream at her captors and try to wrestle away from them, but it faded as quickly as it had come. It did not seem to matter anymore. She was helpless. Rose was still a prisoner.

She felt so stupid for trusting Odette and Nila. That one mistake had cost her everything.

She could still see Miles's eyes like she could see right through him. The anger. The fear. All of it. Miles not being captured was the only thing that brought her any solace. She held onto that thought as tightly as she could and braced herself for what was coming. Whatever it was, she would die. She knew it. It had all been for nothing. When she closed her eyes, all she could see was the flash of the gun that had killed Felix, all she could feel was the terrible heat that had taken Doc Lee faster than she could blink.

Now it was her turn.

The thought was chilling. It crept throughout her whole body until it became her singular focus. The feeling was surreal, and in the strangest way, almost comforting. Comforting to know that no matter what may happen, this would be the end.

They had killed so many others. Her life meant nothing to them.

The door behind groaned again. Rhythmic bootsteps followed. "I have been waiting a long time for this."

Josie recognized the voice immediately as Commandant Reyes's. He drew out each syllable and let the words hang in the air. Josie wrapped her fingers tighter around the arms of the chair.

"Remove her hood at once. Then get out of here."

"You want us to leave, Commandant?" one of the officers countered. "She could be trouble."

"Now," Reyes growled.

A second lapsed. "Right away, sir."

Cold fingers fumbled around Josie's neck as they worked the hood free. Josie blinked as her eyes adjusted. Shadows danced around the room, scattered from the single light dangling directly above her, obscuring the rest of the room. Reyes leaned up against the wall with his arms crossed. He stepped forward, just enough for his face to come under the light. It was sunken, and his eyes lacked the careful cunning she had seen in them before. Josie thought he looked twenty years older from when she saw him last only days before. The day he murdered Felix. But there was something about the way he looked at her now, like she was not a prisoner but a plaything.

"Josie Owens," Reyes hissed. "You have been a hard girl to find."

He walked over to a table she had not noticed before. It was mostly covered in shadows, but she could faintly make out what looked like tools. Reyes slowly ran his finger across them. Then the realization dawned on her. Those were not just tools. They had a much more sinister purpose. They were used for torture.

Now the restraints felt all too tight as she wiggled her arms and legs. Breathing that had been calm a moment ago became faster, verging on uncontrollable. Her indifference about death a moment ago was gone, replaced by the oppressive thought of what cruelty Reyes's tools could do. She focused on steadying her breathing. Reyes was a vulture looking for weakness. She needed to seem strong.

"What do you want?" she asked through gritted teeth.

Reyes chuckled. A deep laugh that dripped of malice. "I find you fascinating. Did you know that? A girl who did nothing but run but somehow, you've become something of a hero to the lower decks. They find your defiance admirable. They need to be shown their place."

He picked up a long thin knife and ran his finger down the spine of it. "Whatever you know from that smashed holomessage would be interesting, I'm sure, and no doubt seditious. But what do I want? In truth, only to make you bleed. To show the rest of *November's Dawn* that resistance is futile."

"Is that what you were doing when you murdered Felix?" Josie said as her anger rose.

"He was disposed of as all traitors will be."

Nausea overwhelmed her. Never in her life had she hated someone as much as she hated Reyes now. "You're going to pay for what you did. People see it now. They won't stand for the lies of the OSD or be their slaves anymore."

"Hardly," Reyes said. "They owe their lives to *November's Dawn*. I will make them see that again."

Reyes's fervent dogma of the OSD made her skin crawl. The last few days had proved the OSD would do anything to stay in power. That drove her belief in salvation on the surface. It was why she couldn't give up. She had the key to the only future where people from every deck would have a chance and a voice in their lives. Reyes and those like him had to be stopped, no matter what.

"Right, because in the darkness below, *November's Dawn* will provide?" Josie chided.

The back of Reyes's hand whipped through the air and collided with the side of Josie's face and only being strapped to the chair stopped her from being sent to the ground. Her lip stung. Saliva slipped down the corner of her mouth. She spit at Reyes's black boots to clear it away. He watched it splatter on his foot and slowly looked at her.

"You're a fighter. You won't go down easily. I respect that." He slipped a white handkerchief from a pocket and leaned down to wipe his boot.

"But it will do you no good here," he roared as he sprang forward.

This time his closed fist connected with her lower jaw.

Josie cried out. The pain was much greater than just a

stinging sensation. A deep throbbing pulsed over and over, sending waves of pain through her head. Dark circles danced in her eyes. The fringes of her vision faded.

Reyes put his hands on his knees. His cruel, sharp eyes pierced right through her. "Down here nobody will hear you scream. Nobody will shed a tear for you. Nobody is coming for you."

He grabbed the long knife again and waved it in front of her face. "Not even the boy you've been running with."

Josie tensed. "Miles will come for me."

Closing her eyes did little to relieve the pain, but it was the only thing she could do to stop the tears from flowing. She had bitten her tongue. The coppery taste of blood flooded her mouth.

Reyes grinned. "Yes, Miles. Miles Thomas if I recall correctly. I hope he does. Saves me the trouble." He nodded toward the door. "I have another room just for him. But first, you and I will be getting more acquainted."

Reyes pressed the long thin knife to her thigh. Its steel was cold. Its wicked gleaming edge begged to be used. Josie sucked in one last gulp of air.

Then Reyes lifted the knife away, she dared to open one eye. He had a curious look on his face.

"You know, I find it strange you stayed so long with the boy. Especially after what he did," he said in an offhand tone.

"What are you talking about?" Every word hurt, but Josie had to know.

Reyes leaned back as a genuine smile crept across his whole face and gave him an impish look. "You don't know?" A cruel look replaced his earlier surprise. "I'll tell you, Josie Owens. And it's going to hurt much more than anything I can do to you. Miles is the one who reported you and the old engineer for possession of the holomessage."

Time stood still. The words rang through Josie's mind over and over. All the pain from her jaw faded behind the torrent of emotions and questions. It made no sense. Miles would never. She trusted him more than anyone. He had saved her that day, risked his life for her.

Reyes had to be lying. She was sure of it. He was trying to manipulate and isolate her.

Reyes saw the conflict in her eyes. "He wanted to do the right thing. Report the trouble he saw." His voice slithered into her thoughts and tried to break them open.

"You're lying," Josie said through her teeth.

"Why would I lie?" Reyes sneered. "Come now, Josie Owens. You must have wondered how we found out so soon. Surely you knew someone had betrayed you. Now you know who."

Josie scrambled as she tried to remember that day. Even if it was only a few days ago, she now found it almost impossible to pull together the loose strands of the memory amid her crowded thoughts. It was blurry, obscured further by the ringing in her ears from the gunshot that had killed Felix.

She dug deeper. To the holomessage itself. To when she told Felix. A soft thud echoed through the memory. Someone had been there. Someone had heard them and turned them in. But the thought of it being Miles was so strange that she could barely wrap her head around it. Then something else came to her. Before the club. When Miles had been inches from her lips, but had pulled away from her. He had seemed so upset, tormented even. Josie felt Reyes's accusation building in her head. Every second it gained strength.

Nausea gripped her stomach like cold twisted fingers. Screaming seemed like the only option left, but she didn't open her mouth. All she could do was look straight ahead at nothing.

The one person she thought she knew, the one constant, was ripped from her.

He betrayed her like everyone else.

Like she was nothing.

"Shall we begin?" Reyes asked while twirling the knife again in his fingers.

Josie stayed quiet, empty. Reyes brought the cold steel against her thigh again. This time the sharp edge was down. This time she ignored it. The blade glided across the top of her skin. The cold and biting steel felt like a thousand tiny fingers all pulling at once. Her leg twitched. It stung, but the pain was a background distraction to what she felt. He applied no pressure. The delicate edge did all the work.

Josie closed her eyes, a tear tumbled down her cheek. There was no reason to care anymore. She had made so many wrong choices. Trusted the wrong people. Doubted the right ones. More than ever her dad's message felt like an impossible burden.

It was all over. There was no mission.

She would hold on for Rose. But it all felt hollow.

The door lurched forward and slammed into the wall. Josie snapped her head up as the knife fell from her leg. The door was outside of the cone of light above her. Squinting didn't help. All she could make out was the hazy lines of a dark silhouette.

"Enough!" the figure boomed.

Reyes stepped back. "First Vicar, you've heard we captured the traitor. We were just getting more acquainted."

Adrian stormed forward, flanked by two P&C officers with two more standing close to the door. He cast a fleeting glance at Josie but didn't stop until he was inches from Reyes's face. Both men were breathing hard. "Get out."

"I am in the middle of questioning a prisoner, First Vicar. Perhaps it would be best for you to leave."

"I never directed you to interrogate her, Commandant Reyes. You were to alert me as soon as she was captured."

Anger flashed in Reyes's eyes. "She has openly defied the OSD and has become an inspiration for lower deck violence. I'm doing what I must to keep order on *November's Dawn.*"

Adrian looked down at Josie's bruised face and the thin cut on her thigh. "That is not your decision to make. You're dismissed."

Reyes's back stiffened. "There is more to be learned from the prisoner."

"Reyes, you're dismissed." Adrian locked his eyes with Reyes. "George," Adrian called, "escort Commandant Reyes from the Pits. I believe his attention is needed on the lower decks."

One of the black clad officers stepped behind Reyes.

"I don't know what your game is, Adrian. But you're making a terrible mistake," Reyes said and stormed out of the room.

As soon as he was gone, Adrian waved away the other officers. The heavy metal doors thumped as they closed again, leaving Josie alone with the First Vicar. She held her breath. One devil traded for another. The First Vicar stood staring at Josie for another moment as he took in the scene. When he was convinced the room was clear, he knelt next to her.

Josie closed her eyes again. It made the pain of the cut feel less real. Adrian's fingers drifted down Josie's arm till they reached her wrists.

But no pain followed.

Instead, the still air filled with the clanking of metal buckles; the pressure on her wrists lessening as the buckles worked free.

"I'm so sorry, Josie," Adrian said in a soft voice. A tone she never imagined hearing from him. "None of this was ever supposed to happen."

"What are you talking about?"

"I promised Serena I would keep you safe. I failed. But you're here now, that's what matters."

"My mom," Josie asked. "You promised her?" The mention of her mom caught her off guard, but she recovered. "You think I'm just going to believe you? That you can walk in here, and I'll go along with whatever you say? I don't know what's happening, but I know it's a trick. I won't fall for it."

"This is no trick, Josie," Adrian said quietly. He finished undoing the rest of the restraints and tied a piece of cloth around her thigh to stem the bleeding. "You don't believe me. I wouldn't if I were you, but I still need your help."

Josie scoffed. She could not imagine in what world Adrian thought she would help him. "Where's my sister? Did you lock her up in one of these rooms too after you kidnapped her?"

"You have it all wrong," Adrian said. "Yes, I arranged for her to be brought to Olympus Deck, but that was only to keep her safe. It's what your mom wanted."

"What she wanted? My mom couldn't even be bothered to make sure Rose was okay. She was all alone when I went back home for her."

"I couldn't let your mom go get her, it wasn't safe."

By the way his expression softened, he seemed to genuinely believe what he was saying but Josie knew better. "I don't believe you."

Adrian paced around the room for a moment before stopping by the wall. "I'll show you." He started typing into a keypad on the wall Josie had not noticed before.

A section of the wall illuminated into a holoscreen shortly after. The display looked like it was from a security camera in a small room. But this one had pristine white walls and was lavishly furnished, nothing like the one she was in now. But it was the center of the room Josie was more interested in. Her sister sat cross legged on the floor, surrounded by plush animals. One caught her eye, Rose's stuffed rabbit, Lewis. Rose looked safe. She looked happy.

"See?" Adrian said. "After the Garden of Tomorrow bombing, I arranged for her to be brought here so she would not be threatened by what's happening on the lower decks."

Josie found it harder to rebut what he was saying, but she still couldn't wrap her head around it. "But Mags. She was attacked by the officers you sent."

"I admit I cannot control every action of my officers as much as I would like. They can sometimes be . . . overzealous. I'm sorry if your friend was hurt; it was not my intention." He glanced around the room. "Now do you trust me enough to leave this place?"

"I still have questions," Josie shot back.

Adrian was typing into another keypad by the door. "And I will answer them. But not here."

Josie considered it for a moment. The First Vicar could not be trusted; she knew that. The OSD had taken everything from her. She was sure there was much he was not telling her but as far as she could tell he had not lied to her yet or hurt her.

If she stayed, Reyes would be back and there was no doubt he *would* hurt her, nobody would stop him then.

She had nothing left to lose.

"Fine. Where are we going?" she said coldly. They were interrupted by a faint rumble that rippled through *November's Dawn*. She had felt similar tremors before, but they seemed to be growing in intensity by the hour.

Adrian stopped while the vibrations continued. He glanced around the room as if expecting something much worse.

When they subsided, he let out a relieved breath. "To my office. Stay close."

CHAPTER TWENTY-FIVE_

"Get out of the way, boy!" a burly man shouted as he stormed down the avenue.

Miles jumped to the side just in time. As he did, his boot caught the edge of a crate, sending his shoulder crashing into the side of one of the ramshackle buildings in the Galley Markets. Flashing red lights and deafening alarms sounded every several moments. His focus was on the chaos consuming the markets from the violent clashes between the P&C officers and the people from Aegean Deck, who were emboldened by Hades Fist and stories of Josie's defiance against the OSD.

An automated voice echoed throughout the massive chamber. "Citizens of Aegean Deck. Vacate this area immediately or risk being fired upon." The message looped over and over.

It was hard for him to wrap his head around the idea of folks being inspired by Josie being on the run. He believed in her completely, but the way he remembered it, the last week had been a nonstop effort to simply stay alive. Far from the glamorized and heroic whispers he had heard in the dark corridors on Aegean Deck, it had been terrifying. But that was the way with stories, they seemed to take on a life of their own. It hardly mattered now though. He had one goal. Find Josie. All he could see was her terror as she had been dragged out of the club by a pair of P&C officers. He couldn't stomach the thought of failing her, not again.

"Psst!" whispered a young girl's voice. "Hey, mister!"

Miles spun around to see a set of small green eyes peeking through a crack in the door of the shack he had fallen into.

"Are you okay?" the child asked. Short brown curls hugged the girl's tan cheeks.

"I'm okay." A weak smile was all he could manage. "You should close the door. It isn't safe out here."

The girl's face scrunched up. "Why're you rubbing your shoulder?"

Miles almost laughed. He hadn't realized he was doing that. "Well, you don't miss anything, huh?"

"Amelia, close the door right now!" a woman shouted.

"But, Mommy, he's hurt."

A second set of eyes, much higher than the first, appeared in the crack. They studied Miles for a moment, as if assessing the risk. "What're you doing out there?" Then they narrowed. "You're not part of Hades Fist, are you?"

Miles shook his head. "No, ma'am. I'm just looking for a friend."

The woman's eyes tracked up and down again, then her scowl softened, and she disappeared into the house. Miles sighed. Her mistrust didn't surprise him. Before he could turn away, the door screeched as the woman pulled it back into the shadow of the shack. Her head popped back out while she surveyed the path. "Quickly!" She beckoned him on. "I don't want to attract the P&C's attention."

"Right," Miles said, feeling half-ashamed for taking so long already and went inside.

Rusty walls gave the small room an orange hue. It was filled with broken furniture and other scraps too worn to be wanted by anyone else. Miles figured the woman spent her time fixing the various odds and ends trying to turn a profit. It looked like bleak work.

"Come, sit down," the woman said and motioned to a crude metal stool. The young girl, Amelia, jumped up on another stool, and stared at Miles, determined not to miss anything.

Miles was too anxious to sit. He didn't have time. But wandering around the Galley Markets had gotten him nowhere. He needed information. "Thank you for letting me in. You didn't have to. I'm Miles." He looked at the girl. "I know you're Amelia, but what's your name, ma'am?"

"I'm Amara." She sighed. "You said you were looking for someone?"

Miles straightened. "Yes. My friend. She was taken by P&C officers."

"Then she's as good as gone, I'm afraid."

"We can help," Amelia chimed in.

"Amelia," her mom shot back. Amelia sunk down in her stool. "I'm sorry, but the P&Cs are not tolerating anything anymore. The weapons they have . . ." She shuddered and closed her eyes.

"She's not gone," Miles whispered, almost to himself. He couldn't stomach the thought of Josie being gone. "I know she's not on Aegean. I need to find Marcus Abbott. Have you heard of him?"

Amara's eyes flashed with fiery recognition. "And why would you need to find him if you aren't part of Hades Fist?"

"Because they're the only ones who can help me find my friend."

Amara mulled it over. "Fine, but then you need to leave. Last I heard, his filth was holed up in Bingo's Secondhand

Supply over on the other side of the markets. No doubt hiding from all the fighting he's caused. Coward."

Miles sucked in a breath of air. She wasn't wrong. He had seen the wreckage left from the riots. Both sides held nothing back, and he figured it would only get worse. But at least now he had a lead.

"Thank you, Amara." His eyes moved to the girl who was standing at attention. "And you too, Amelia. You were very brave."

Amelia grinned a toothy smile.

A loud crash echoed from outside. Followed by a string of angry voices and screams. The shack shook gently from the force; dust and small rust particles fell from the walls. Amelia covered her ears.

Amara reached across the table to her daughter and put a hand on her shoulder. "It's okay. It'll be over soon." She looked back at Miles. "Hades Fist be damned. They're all fools, so caught up in themselves that nobody thinks about the people who will get hurt along the way. Nothing ever changes down here."

"You should leave. It will only get worse."

"We have nowhere else to go. Everything we have is here."

Miles nodded solemnly and stood from the table. He feared that was what she would say and only wished he could help them, but he had nothing to offer.

Amara wrenched the door free again. "I hope you find her, Miles. I truly do," she said as he stepped out.

It was easy enough to find his way to Bingo's Secondhand Supply. It was one of the bigger shops and had its own neon signs pointing the way. The trouble was trying to avoid the pockets of fighting spread throughout the chamber. If a P&C caught him, there was no chance he could get out of it. Part of the OSD's effort had been to restrict access to the markets and brand anyone remaining inside as traitors who were aiding the terrorists. The Galley Markets was not known for its cleanliness or glamor, but now the fighting had left it shattered and broken.

The shop was just around the next corner across one of the wider avenues of the chamber. An overturned table blocked the path and gave a good spot to see if the way was clear ahead. Miles slid up against it and glanced over. The hairs on his neck prickled. On the other side of the table were two small piles of what looked like dust or some sort of powder. It was eerily familiar. He jumped over and touched the powder. It was soft and crumbled when he rubbed it between his fingers. Then he remembered. Nausea gripped his stomach as he realized what the piles of dust were. These were people, blasted down by holorifles. Miles closed his eyes as he gently rubbed his fingers off on his shirt, trying to be as respectful as he could, as if such a thing mattered now.

"Stop right there, boy!"

Miles turned and saw a P&C officer running toward him. The officer didn't have his holorifle pointed at him, yet Miles knew it would only be a matter of time. They had been given the order to shoot first and ask questions later. Beads of sweat rolled down Miles's neck. He would do whatever needed doing to get back to Josie. A handful of seconds were all that separated him from the officer. It was now or never.

He waited until the officer was only steps away, making it appear he would come peacefully. At least that was what Miles hoped the officer would think. All that mattered was that the holorifle stayed strapped to his back.

Miles spun on his foot and crouched low. Now was his chance. The officer had taken the bait and his eyes flashed with fear as he recognized what Miles was doing. With all his strength, Miles sprang up toward the officer's chest and throat.

The only part of the officer's body not covered in tactical gear was his neck. The meaty part of his palm collided with the underside of the officer's jaw.

The officer choked and grasped his throat. The impact sent him staggering backward, where he tripped on a loose pipe. The officer's head snapped against a metal wall with a sickening crack. His body crumpled on the ground. Miles fell to his knees next to him as the shock of what had just happened set in. The man was dead. The nausea grew again. He had been forced to choose and had killed a man because of it.

What worried him the most was that he knew he would make the same decision every time.

The officer had been alone, and Miles didn't hear anyone else coming. He couldn't stomach the thought of sitting next to the body or piles of dust any longer. He kicked the holorifle away in disgust then jumped up and ran toward Bingo's storefront. He was close. It was all he focused on. He pushed harder, eager to be out of the open and away from prying eyes and slowed only enough to grasp the door handle to wrench it open.

Momentum carried him past someone standing just past the door.

The inside was lit with a dim blue light that couldn't pierce the thick shadows in the room. Several figures turned away from a rickety table in the center.

"An unexpected surprise." Marcus Abbott pulled back his hood.

Miles glanced around the room. As his eyes adjusted, he recognized others. Tai and Joshua stood close to Marcus. Matias and three more he didn't recognize were not far behind.

"Marcus," he said in a low voice.

"Miles, are you okay?" Tai said and rushed over to help steady him.

"I'm alright, Tai. Thanks."

"Our wayward Miles. The last I saw you, you were determined not to leave the side of young Miss Owens," Marcus said in a dry tone. "And yet here you are. Have you finally come to help the cause?"

"I'm not here to join you."

Marcus's eyes narrowed, and his voice deepened. "Then why are you here?"

"It's about Josie. She's been taken."

"Taken?" Tai repeated. "What? How? What do you mean?"

Joshua put his hand on Tai's shoulder. "Miles, what happened?"

"P&C officers. I was able to get away, but they took Josie," Miles continued. "I have to find her. Will you help me?" He looked around the room at everyone. Each one deflected his gaze when it came to them. Silence engulfed the room.

"Please. You must help me. They only caught her because of me. I can't do this on my own. Josie needs help. She needs us now." The words died out. Leaving the space quiet enough he could hear his own heartbeat. Miles had swore he would not beg, but that distinction didn't matter now. He would beg if he had to. Josie would do the same for him.

He looked back at Marcus. His expression betrayed nothing, but Miles knew this was his ploy. He liked to see how things shook out before taking a stand. It was just that now, with every second wasted, Miles could feel Josie slipping away.

"We'll help you," Tai said finally. She glanced around the room sheepishly. "Josie's one of us."

"What else do you know? Details," Joshua said.

Miles let out a long breath. They had a chance now. "We were at—"

"No," Marcus boomed.

"No?" Tai's eyes fixed sharply on him.

"What concern is it of mine if she got herself captured? Josie knew the risks and will live with the consequences."

"You can't be serious," Tai countered.

"Sir," Joshua stepped close to Marcus. "We made a deal with her, and as much as I hate to admit it, she delivered."

"Aye, she did," Marcus snarled. "And I gave her a chance. She threw it away willingly. I will not risk everything I have sacrificed for the sake of one person. Not when I'm so close."

"You've sacrificed?" Joshua edged back with disbelief scrawled across his face. "What about the rest of us? Or Doc Lee and all of those who've died fighting on Aegean for the cause. Haven't they sacrificed? You don't even care that they died. Only that they fought. And here we are holed up in a ruined building because you won't give the order for us to fight the P&Cs in the streets and protect the people that need us."

"Watch your tone, boy," Marcus growled. "Their deaths were necessary to free us from oppression. But my ambitions are greater than just Aegean Deck. We will stick to the plan and leave tonight. That's an order."

"Then you go without me," Joshua said quietly.

"What did you say?"

Joshua met Marcus's gaze. "I might not have thought the highest of Josie. She's naïve and stubborn and has an infuriating knack of not listening. But she fought for us. She believed we could be better. I won't sit back when I know I can help. That's what a coward would do. No one else is going to die."

Nobody moved. Nobody dared even breathe. The look of pure anger on Marcus's face was terrifying. Miles kept a straight face, but he felt a sense of pride watching his brother stand up to Marcus. It gave him hope.

Everyone in the room stood at perfect attention, waiting for any indication of what might happen next.

"If you leave, there's no coming back," Marcus said, punctuating each word with deadly calm.

"I know," Joshua replied quietly. He turned to Miles and Tai. "Let's go."

Miles knew better than to wait any longer. When they got to the door, Joshua stopped short. "Matias, are you coming?"

Matias looked down at the ground and then back to Joshua. "I can't." His usually deep voice was thick, as if each word was an effort. "I have to see this through."

Seconds passed. Joshua's lips moved silently around words that never came, replaced instead by a shallow nod toward his friend who returned the simple gesture of understanding.

"Joshua," Marcus called, "I'm letting you go freely and unharmed because of the loyalty you've shown me in the past. That grace will not be extended a second time."

Joshua said nothing and pushed through the door, back out to the open chamber of the Galley Markets.

"I'll never be able to thank you enough," Miles said once outside. "I would have understood if you stayed."

"Look around you, Miles," Joshua said as he gestured at the wreckage of the Galley Markets. "We grew up here. Our whole lives were here. Mom didn't fight for us her whole life for me to turn my back now. This is Marcus's war. This isn't what I wanted."

Miles would tell Joshua and Tai about the plan to return *November's Dawn* to the surface on the way. Every second they wasted now put them further from Josie.

CHAPTER TWENTY-SIX_

THE PIERCING GAZE of Cornelius Graham fell directly on Josie from above Adrian's desk. Part of her was in awe about sitting in the room where Cornelius Graham had worked and given life to *November's Dawn*. But the worst thing she could do was lower her guard now that she was in the heart of danger.

"You said you needed my help. What did you mean?" she asked.

Adrian glanced up at the portrait of Graham. His face was pale and sunken, but a deadly seriousness flashed in his eyes. "First, I need you to denounce Hades Fist and the riots they have sparked. Then I need to know what you learned from the holomessage Felix gave you."

Her jaw clenched. Asking her to betray her friends infuriated her. Hearing him say Felix's name made her feel sick. "No."

"Josie—"

"If that's what you want, then just send me back to the Pits."

Adrian slammed his own glass on the desk. "I very well could."

Josie kept her eyes locked with his. Then his scowl broke. "I'm not an evil man. I know you think so. In fact, many do. But I have devoted my life to protecting *November's Dawn* and every soul aboard it."

"As long as those souls are from Olympus Deck."

Adrian licked his lips before continuing. "Regrettably, in any system there are those who sacrifice more than others. The history of humanity is a history of great and necessary sacrifice. I'm doing what I must to ensure we're not the end of humanity. Do you know why *November's Dawn* has survived all these years under the waves?"

She looked away rather than give an answer. It sounded like the start to an OSD lecture—one she didn't want to play into.

"Order. Order is why we survive. See, *November's Dawn* is an organism. It lives and breathes and walks on the floor of the seas and every one of us is a vital part of the whole. When one part is broken, the whole system is in danger. Order makes sure broken pieces are removed. If Aegean Deck stops producing food, clothing, and provisions, we die. If Delos Deck stops teaching our children and training many of the scientists and engineers who work throughout the ark, our systems will fail, and we will die. If Olympus Deck was no longer able to innovate and pass ideas across every deck, if we were no longer able to pilot the ark itself, chaos would spread, and we would die. Every aspect of our lives is governed by that fragile order. Hades Fist has the self-righteous belief they can strip away order. That people will naturally govern themselves in a fair system. But how can that occur when we are constrained by the limitations of *November's Dawn?* When supplies are low, who in the system decides who receives and who must go without? Our existence is bound by the waves we live beneath, and that reality governs our way of life. This movement in the lower decks must be snuffed out or we'll all suffer."

"You don't need my help for that," Josie said. He was a smooth talker. Part of what he said she might even agree with, but betraying the lower decks was not an option.

"That is where you're wrong. Like it or not, Josie Owens, but you've become something of a hero to this movement. I suppose it was my mistake in creating such a show of trying to find you. It gave you a platform to stand up against the OSD. But your actions carry weight, so would your denouncement of the riots." He stopped for a moment and ran his fingers through his hair. "I'm doing everything I can to protect the people. It's the only part of my job that matters."

"Then give up your power. Let the people have a voice for once. Not just those from Olympus Deck."

He looked to the side, as if almost contemplating it. The office shook as another tremor worked its way through *November's Dawn*. They were becoming more and more frequent. Then his expression hardened again. "No. *November's Dawn* faces bigger threats than rebels."

Now Josie was curious. "What could possibly be more important than half the ark rioting?"

The sunken look returned on Adrian's face. He seemed to shrink at her words. "The death of us all."

"What?" That was the last thing she had imagined hearing.

Adrian looked up at her. "Did you feel that just now? The shaking?"

"Yeah. Why?"

"It's caused by the ark smashing through rock formations as they move. They've been getting more severe. It means we are nearing the Obsidian Trench."

"What does that have to do with anything? I thought that was the point of your celebration."

He swallowed. "Our navigational computers have been crippled. We're stuck on our current course and unable to turn. When *November's Dawn* reaches the Obsidian Trench, we will walk straight into its depths. No one will survive it."

The finality in his voice sent a shiver down her back, but she knew better than to trust him. This was a trick to make her believe he fought for the good of the ark. But what if he was telling the truth, albeit bluntly, and they were all in terrible danger. "How can I possibly believe you?"

"You'll have your answer when we reach the Obsidian Trench. If we have any chance at fixing the problems plaguing us, the fighting must stop and you must tell me what you learned from the holomessage. Any piece of information could be the key."

Silence settled in the office. He wanted her to betray not only her friends but also her dad.

She heard his voice from the holomessage. That *November's Dawn* was meant to rise to the surface again. On the surface, they would never have to worry about canyon trenches on the ocean floor. They could create a better future where the people had the power to be free. But if she trusted Adrian and he was indeed lying, she would sacrifice everything for nothing.

Josie's conflicted thoughts hammered in her head. Every time she thought she got close to an answer, some reasoning pulled her in a different direction. The ear-piercing memory of the gunshot that killed Felix grounded her. Finally, she gave up and went with what her heart told her.

"I won't do it."

Adrian looked like the breath had been stolen from him. Then he stood. "George will take you to a room." He walked to the front of the office. "I pray you reconsider," he said and walked out.

Josie was in a daze. Two P&C officers in full jet-black gear stepped to either side of her. They didn't bind her wrists, but she got the distinct feeling she was still a prisoner.

So be it.

She took one last look at the portrait of Cornelius Graham. Then she noticed it. Set underneath the picture was a series of intricate symbols. To anyone they would look like a string of decorative styling, but Josie felt the symbols shared a strong resemblance to something she was very familiar with.

The Heart of the Dawn necklace.

The guards pushed her out of the office before she could get a better look. They led her down a passageway just as luxurious as Adrian's office had been. They stopped at the far end of the passageway, in front of large white doors. Wordlessly, one of the officers opened it and beckoned her in. It was a room like the one she had seen Rose in. A bed was on one side. She sunk into it as she sat down. The room was not uncomfortable and dark like the Pits had been, but a cell all the same. Pulling the Heart of the Dawn necklace out of her shirt gave part of the room a faint red glow. Its heat radiated into her open palm. She saw her dad's face again in the holomessage.

Adrian had asked her about the holomessage. That was strange.

Nobody had more access than he did. He *had* to know the true purpose of *November's Dawn* was to return to the surface when it was safe. Nothing else made sense. Maybe it really was just a way to get her to tell him what she knew and be his puppet.

She almost wished Miles was with her. He would have some ideas about it all. But that was over now.

He was the reason Felix had died. He was the reason for everything. Commandant Reyes's twisted laughter echoed in her ears and the terrible nauseous feeling crept through her abdomen again.

But even as those thoughts passed, new ones took their place. And they only made her feel guilty. She had condemned Miles but still didn't know why he had turned her in.

Something drove him to do what he did. Something bad.

Then tears fell. Nobody was coming for her. Her chest tightened in-between labored sobs. She was alone. She had failed everybody who put their trust in her. If she was lucky, sleep would stop the pain for a while.

But what did she care now? At least the pain wouldn't leave her.

Her eyelids fell and sleep embraced her.

Dreams took her. She watched as a young Odette and Nila ran through an empty passageway toward her. Josie turned and ran in the other direction. She just wanted to get home. Tears stung her eyes and made it hard to see. Odette laughed and said nobody liked her. Nila said she never was her friend for real. Josie just wanted it to stop.

Finally, she was home. Her mom stood at the kitchen counter in their small cabin. The tears just kept coming, but at least her mom was there; she would help. Josie sniffed as she pulled on her mom's shirt. Between hiccups she told her mom what happened and how horrible Odette and Nila had been to her.

Her mom frowned. "Well, have you talked to them? Asked them to stop calling you names?"

Josie was crushed. She stood looking down with her hands jammed in her pockets. Of course, she wanted them to stop. Maybe her mom didn't understand. If only she could explain it better.

"Maybe you should stay away from them for a while," her mom added flatly.

She looked up, the tears still glistening in her eyes. Slowly, she reached her arms around her mom in a one-sided hug. Her mom loosely set one free arm on her shoulder. More than anything, Josie wanted her dad—he always gave her the best hugs—but he was gone.

Knocking at the door jolted her awake. Josie pushed herself up.

She was a prisoner. Why would they be knocking? Several seconds passed. Then the door hissed and opened. Josie clenched her fists around the sheets of the bed. A woman stepped through.

Josie thought she was still dreaming. She had to be.

"Mom?"

"Oh, Josie," Serena said smiling and rushing across the room. Right before the bed, she stopped and looked down. Instead of immediately joining her daughter, she lowered her head and asked, "Can I sit?"

Josie scrunched her legs up close and nodded. She was still not fully convinced she wasn't dreaming. "What're you doing here?"

"Adrian told me they found you. I was so relieved. I came right away." Her eyes settled on the bandage on Josie's leg, then made their way down to her bandaged foot. "Are you okay?"

"I'm fine." Josie shied away awkwardly. Part of her was glad her mom was there, but she didn't know what else to say as she had not been close with her mom for years. "The First Vicar let you in?"

Serena's eyebrow raised. "Well, yes. You're safe now. Adrian promised me you'll be safe."

Josie's head spun, and her face flushed. "Safe? I'm a prisoner. They killed Felix. I tried to keep Rose safe, and they took her too. Everything is so wrong."

"I'm sorry, Josie. I'm so sorry I wasn't there to protect you. I should have been at your party on Engineering. I never should have put you in a position where you had to make those choices for Rose. And not a second goes by where I don't regret it." She spoke slowly, as if fearful of each word. "But you're here now, that's all that matters."

Josie looked away. It was just so hard for her to lower her guard and let her mom in. For some reason, that was how it had always been. She understood why her mom had been forced to take the job on Olympus, but even now, when Josie felt more alone than ever, she couldn't let her mom in. She glanced back, seeing the longing in her mom's eyes only added to the pain but no words seemed like they could help now.

Serena gently put her hand on Josie's leg and gave a slight squeeze. "Well, I won't bother you anymore." She walked to the door. "I'm just so glad you're okay, Josie. I love you."

Josie knew what she wanted; she just didn't know if she had the strength to do it. Her mom was about to leave and then her chance would be gone. "Please stay," she said, the words tumbling out. "I mean, if you want."

Her mom smiled. It was the warmest thing Josie had ever seen. "Of course, Josie. I'll stay as long as you like."

Josie shifted so her mom would have more room on the bed. Saying those words, simply asking her to stay, had relieved so much of the weight on her chest. Her mom slipped back onto the bed. This time more relaxed.

"I can't imagine the strength it took to go through what you did. That's courage I've never had," she said.

A thousand thoughts of all the danger she had faced flashed in her mind. None of that had felt as hopeless as she did now. "I don't feel strong."

"You never do at the time. In the moment, everything feels like it threatens to tip the scale. Makes it where one minute you're breathing and the next your head is underwater. The strength is to continue. The courage is to keep fighting for yourself and those you love." As her mom spoke, she seemed to get lost in her words like she was talking to herself as much as to her daughter.

"How can you say that when you work for Frost?" Josie looked away.

Serena cupped Josie's hand in hers. "I've only ever done what I had to do to protect you and Rose. I know I've made so many mistakes along the way. I tried to steer you from making the same mistakes I did when I should have just listened. When I should have just been there for you. Been a mother. A friend."

Josie could hear the tremble in her mom's voice. Her throat tightened, so she kept her eyes locked on a small smudge on the wall. "So why did you do it?" She was not sure why she asked. It was clear why her mom had done it. Some part of her just wanted to hear her mom say it out loud. Then maybe she could try to move past it.

"After your dad's accident, we had nothing. Rose was so little and you were just a child yourself. We were going to lose the cabin. I worried every day simply about surviving to the next. Adrian stepped in and gave me a job, a means to protect my family. I don't know what I would have done without him."

Josie swallowed hard. "I get it. It just hurts."

"I should have trusted you sooner, Josie. But we had to be very careful. There are some on the ark who would not take kindly to the First Vicar showing so much favor."

Then a thought crossed Josie's mind that made her forget everything else. "It wasn't an accident that killed Dad." It was all she could do to keep her voice steady. "Someone was after him."

"Why would you say that?" her mom asked, her voice now poised with striking calm.

Josie closed her eyes, forcing a tear to break free and tumble down her cheek. "He left me a holomessage from right before the accident. He said they were after him. The OSD, Frost, he did this."

"No. No, that can't be."

"Mom," Josie said and put a hand on her mom's leg. "It's true. Dad said it himself."

Her mom seemed caught in a trance. Josie wasn't even sure if she heard her. Then her eyes focused. "No, Josie. You have it all wrong. Adrian wasn't after Dom. They were friends. They worked in secret on reforms that would have changed *November's Dawn* forever."

"But why would Dad say that then?" Josie said, her voice rising sharply. She yanked up the Heart of the Dawn necklace from under her shirt. "Why would he leave me this?"

Her mom gasped as the red glow danced across her face. Recognition set in her eyes. "Dom showed me that once. He said he found it with Marcus in one of Cornelius Graham's old storage compartments."

Hearing Marcus' name made her skin crawl. "Mom, I need to know everything you know."

"I really don't know much, Josie," her mom said and looked at the necklace again. "Dom was obsessed with this. He found documents that described the ark as being capable of some sort of transformation. He said the necklace was the key to activate it."

Josie could hardly breathe. That confirmed what the necklace did. The only question left was where to do it from. The bridge was still the best bet. "And Marcus didn't care about any of this?"

"Marcus and your dad were different people, Josie. I remember they argued about the necklace. Marcus thought it was all fairytales and a distraction from the real work. I think Dom gave up trying to convince him."

"It's not a fairytale." Josie held the necklace in her palm. A sinking feeling settled in her stomach. Marcus was with her dad the day of the accident. He had known about the necklace. What if he wanted to keep it a secret? She couldn't believe Marcus would abandon his cause, but something wasn't adding up. She wondered what other secrets he had.

Something felt very wrong.

Josie slid the necklace back under her shirt. "Mom, this isn't all a coincidence. Dad was murdered. Don't you want to find out why?"

Serena took her hand "We're going to find out." Then, without warning she jumped up from the bed. "George!"

The door slid open and a P&C officer burst through with one hand wrapped tightly around his security baton. "What is it? What's wrong? Are you hurt?" He eyed Josie still sitting on the bed.

Serena frowned. "No, we're fine. I need you to get Adrian. I need him here now."

He looked back and forth between them like he weighed the repercussions between disturbing Adrian and angering Serena. "Fine, wait here."

Apparently, Adrian was less threatening. What did that say about Josie's mom?

"What's going on?" Josie asked.

Her mom's pained expression furrowed her delicate features. "I'm not sure, Josie. I'll tell you everything, I promise. But first I need to see Adrian."

Josie wanted to push it further, but her mom's seriousness gave her pause. Whatever was worrying her was obviously important. Josie was closer now to the answers she had been looking for her whole life. The only thing left was to wait a little longer.

Thankfully, it was not long before she heard echoing footsteps and low voices from beyond the door. The First Vicar stepped in and closed the door.

"Adrian, thank god," Serena said as she stood up and went to him.

A cautious look from Adrian toward Josie stopped her mom in her tracks. "George said it was urgent," he said in a low voice, one Josie had not heard him use with anyone else.

"It is," her mom whispered. She looked over at Josie. "Tell him what you told me. About Dom."

Josie looked down while fidgeting with her fingers. This was it. If she said something now, there was no going back. Adrian eyed her expectantly. Josie looked at her mom again and nodded. "The holomessage, the one you want to know about," she started.

Adrian was invested now. He moved closer to Josie.

"It was from my dad. He said someone was after him."

Adrian leaned down and grabbed both of Josie's arms. Sharp and focused eyes narrowed on her. "You're sure of this?" He sounded almost frantic. "Josie, you're sure that's what he said?"

Josie frowned. "Well, yeah." Now she was annoyed. "So you're telling me you weren't after my dad?"

"No," Adrian whispered and shook his head slowly. "Did he say who was?"

Now Josie was the one to shake her head. She had just assumed it had been the OSD. Adrian seemed different, guilty almost, not like he was lying but as if he were truly sorry. His reaction was genuine, if nothing else she was sure of that.

The thought of him and her dad being friends was bewildering. And now to find out they were working to reform

November's Dawn? What if she had been wrong this whole time, and Adrian could be trusted? She didn't see another way out anymore. Taking that chance was the only option left.

"Adrian," Serena said and stepped close to him. "What does this mean?"

"It's what I've feared. Someone has been working against me. Against us." Gently he took Serena's hand. "Stay here. I'll be back soon."

"Wait!" Josie shouted. It was now or never. She still didn't fully trust Adrian, and she had come to regret her quick willingness to trust far too often, but she felt he was blindly walking into something dangerous without her help. "You wanted to know about the holomessage, right?"

Adrian turned back to the door. "It'll have to wait, Josie. I must get to the bottom of this." He looked again at Serena. "The door will be locked. You'll be safe 'til I return."

As soon as he was gone Josie eyed her mom. She could see the worry in her creased brow. Everything was confusing and the timing could not have been worse, but Josie had to know what that touch meant.

"Mom?" She hesitated. "You and Adrian. You're not together, right?"

Her mom laughed. The sort of involuntary laugh someone does when nervous. Her face flushed, but she shook her head all the same.

CHAPTER TWENTY-SEVEN_

Hurried footsteps echoed through the passageway. The more Adrian thought about it the more he could feel his anger growing and the faster he walked. A lifetime of service to *November's Dawn* had led him to this moment. A singular point where he had the chance to save them all and now he knew without a doubt, he had been betrayed. What Josie had told him confirmed the suspicions he had.

And he was certain Director Clarke was part of the conspiracy.

He cursed himself for not seeing it sooner. This was going to end. It was his duty.

Another tremor forced him to steady himself against the wall. Yet another sign their time was quickly running out.

"Did you alert Reyes?" Adrian called over his shoulder to George.

"Yes, First Vicar. But I haven't heard back from him."

"Send it again," Adrian ordered. "I'll need him."

"Yes, First Vicar," George said in an uncomfortable voice. "I know it's not my place, but are you well, sir? It's just I haven't seen you this mad for quite some time."

"You're right," Adrian said without missing a step. "It's not your place." A cold silence followed, then he thought better of it and stopped. "George, you have served me well and over the years I've come to rely on you a great deal. But something is happening now, something terrible and I intend to put a stop to it. Can I count on you? Do I still have your loyalty?"

George eyed him curiously. "Of course, First Vicar. I have seen it myself. Nobody is more devoted to *November's Dawn* than you." His cheeks broadened into a grin.

Adrian smiled, then the fleeting amusement faded. It was true. Nothing would stop him from doing what he must to protect *November's Dawn*.

The passageway tracked off up ahead and led to a larger and more opulent corridor. Large decorative letters adorned one side of the wall: *Offices of Industrial Cannery Limited*. It was late in the day, so there were only a few people still milling in and out of the various offices and support rooms off the corridor. His target was directly ahead. The largest of the offices, its broad double doors were flanked by thinly veined alabaster sculptures of ancient Greek gods. He stopped just before them.

"Wait here. Send in the commandant when he arrives," Adrian ordered. He took a deep breath and turned back to the door. There was no going back now. After a few seconds, his face relaxed as he put on a look of indifference and control. The look of the First Vicar. He raised his fist to knock, but before he could, the doors hissed and slid open.

"Ah, Adrian," Director Clarke's voice carried. "I thought that was you I saw coming through my offices in such a rush. Do come in."

Adrian stepped into the stately office as the doors slid shut behind him. Clarke sat behind an ornately carved wooden desk. Adrian never took his eyes off him. He didn't know the full extent of the conspiracy, but this was the start of stamping it out. The reforms he had been working on with Dominic Owens would have drastically changed the corporate culture of the ark. Nobody else had the influence and ambition, or more importantly, more to lose from that than Director Clarke. The only question was what else Clarke had been up to but first he needed answers about Dom. He wanted to know what happened to his friend. "Don't patronize me, Clarke. We both know why I've come."

The smile faded from Clarke's face, replaced now with a sharp gaze and menacing scowl. Even at his age, the Director looked a formidable man. But Adrian stood taller. He was the First Vicar. *November's Dawn* was his to protect from any threat, no matter where it originated.

Clarke drummed his fingers across his desk. "Then perhaps this will be a shorter visit than I anticipated."

Adrian walked over to a large bookshelf and gazed at the leather-bound volumes from the old world. "That is up to you, Director. Confess your sins against the OSD, and I will consider letting you live."

Clarke smiled and motioned to the chairs in front of his desk. "I think not. Please sit."

Adrian studied him for a moment before taking the offer to sit. Clarke had not denied his betrayal, but his equally confident tone was unsettling. In his mind, Adrian saw Dom's face as vividly as if he were standing right before him. He owed it to his friend.

"The reforms. How did you know what Dom Owens and I were planning? You couldn't have orchestrated this treachery on your own. Who else is involved so I can end this once and for all?"

Clarke frowned like he was genuinely confused then held up his hand. "Ah, Adrian, wait a moment. Let everyone arrive before we continue. Commandant Reyes, please join us."

Adrian glanced behind him. The office door was still closed. He was sure he would have seen Reyes's arrival. Then he heard shuffling from another smaller room just off the main office. Commandant Reyes came through. He stood in perfect military form off to the side. His eyes were locked straight ahead. A cruel smile crept across Clarke's face when he noticed Adrian's confusion.

"Now, where were we?" Clarke said.

Adrian's mind raced. Reyes must have arrived before he did. "What's going on?" He gripped the arms of his chair. "Commandant Reyes, why did you not respond to my message?"

Reyes's stoic eyes glanced toward Adrian, but he didn't answer. Adrian swallowed dryly. Something was terribly wrong.

Clarke chuckled. "Do you see it now, Adrian? Your time is up."

"You would threaten me?" Adrian roared and stood up. He needed to take control of the situation. Fast. "I'm the First Vicar of the OSD." He spun toward Reyes. "Commandant, I order you to arrest Director Clarke on charges of treason and murder."

Nobody moved. The three men stood silently as if locked in an internal battle of wills, all waiting to see who might fold first. Every second that passed added to the doubt growing in Adrian's mind and solidified the terrible unease. Reyes still made no motion to follow his order.

Adrian had been played. The revelation was crushing.

Clarke circled around his desk. "You are weak, Adrian. I have always suspected it, but these riots proved it. You don't have what it takes to lead. You were gifted the most powerful position in history, and what have you done with it? Nothing. It was a position that should've never been yours. *November's*

Dawn demands an iron fist and that is something you cannot provide any longer. But we—" He motioned to himself and Reyes. "We can, and we will regain control."

Adrian shook his head. He tried to make sense of it all. "No. No, it doesn't make sense. What you've done . . . You've been planning this for years. The riots alone didn't push you to this treachery."

"True enough. I've known for years what this would come to," Clarke said and shrugged. "But it was your most recent failures to stop the terrorists that showed Reyes your inabilities."

At this Reyes turned to Clarke. "What are you saying? You've been planning this?"

Clarke frowned. "This is not the time for doubt, Commandant. We have come too far."

Reyes's eyes sharpened. "No, you will tell me the truth now."

Adrian stepped back, as the tensions between the two men rose and their focus shifted from him. This was his chance. "George!" he shouted.

At his call, George emerged through the door. His hands gripped tightly around the holorifle he carried.

Adrian didn't waste a second. "They're traitors! Shoot them!"

George frantically glanced around the room to assess the situation and find his bearings. The split-second hesitation was all it took. Before Adrian could say another word, an ear-shattering crack echoed in the room.

George fell.

Reyes stood with his arm straight out, faint wisps of smoke trailed out of the pistol in his hand, still trained on the spot George had fallen. A sulfurous fume permeated the office.

"Now do you see, Adrian?" Clarke gloated. "*November's Dawn* has no need for a First Vicar. It needs only one who will hold it in complete control. Then the companies can flourish, and everybody will know their place. I am that authority."

Adrian spoke through gritted teeth. "So you did this all for money? The companies already have a monopoly on everything aboard the ark. What more could you want?"

"*November's Dawn* only exists because of the cooperation of the companies. It is time we had the final say in its rule."

"There's no way the other Directors will go along with this. Your company will have too much power." Adrian grasped at any logical argument he could find.

"Maybe at first. But once they see the stability I create and the potential for profits, they'll come around."

"It will never work. Leadership is not something to be taken as a prize and squandered on petty men. It's duty." He turned to Reyes. "You've doomed us all."

Reyes shook his head. "I've saved us. Like I always do."

Clarke's earlier gratification faded. "I had hoped you might see reason. See that this is the only way forward and that you might accept your new place. But it's clear now this will go nowhere. In time you'll see this is the best future for *November's Dawn*. After all, you really don't have a choice."

He looked to Commandant Reyes who had resumed his military posture. "Reyes, take him to the Pits; we'll need him later. But now we must move quickly to take power before *November's Dawn* devolves further."

If it was even possible, Reyes's posture stiffened more at the order. Adrian watched him intently. For one brief second, he hoped the commandant might see the danger of his actions and remember his loyalty to Adrian, but then Reyes looked at George's crumpled body and his jaw clenched.

"It will be done," Reyes said.

The words fell like the crushing tides that raged above. It was over.

CHAPTER TWENTY-EIGHT_

Josie paced around the room one more time. She felt helpless being stuck so she went over everything she knew over again.

"Mom, I'm telling you. Dad knew a way for us all to return to the surface." She gripped the Heart of the Dawn necklace in her hand and thrust it at her. "And this is connected to it all. Somehow."

"You sound just like he did," her mom said. "I want to believe it, Josie. It's just . . . Why didn't Adrian say anything?"

"That's what I thought too." She looked sidelong at her mom. "Maybe he's not as trustworthy as you think. Why didn't he go ahead with the reforms after Dad died?"

"It's not that simple," Serena said. "After Dom's accident, Adrian felt he no longer had the support to push through the changes. Your dad was popular, folks listened and looked up to him. He would be so proud of you, Josie. I know it."

Josie looked away. "I just wish I knew more about him."

Serena gently put her hand on Josie's shoulder. "Most of your life I haven't been able to tell you the truth, even when I knew you wanted to know more than anything. It broke my heart, but it just wouldn't have been safe. When this is over, I'll tell you all about him."

"I'd like that," Josie said. "Thanks, Mom."

Josie was still uneasy about being locked in the room. Her mom seemed to share her tension and was busy twisting her hair around a finger. She caught Josie's glances.

"Would you like me to braid your hair?" Serena asked.

Josie thought about it for a moment. Her hair had come undone from getting captured. It hardly seemed like the time. But then again, what else were they going to do? The door was locked.

She shrugged. "I guess."

Her mom smiled. "Come sit in front of me."

Slowly at first but then with more confidence, her mom wove her fingers through Josie's tangled hair. Try as she might, Josie couldn't remember the last time she'd been with her mom like this. It had definitely been years since she had let her mom braid her hair. She closed her eyes and silently winced when her mom pulled too hard, but it didn't hurt as much now.

"Mom?"

"Sorry, am I hurting you?"

"What?" Josie said. "Oh no, it's just I wanted to say I'm sorry."

Her mom's fingers stopped moving. "You don't need to apologize for anything."

Josie turned around to face her mom. It was now or never. She was so tired of the anger she had carried for years about what her mom did. Anger that had made her unable to see the struggles her mom endured for her and Rose. Now that anger had faded and guilt crept in.

"I do though. I've always tried to play the victim in Dad being taken from us. Like I was the only one hurting. And I mean, I was hurting. I still am. But I never stopped to think about what it must have done to you. You were all alone raising a family and instead of trying to help pick up the pieces, I blamed you for it all. It wasn't fair. I'm sorry it's taken me so long to see it." Josie bit her lip to stop it from trembling.

Without saying a word, Serena pulled Josie into a hug. It was an embrace that reminded Josie of the ones she would get from her dad. She let herself be completely taken by it, and all she felt was love for her mom. Both of their eyes glistened now.

Josie stood after a few more moments. "It's been a long time since Adrian left."

Serena's brow creased while she thought. "I guess it has been a while."

"Something doesn't feel right," Josie said and eyed the door.

"Josie, he said to wait till he comes back. We should be patient."

"No," she muttered. "We've been in here long enough." Once at the door, she raised her fist and struck it. "Hello! Hello! Let us out now!"

Josie waited for a few more seconds. Nobody answered. She didn't hear anything on the outside, but she wasn't sure if she would be able to anyway. Maybe the door was soundproof. She knocked again anyway, this time much harder. "You have to let us out! I'm telling you—" A loud crash cut her off. Followed by a reverberation from the other side. Josie put her ear to the door.

"Get back, Josie!" Serena said.

Before Josie could respond, the door hissed. The telltale sign it was about to open. Now Josie did jump back several paces. When the door slid open fully, a dark mass fell toward them and slammed to the ground.

Her mom gasped. The lights in the room lit up the black uniform and gear of a P&C officer lying face up on the ground. A tactical helmet covered his face. He wasn't moving. Another officer stepped through, this one in full gear as well, but he just stood there. Josie held her breath. Then the officer reached up and unbuckled the clasps on his helmet. Josie almost fainted when she saw his face.

It was the last person she ever expected.

Josie inhaled sharply. The cool air flooded through her lungs again. "Miles!"

"Hi, Josie," Miles said and nodded toward her mom. "Hello, Mrs. Owens. Are you both okay?"

Josie grappled with what was unfolding in front of her. Her initial joy of seeing Miles quickly faded as she remembered what he had done. She had a hundred questions and couldn't bring herself to ask a single one. "I, well, yeah . . . We're fine."

"Miles, how did you know we were here?" her mom asked.

"I'll be happy to answer any questions you have." Miles motioned to the officer on the ground. "But we need to leave."

"We're not leaving," Josie countered.

"Adrian told us to stay here until he came back," Serena said.

"Then we had better be out of here even quicker. The First Vicar has been arrested."

"What?" Josie and her mom said in unison.

Miles nodded as he glanced back out to the hallway. "Director Clarke is calling the shots now. Well, Clarke and Reyes, I guess. Come on!"

Josie exchanged a worried look with her mom. If Adrian had been arrested, they were vulnerable. She groaned as she followed Miles out.

"Wait," her mom called out. "I can't go."

"What do you mean? Mom, you can't stay here," Josie said, spinning around.

Serena shook her head. "If what he says is true, our family

is in more danger than most. Director Clarke will not leave loose ends. I have to get Rose."

"We'll go with you," Miles said.

"No, it'll be safer if it's just me. Go with him, Josie. You know what you must do."

Josie wrapped her arms around her mom. She felt closer to her than she had in years. The thought of separating again scared her, but she knew her mom was right. There was no more time. "I-I love you, Mom. Be careful, please."

Scattered tears pooled in her mom's eyes. She blinked them away. "I love you too. Don't worry, I still have a few friends. Rose and I will be fine. It's you I'm worried about."

"I think I'm starting to get the hang of this. Running for my life, I mean."

Her mom's face went white.

Josie grimaced awkwardly. "It's a joke, Mom."

Serena sighed and seemed to breathe again. "Right, yeah. Still, just be safe."

Josie nodded and followed Miles out of the room. Serena made her way down the other end of the hallway. Josie prayed she would get Rose and be okay. With any luck, they all would.

"You ready?" Miles said, the holorifle across his back. "I kind of know my way around here now. We have to get to the bridge before Clarke and Reyes. They're planning something big. This is our only chance to stop them."

"Stop," Josie said and closed her eyes. The pain of seeing Miles act like nothing was wrong was too much. "I just can't."

Miles touched her hand. She hesitated just enough for him to notice.

"How did you find out?" he asked quietly.

"Reyes told me when he was torturing me. I had to find out from the same monster that killed Felix." Her voice was steady, which surprised her. It carried a sharp edge she found fitting and somehow made her feel like she was in control of the situation.

Miles's eyes glistened in the low light. "I'm so sorry, Josie. I never meant for any of this to happen."

"How could you, Miles? I trusted you. I thought I meant something to you. But I don't. Everything you said to me was a lie."

Miles looked stunned. "I didn't lie to you. All those moments were true. There hasn't been a single second where I haven't regretted what happened."

Josie fumed. She nearly screamed at him. That would attract attention though, so she was glad she stopped herself, but that did little to stop the pain. She felt the twisting sting of everything all over again. "Then why did you do it?"

"Because of my mom. I did it to save her."

"Save your mom? Miles, what are you talking about?" Josie thought about it. Mrs. Thomas had a sickness that would kill her. But the day of the garden explosion, she had been feeling better.

It all made sense.

Miles's eyes met with hers, and he nodded slowly. "The medicine my mom needed. They gave it to me in exchange for turning you in. It was my fault I went to them. I thought it was the only way. I was just so desperate to get her the help she needed that I saw my opportunity and I took it. And Felix . . . It's all because of me." He cradled his head in his hands. "I never meant for any of this to happen."

Josie was at a loss for words. It was all too much to process. They had bigger problems, and time was running out.

Josie leaned against the wall. Was this what she was looking for? A way to explain what happened, to somehow prove Miles really did care about her? Part of her wanted to run to Miles and hug him, but the other part was not sure if it was enough for her. Felix had been murdered because of him.

But as much as she hated it, she started to understand something. Would she have done it any differently? She would do anything for Rose if she was in danger. Could she blame Miles for trying to save his family? Hearing the truth did make her feel slightly better. She just wished he had told her before.

Before she could think of anything else to say, a resounding thud echoed down the hallway. Their heads snapped toward the disturbance. Miles reached across her body and pushed them both up against the wall.

Whatever else they needed to say would have to wait.

Two fully clad and armed P&C officers came into view, their dark visors and readied holorifles made for a menacing look. Their attention seemed to be on the room Josie and her mom had just been locked in, a fact that sent cold shivers down her spine. Miles put a finger to his lips and pointed toward a small grate.

Once inside the maintenance shaft, they wove their way through tight passes of low beams and pipes while working to avoid the expanse of cable and wire bundles.

"How do we get to the bridge?" Josie whispered as she ducked under another steam pipe.

"The P&Cs cutoff the way I wanted to go." He paused. "From here, our only option is one of the bathyspheres that ride along the outer hull of *November's Dawn*."

"Bathyspheres?"

"Yeah. They're like elevators that move on the outside of the hull. Who knew right?"

They came out into a passageway that was far more utilitarian than the rest of Olympus Deck. Gone were the sleek white walls and decorative coves. Now they were surrounded by the pipes and metal walls she was much more used to.

Judging by the eerie creaks and groans coming from the walls of the passageway, they were very close, if not right up against, the outer hull of *November's Dawn*. Miles stopped in front of a large metal hatch with a great spinning wheel which held the locking mechanism in place and created a seal strong enough to endure the massive pressure variations that occurred.

"Here it is," Miles said. "I'm glad I spent some time looking around up here. Or else we never would have made it out of there."

A cool blast of stale air rushed out of the bathysphere as the hatch creaked open. The small circular chamber of glass and metal looked as if no one had been inside for years, if not longer. Once inside, Miles pushed the heavy hatch closed.

An analog console protruded off one side of the sphere, lit up with an array of buttons and lights, nothing like the holotech screens and controls that were found almost everywhere in *November's Dawn*. Dust covered everything. Miles wiped his thumb across the buttons and switches, revealing faint lettering. Josie inched forward to see but decided to let Miles figure it out.

She busied herself with looking into the inky darkness of the ocean instead, as if it could possibly offer her anything different than it had for her whole life. Only this time, she pictured what it all might look like on the surface. Even just imagining it seemed alien. She had seen photos of what it looked like before the war but there was no telling what it would be like now, after years of tectonic movement. Yet, they had a better chance returning to the surface than they did staying in the deep forever.

Still, what if she was wrong?

Miles grunted as he worked to bring the bathysphere to life. "Damn it."

"Is everything okay?"

He punched at a few more buttons, but nothing responded in kind. He ran his fingers through his hair. "I thought I knew how to get this moving. Some engineer I am."

Josie moved beside him and looked at the controls. It was an older system. Felix had shown her something similar in the past. "It's okay, Miles. Let me look."

Miles sighed. "Yeah, okay."

Within minutes, Josie had the bathysphere controls lit up and running. They stood silently as the bathysphere crawled along the outer hull of the ark. It was far slower than any of the elevators.

Josie's hand drifted up and wrapped around the Heart of the Dawn necklace. It was important beyond measure, that much was clear. Now she just needed to figure out how to use it.

"Miles," she said as she pulled out the necklace. The shimmering light coming from the magnificent red center of the Heart of the Dawn radiated throughout the small chamber and gave everything a golden hue. Josie quickly explained to Miles what her mom had told her.

"Are you sure this is the right thing to do?" she asked. "I mean, taking *November's Dawn* to the surface affects every one of us. It just seems like a decision bigger than just one person."

"It is. But what other choice is there? Do you think the Directors would allow a fair choice? I mean, would Marcus let that happen? I don't think all this will ever end as long as we're stuck on the bottom of the ocean. We need a fresh start. You can give us that."

"Yeah, that's what I thought."

Miles then quickly explained what happened on Aegean Deck after she was captured and the falling out he had with Marcus and how Joshua and Tai had left with him.

Josie had her own suspicions about Marcus, and this made

her dislike him even more. She couldn't shake the fact that Marcus had been with her dad the day he died and knew about the necklace but never said anything. What was he really capable of? He had to have help from someone, someone close to the OSD. She doubted it was Reyes. He had always seemed too devoted to his duty. But who?

One thing was for sure, they weren't fighting for the same future. She took a deep breath and looked back out of one of the viewports.

"Miles, I'm worried about Marcus. If Director Clarke and Reyes have taken everything over, there's no way Marcus is letting it all happen. We have to be ready for anything."

"We will be."

She was glad Miles was with her. Even after everything.

"Have you been to the bridge?" Josie asked. "We have to stop whatever Clarke and Reyes are planning. Then we still need to find where to use the necklace. It must be a type of data cartridge that overrides the ark's programing."

Miles nodded as he thought it over. "That would make sense. Whatever it is, we'll find it. You know, once you get to Olympus Deck, their security really isn't as good as you'd expect. I guess they don't imagine anyone from Olympus Deck would have ulterior motives."

Josie tried to put on a brave face, like she was confronting her destiny head on, but she was terrified of what was to come. Adrian had been reasonable, and if what Miles said was true, Director Clarke was ruthless, and she knew all too well what Commandant Reyes was capable of.

But there was still a chance. She could still make everything right.

CHAPTER TWENTY-NINE_

THE BRIDGE WAS JUST as impressive as Josie imagined it. A series of chambers filled with balconies and catwalks offered unparalleled views of the outside ocean. Josie had seen the lights shining out from the bridge into the endless darkness even while they had been in the bathysphere. Almost every space in the chamber itself was taken up by expansive networks of holoscreen displays, controls, and mechanisms.

Everywhere she looked, she tried to find a control panel or anything that could relate to the Heart of the Dawn, but so far nothing matched. A terrible part of her was almost glad she hadn't found it yet. It gave her time. Precious moments before she had to decide the fates of everyone.

The bridge was eerily silent. So far, from where Josie and Miles crouched behind a series of forgotten shelves, she had not seen anyone. Not even any of the multitude of pilots she figured were needed to properly run the place. Though she couldn't decide if this made her feel better or worse about the whole situation.

"We should be looking for a control panel for the necklace," Josie huffed.

"Let's just be careful," Miles said. "We don't know what Reyes and Director Clarke are doing. We can't let them take over the ark. Let me see if it's clear."

Josie nodded and watched as Miles propped himself on a shelf that gave a good view. She couldn't help but notice something different about him. He seemed more confident with himself—or more at ease. She wondered if something else happened when they were apart that he hadn't told her.

The large double doors of the bridge opened. Miles threw himself back down to the ground and out of sight. Footsteps sounded from beyond the door before it was even fully open. Several pairs of footsteps.

"Tie him up over there," a low voice commanded. Josie didn't recognize it.

"What's your move here, Clarke?" another responded.

That voice she knew as Adrian's.

Josie peeked through a crack between stacks of old data cartridges. Adrian's hands were tied, and he was led by a masked P&C officer. An older man stood in front. The source of the low voice, she reasoned. Commandant Reyes skulked behind. Her first impulse was to jump out and attack him, but that thought quickly faded as she saw another P&C officer come through the door.

Thankfully, nobody bothered to look over at the musty corner Josie and Miles hid in, but there was no way to find the control panel now that others were there.

They moved as a group toward the circular deck at the front of the bridge. Josie and Miles followed slowly behind them. The P&C officers threw Adrian into one of the auxiliary chairs around the chief helmsman's spot and secured him with magnetic cuffs.

Josie crept to the base of the deck and slouched behind a large panel of blinking buttons and switches. Miles scowled, but there was no chance she was going to miss what was happening. They were in a perfect spot, within earshot yet still far enough away to be unnoticed.

Director Clarke and Adrian argued.

"I won't do it," Adrian said flatly.

Director Clarke chuckled. "You will transfer operational control of *November's Dawn* to me. Your life depends on it."

Josie exhaled a controlled breath. She hated the thought, but Adrian didn't know what her dad's holomessage was about. At the very least, Clarke couldn't force that information out of him.

Adrian refused to acknowledge him, instead turning to his former commandant. "Reyes, you know the danger the ark faces. If we can't get the navigational issues solved in the next few hours, we will all die."

"One problem at a time, Adrian. Right now, you're my biggest concern. I'm confident the techs will fix the navigational problems. No doubt you simply couldn't find the right means of motivating them."

"You may kill me, but the people won't follow you. Look around. *November's Dawn* is in chaos. Even the bridge is deserted. And I'll bet that by now, Hades Fist is better situated to take control than you two are."

Again, Clarke laughed, this time a throaty gurgle that echoed in the empty air. "We shall see. The question right now is what you will do. Transfer control, and I may be merciful."

Reyes stepped forward. "He needs to make an announcement to the whole ark explaining he is giving up leadership."

"What?" Director Clarke said. "Why?"

"Because he's right. The OSD leads the hearts and minds of the ark. They need to know the First Vicar is gone, that he failed us all and new leadership has risen."

"How fitting that the reign of the First Vicar should end

with his own tongue. A final sermon of sorts?" Director Clarke emphasized each word.

"The people will see right through you," Adrian said.

Josie smirked. She didn't know Adrian's endgame, but he was rattling Clarke. For a moment, she thought back to her conversation with Adrian a few days ago in the Observatory when she remained defiant for the sake of her own beliefs. She felt Adrian was doing the same now. She could appreciate that. It endeared him to her.

"What people? Serena Owens? You thought you could favor a wretched family from the lower decks and nobody would notice? Well, I did, Adrian. She will be dealt with. The daughter. The mother. Even the young one." Clarke glanced at Reyes. "Reyes will see to that, I'm sure."

Adrian dropped his head. "All these years I trusted you."

"Enough," Clarke boomed. He pushed a button and a holo-screen panel lit up. "Transfer control or die now." His words were punctuated by a holorifle aimed directly at Adrian's head.

Silence engulfed the room. Then Adrian spoke softly, "Spare Serena and her family and I'll do it."

Josie took a deep breath. Hearing Adrian pleading made her feel like she had been punched in the stomach, which surprised her. Considering how she felt about the man, she should have been fine with what was happening to him. But seeing him bargain for her life above his own threw out every doubt she had.

However misguided, Adrian was trying to save her.

She had to do something. It was now or never.

Josie was coiled low and ready to strike. Miles desperately reached out to stop her. Before he could, Marcus Abbott joined the party on the bridge.

Marcus pulled Josie back just as she started to jump out of their hiding place. The toe of her boot smacked against the paneling that shielded them from sight. A resounding thud echoed from it.

Heavy footsteps thundered down the stairs from the deck. Before any of them could move, two P&C officers trained their holorifles right on them. Commandant Reyes stood at the top of the platform. His shadowy figure was outlined by the bright orange light of the holoscreens around him.

"It appears we have snared some rats," he said coldly.

The P&C officers motioned with their holorifles for Josie, Miles, and Marcus to climb the stairs to the top of the deck. Nobody offered any resistance.

They all knew it was over.

Josie glanced at Marcus. The leader of Hades Fist had a smug look on his face, like he'd wanted this to happen. There was only one reason that would be the case. And it confirmed every suspicion Josie had about the man.

And made him far more dangerous.

It made her blood boil. If he had not grabbed her, this would not have happened. She wasn't sure what she'd been trying to do in the first place, but he had robbed her of her chance all the same.

An awful hollow feeling grew in her chest. Regret. She had a chance and didn't take it.

Everyone would suffer for it.

Adrian perked up as they made it to the top of the deck as if curious to see who the interlopers were. When their eyes met, the light faded from his.

"No," he whispered.

The desperation written on his face crushed Josie. She swallowed but found her throat had gone dry. All she could do was mouth the words.

I'm sorry.

His expression changed, as if questioning why she could

possibly be sorry. Like he was saying he's the one who screwed up.

"I knew we'd see each other again," Reyes smirked. He looked Josie up and down and then turned to Marcus. "And you've brought the king rat himself. You've made my job a hell of a lot easier. Fitting since it was you who sparked this chaos. The girl who resisted and the leader of Hades Fist, taken down in one swift stroke."

The P&C officers lined Josie and Miles up next to Adrian. Josie winced when the officer behind her kicked the back of her knees. Her face nearly smashed into the floor, but she caught herself just in time.

Miles received a similar treatment. Marcus was the only one still standing. The other officer held out cuffs toward the leader of Hades Fist but made no motion to cuff Josie or Miles.

Marcus only smiled. "Those won't be necessary."

Reyes stormed close, until their faces were mere inches apart. "For what comes next, I assure you, they're necessary."

"Calm yourself, Reyes. I've waited a long time for this," Marcus said.

"What're you talking about?" Reyes sneered. Then a curious look overcame him. Nobody on the deck moved. It was like each one worked to figure it all out.

"Because they've been working together," Josie said before she realized. Everyone looked at her. It all added up toward one outcome. After her mom told her Marcus knew about the Heart of the Dawn, she was sure of it. Marcus had played both sides.

"No, we haven't," Reyes barked.

"Not you," Josie said and pointed at Director Clarke. "Him. Marcus has been lying to us the whole time. He never cared about Hades Fist or the ark. Only himself."

Reyes spun toward Clarke. "Tell me she's lying. Tell me you haven't been working with Hades Fist?"

"The girl put it together. There's no reason to lie now, my dear Commandant." He turned to face Marcus. "Although I was not expecting this visit so soon."

Marcus brushed past Reyes. "I caught wind of your little coup on the bridge, and I wanted to make sure you stuck to the arrangement."

"You were there when my dad died," Josie said quietly as she looked up from the ground and met his eyes. It took every ounce of control to not lash out at him. She didn't want to reveal the Heart of the Dawn, but she had to know the truth after all this time. "Did you kill my dad?"

"What are you talking about? That pressure breach almost killed me too." He motioned toward his injured leg. "It was after the accident that Clarke and I came to our little deal."

"It had to have been you," Adrian said as he put together the pieces as well. "You were the only other one close enough. You found out about the reforms and you killed Dom to stop it."

"Enough!" Marcus roared as his anger boiled over. "I don't know why they've kept you alive, but you die now." He reached for the nearest holorifle being held by one of the officers.

Josie's heart hammered. Marcus would kill Adrian. She was sure of it. "You can't kill him! You still need him to take control of the ark."

"You've been a nuisance since the day I met you. You're next." A wild look flashed in Marcus's eyes as he looked at Director Clarke and Reyes. "If we're going to rule *November's Dawn* together, then he dies now."

"Rule together?" Reyes spat. "You're a parasite from Bottom Bays. You know nothing about the order of the ark. Order that I have spent my life protecting."

Director Clarke held up a hand. "Commandant, please."

"This is a partnership?" Marcus said as he motioned to

himself, Reyes, and Clarke. "Don't forget, Director, I control the lower decks now. Without Hades Fist, you have nothing."

"I understand." Clarke watched him for a moment then reached into his jacket. "I didn't want to do this so soon, but you leave me little choice."

Director Clarke removed the dark silhouette of a pistol and aimed it directly at Marcus's chest. His hand shook, but only for a moment.

Two ear-piercing blasts echoed throughout the bridge.

Marcus's eyes went wide, and his large stature made him fall to his knees rather than backward. A blood-curling gurgling came from his chest. "Why?" he muttered through a mouthful of blood.

Clarke's stare hardened. "You were only ever a means to an end, Marcus. Surely you should have seen that."

But it was too late. Marcus's expression glazed over. His face a picture of fatal confusion.

Once again nobody moved. Everyone battled combinations of confusion, fear, or in Reyes's case, rage.

Josie held her breath. She had no idea what was going to happen next. Beside her Miles postured with striking calm. It seemed like every person left on the deck waited. Adrian rattled his wrists around in his cuffs, trying to seize his chance, but it was no use.

Director Clarke wiped his forehead with the back of his hand, leaving a trail of glistening sweat along his receding hairline. Gone was his composure from before. Shooting Marcus had rattled him, but he was still deadly focused.

"Well, that was a nasty bit of business—"

A bone crunching crack stopped Director Clarke dead in his tracks. His eyes rolled to the back of his head. Then he fell, unconscious. His face smashed flat as spittle dripped from his open mouth.

Commandant Reyes stood behind him, holding his own pistol like a club.

"Reyes," Adrian said slowly. "You can still stop this. Unbind me, and we may still have a chance to save *November's Dawn*."

"Shut up," Reyes sneered, his eyes flashed with anger. "Helmsman Ido is a fool. The same as you. You knew about the threat the Obsidian Trench posed, and you did nothing. I will shut down *November's Dawn* before we reach the Trench."

"That's a death sentence. It would only be a matter of time before the next seismic event ripped the ark apart."

"I'll take that chance." Reyes's voice was cold and calculating.

In that moment Josie knew without a shadow of a doubt that taking the ark back to the surface was the only future. Otherwise, people like Reyes would always try to take back control and rule with an iron fist.

No matter what, she had to fulfill her dad's dream. It was her dream now.

"You would kill us all just to satisfy your own ambition!" Adrian shouted.

"No. You don't see it, do you?" Reyes's eyes flashed, clearly becoming more unstable by the minute. "I'm the guardian of *November's Dawn*. I know now I'm the only one with the strength and will to lead. For years I've protected her and done what you could not. Preserved order and our way of life. Anticipated obstacles. Removed threats. Like I did five years ago."

Adrian looked at him with wild eyes. "It was you? You murdered Dom?"

Reyes licked his lips with grim satisfaction. "Aye. Those reforms would have destroyed decades of peace aboard *November's Dawn*. You, of all people, should have known that.

It was simple enough to orchestrate really. Those ideas needed to die. And so they did, alongside Dom Owens."

Josie's mind raced as she tried to process. She'd been wrong. It wasn't Marcus after all. A dreadful sensation rippled through her stomach. Reyes was smiling right at her. The death of her dad, and of Felix, flashed in her mind. She finally knew the truth. After all these years, there it was. Standing squarely in front of her was the man who had taken everything from her. No amount of understanding or experience could have prepared her for this moment. It was a simple thought, one overriding directive. It focused her and dulled all other emotions.

She wanted him to die, and she was going to be the one to do it.

The only thing that stopped her from moving was the barrel of the holorifle pressed firmly against her back.

But all she needed was one chance. One moment.

"You should be thanking me, Adrian," Reyes continued. "He was a pest to be removed."

Every word Reyes said drove Josie deeper into her rage. "You're a coward, and you're going to fail. Nobody will follow you," she whispered.

"Josie, no!" Adrian warned. He was still working to loosen his cuffs. The rattling was louder and more persistent now.

"What did you say, girl?" Reyes said, his voice now cut with anger.

"You're not half the man my dad was." She glanced at Adrian, hardly believing the words she was about to say to Reyes. "And you're not half the man Adrian is. In the end, nobody will remember your name."

She had no idea what her endgame was, only her anger seemed to matter now.

Reyes sucked in a breath and backhanded her. Josie hadn't

anticipated the blow, and it sent her to the ground. The warm coppery taste of blood flooded her mouth.

Miles jumped forward but the officer held him firm.

Reyes straightened and looked down at the pistol still in his other hand.

"Say hello to your father for me." He pulled the hammer back. It clicked into position.

Josie stared directly at the barrel. It was over.

Oddly, the prospect didn't frighten her nearly as much as it should have. Time seemed to move slower. In that moment, all she experienced was a gentle calmness and clarity of thought which seemed impossible only moments before.

No, she didn't feel fear, only regret, a longing for all the things she wouldn't get to do and all the things she should have done but never could. Regret that Reyes would go on to enact his iron grip on *November's Dawn* and she had not been strong enough to stop him. She had the chance to avenge her dad and Felix, to free all of *November's Dawn* from the oppression life under the ocean demanded. The chance was gone now.

Miles struggled against the P&C behind him, but it was no use. Josie looked at him one last time. Desperation and terror danced in his eyes. She tried to look strong. She tried so hard to tell him everything in that last look. The only thing left to do was to accept it. She focused on the pistol then closed her eyes.

This was it. She was sure of it.

But the hammer never fell, and the shot never came.

Footsteps thundered up the stairs and reverberated through the platform. The split-second distraction was enough for Reyes to take his eyes away. Shouting then came from the stairs. Josie looked over too.

All at once Joshua and Tai raced up to the deck. Each armed with holorifles held snugly to their shoulders. Within seconds, they had each fired a shot. The blasts came deadly close to her and Miles. The storm of light and heat was all too familiar and forced her to shield her face with her hand, but this time it didn't take her by surprise. Miles fell backward to avoid the fire.

The convulsing spasms of energy smashed into the two P&C officers right next to him. Instantly, their bodies exploded into a billowing cloud of ash and dust. The gut-wrenching odor of burning flesh and hair seared her nostrils.

Reyes still held his pistol with a blank expression, as he tried to process what was happening. The delay was all Josie needed as she sprang at him, trying to take him down. Miles saw it too as he regained his footing and charged forward. Their eyes met in a single, perfect moment of understanding and purpose.

But Reyes was a hardened and capable soldier. His surprise was short lived, and their chance faded. Pure rage boiled in his eyes. He brought the pistol back up toward Josie's chest. Several steps still separated them. Miles was farther still.

Josie registered it too late. She was already fully committed. All her momentum took her forward, toward the gun and certain death.

Reyes squeezed the trigger. Nothing would stop him now.

She kept her eyes open this time. Tendrils of fire erupted from the barrel as the bullet hurled to its target. But someone jumped in front of her, shielding her from the bullet destined for her heart. The round slammed into the figure's torso with a sickening thud and he crumpled on the floor.

Josie's whole body tensed when she finally saw who it was. She could barely even make herself breathe.

Adrian had thrown himself in front of the bullet to save her.

His body lay where it had fallen. A thousand thoughts

flooded her mind but only one mattered, stopping Reyes once and for all. Her gaze flicked up at the commandant.

This time, Reyes's surprise lasted longer.

Josie seized the moment and jumped over Adrian, closing the final gap between her and the commandant. He had no chance to realign his aim this time. Her body smashed into his just as Miles reached him too. Even against Reyes's strength and stature, their combined weight drove him to the ground. Miles pinned his arms and punched him twice, once in the stomach and another more feral blow to the face. Josie wrestled with his strong grip as she tried to claw the pistol from him.

Even fighting the two of them off, Reyes was tenacious and dangerous, and it took another savage punch from Miles for his hand to open just enough for Josie to pry away the gun. As soon as it was free, she jumped off him and pointed it directly at him. Miles backed off as well.

She glanced back to Adrian where blood pooled beneath him. Miles saw the concern on her face.

"I'll check on him," he said softly.

Josie nodded. Her eyes sharpened as she turned back to Reyes, who was now on his hands and knees. Blood dripped from his face. She aimed the barrel directly at his head and pulled the hammer back.

Reyes heard the click and stopped moving. He sat back on his legs and lifted his head up to her. The barrel now sat centered on his forehead.

"So," he said, sending more droplets of blood to the ground. "You've finally done it. But I wonder, do you have the heart? Can you kill a man, Josie?"

Josie's knees shook, but her breathing was deadly calm. Joshua and Tai moved to either side of her, their holorifles at the ready, waiting for whatever might come next. Behind her, she could hear Adrian wheezing as he struggled to breathe.

But he was alive. That's all that mattered.

She looked into Reyes's eyes and saw nothing. They were emotionless and cruel. A deep-seated anger raged as she held the pistol to Reyes's head. This was the man who had taken everything from her and destroyed her family. She could avenge all their sacrifices.

It was only because of Adrian that she was still alive. Reyes was evil. Simple, pure evil. No amount of understanding could account for it. He deserved to die.

Before she had been powerless, but now she was in control.

This very same pistol had been used to murder Felix. It was almost fitting that she aimed it now at Reyes's head, the same way he had done to her friend. One shot was all it would take. Then it would be over. Reyes would never hurt another person. Slowly her finger slid closer to the trigger, gliding involuntarily until the cold sliver of metal was poised firmly against her pointer finger. Maybe it would finally bring her peace.

One gentle squeeze. One last breath.

"Don't do it, Josie," Adrian called. His voice was frail and labored but rang with purpose.

She looked over to see him rolled on his side. Sweat glistened on his forehead and through a grimace of pain his eyes gleamed with a determined and hopeful spark she had never seen before.

"This isn't you. Your dad . . . Felix . . . They wouldn't have wanted this for their little fox," Adrian continued.

Josie stepped back in shock. Her old nickname. Words she longed to hear so badly. Only she never expected to hear them from the man she had hated for so long, but who had a much greater impact on her life than she'd ever imagined. He was a good man who'd risked everything to save her.

She heard her dad's laughter. She felt Felix's calloused

hands guiding hers. She remembered all their love. And she loved them back. Killing Reyes would not bring her closure.

It would not bring them back to her.

All her life she had borne the pain of losing her dad and never truly saw the people still there for her. But Adrian was there now, as was her mom and Rose and even Miles. They were all still there. They needed her, and she needed them.

Slowly, the anger faded. A new sense of peace and love replaced it. It built in her and gave her hope she had never experienced so strongly before. Perhaps she had never truly understood it, but she did now. Tears fell gently down her cheeks. She didn't bother wiping them away.

Miles stepped close to her. "Josie," he said in a voice just for her.

She turned to his outstretched hand and closed her eyes. Felix and her dad smiled at her and gave her strength. Slowly she placed the pistol in Miles's palm and took in a precarious breath.

Miles slipped the gun away and looked back at her with longing eyes. He wrapped his arms around her and pulled her close.

Josie burrowed her face in the crook of his neck and quietly sobbed, but they weren't tears of sadness. For the first time ever, she embraced herself, all of herself. She felt stronger than she had ever been before.

After a moment, they pulled apart. Miles balled his fist and one swift punch cracked Reyes across the face, knocking him to the ground.

"That's for my family," he whispered.

The bridge shuddered violently as the ark's massive metal legs crushed another rock formation, reminding them of their fate if they could not figure out how to get *November's Dawn* to turn away from the looming Obsidian Trench.

CHAPTER THIRTY_

Everyone stood on the central deck as they grappled with the aftermath of Reyes and Director Clarke's attempted coup. Josie and Miles had discreetly looked around the bridge for anything relating to the Heart of the Dawn.

There was nothing. But they hadn't had time for a more thorough search.

Josie now watched *November's Dawn* lumber onward through the ocean from the observation deck. Miles stood silently next to her.

She could still feel the tension between them that came from everything they needed to say, only she couldn't bring herself to do so in front of everyone when they were running out of time. Miles didn't seem to be able to either.

Commander Rexus, another high-ranking P&C officer that Adrian trusted, had come to take Commandant Reyes and Director Clarke to the Pits. Josie had been glad to be rid of them. She couldn't stand to have Reyes's small, cruel eyes on her.

Joshua and Tai were huddled in a tight circle, whispering

anxiously about Marcus. His death opened a power vacuum in the lower decks, but they had a much bigger problem.

They would all die if they couldn't fix the navigational computers.

A nurse finished treating Adrian's bullet wound. He grimaced when she pulled the bandage tight over his abdomen but offered no complaint. Josie had begged him to get further medical care, but he had refused, saying he wouldn't leave when the danger was still so close.

"How long before we reach the Obsidian Trench?" Josie asked.

"Not long. Hours at best. It was never supposed to come to this," Adrian said.

"Yeah? Then what was it supposed to come to?" Joshua interrupted. He had the most trouble accepting peace with Adrian, the man he had spent so long fighting against.

Adrian's eyes darkened. "I understand your frustration, Joshua. I had planned to devote all our resources to finding a solution, but certain other events transpired that required my attention instead."

Joshua picked up on the insinuation and backed off.

"But there must be something we can do. It can't just end like this," Tai said.

"There is." Josie reached for the Heart of the Dawn necklace. She had to trust everyone now. There was no time left. Golden light bathed the deck as she pulled the necklace over her head. Everybody's eyes fixed on it.

"What is that?" Adrian asked while craning his neck further from the chair to get a better look.

She walked closer to show him. "It's called the Heart of the Dawn. My dad gave it to me."

"Dom gave you this?" Adrian asked. "Did he say what it was for?"

"It's the key to save *November's Dawn*."

"He knew about the navigational problems?"

"No, you're not getting it. He wasn't talking about the navigational problems. He believed there was a better future out there." Josie gulped as all eyes stared at her. What she was about to say would seem like madness to them all. "The real purpose of *November's Dawn* wasn't to stay under water forever. The ark was meant to return to the surface again. We can rebuild and have a chance to start over, make things better than they were before." She felt strange describing it like that, but it was how her dad explained it.

Nobody spoke for a few moments while they tried to grapple with what she told them.

Then Adrian frowned. "No, I don't believe it. I'm the First Vicar of the OSD. If this was our true purpose, I would have known." He looked at Josie. "How did Dom know?"

"My mom said he found the necklace and documents about it in one of Graham's private storage rooms."

"How did he get access? Why didn't he tell me?"

Josie shrugged. She had her own questions, but now was not the time to add her doubts to the fire. "Adrian, this is a chance to save the ark. Maybe our only chance. Do you honestly believe Helmsman Ido will fix the computers in time?"

Adrian sat back in his chair while his breathing became more ragged.

"What do we even know about the surface?" Joshua asked. "It could be more dangerous than it is down here. Worse, what's to stop us from becoming as bad as they were before the great war?"

Miles stepped forward. "We don't have a choice. The ark is walking into a trench. Into certain death. And I understand why you're worried, but we won't let that happen. Look around you. We know what will happen if we stay down here. Even with change or reforms or whatever you want to call it. Eventually things will go back to the way they were, with people in power at the top and everyone else below them. We know the mistakes of the past. We won't make them again on the surface."

"That's a nice idea, little brother. But I'm not convinced."

"Don't be stupid, Joshua," Tai quipped and pointed to where Marcus's body had fallen. "Hades Fist was a lie. We were all tricked by Marcus. All he wanted was power. I say we go up."

"We can't make this decision for everyone. There should be a vote. All of *November's Dawn* should decide," Joshua added.

Josie clapped her hands together in frustration. "There isn't time. Haven't you been listening? *November's Dawn* is headed in one direction, toward a massive trench that will kill us all. If we power down the ark, we might live five years, we might live five months, depending on seismic movement. But we know how it ends. Our only real chance is to go up."

"We're split then," Joshua said.

Another tremor shook the bridge as the massive metal legs of *November's Dawn* smashed through another field of rock. Outside the viewports, the clouds of dust and debris blocked everything from sight. A barrage of rubble and coral fragments bounced against the thick glass. Luckily, it held firm. Josie wondered for how long.

"No, it's over." Everyone stopped and looked at Adrian. "I cannot tell you what we will find on the surface, but perhaps it's time. Do you have any idea how to use the necklace?"

Josie held out the Heart of the Dawn and smiled. Since they hadn't found any sort of port for the necklace on the bridge, Josie had started to think about the matching decorative symbols under the portrait of Cornelius Graham. "In the office of the First Vicar."

Adrian nodded. "Let's go then."

Josie reached out to him hesitantly. It still seemed such a strange thought to care about what happened to Adrian after spending so much of her life hating everything he stood for. But he had proven the man he was, a friend of her dad and an important person to her mom. She put her hand on his. "Thank you, Adrian."

"You remind me of him so much. You have the same look in your eyes. Courage and hope. He would be so proud of you. I know it," Adrian said.

She tried to speak but her throat tightened, the precarious first warning sign of tears to follow. Something she didn't want the others to see. The only thing she could do was nod and turn back to the stairs.

There would be time for them to get to know each other more, but now she had a duty to the entire ark.

Joshua stepped forward. "Tai and I are going back down to Aegean. With Marcus gone, folks are going to be scared. It'll be chaos until this is all sorted out." Then he looked at Josie. "I still don't think this is right. But you haven't messed up too bad so far. Don't ruin that streak now."

Josie nodded in return. She didn't agree with everything Joshua had done, but she understood it and he had proven himself when it mattered.

Commander Rexus was waiting for Josie, Adrian, and Miles outside the main doors of the bridge. He was a well-built man with a squat face and a thin mustache that made his upper lip look dirty. Even though he had been a subordinate of Commandant Reyes, he had not hesitated for a moment when Adrian had ordered him to arrest his superior.

"To my offices, Commander. We must hurry," Adrian said.

"This way," Commander Rexus said in a gruff but not unkind voice.

They quietly snaked their way back through the many passageways to Adrian's suite of rooms. Commander Rexus stopped and saluted the P&C officer standing guard outside then typed in the necessary codes to open the door. Before he could hit the final key, a loud thud startled them.

Josie turned to see Adrian slumped against the wall, clutching his abdomen.

"I just need a moment," he said, between labored breaths.

Josie touched his arm. "You need more than that. It's okay, we can take it from here."

Adrian looked between Josie and Miles and smiled slightly. "I don't doubt you can. Find me when it's done."

Josie nodded and Adrian did the same. There was no time left for anything more. Then Commander Rexus helped Adrian down the passageway, leaving Josie with Miles. She turned to enter the office.

"Josie, wait," Miles said.

Josie gulped, knowing he wanted to further explain why he had reported her to the OSD. He had told her what happened, and she believed him. The more she thought about it, the more she was relieved to finally know. If reconnecting with her mom had proved anything, it was that she could not just hold a grudge without understanding.

She was still hurting, but at least now she could understand the terrible reasons behind it and the unbearable choice Miles had been forced to make. At least she knew now that it was not because he never cared for her. All she wanted was to have him in her arms again, to feel his warmth, to hear the rhythmic rise and fall of his heartbeat and to never let him go.

"I know there's no time. If this doesn't work . . . I just need you to know—" Miles started.

She put a finger to his lips. "I can't promise you I'll just get over it, but I can tell you I don't hate you. You did what you had to do. I understand that."

"You do?"

"Well, I'm trying to," Josie admitted. "I mean it was for your mom."

"Yeah. She needed the medicine so badly. I just didn't know what else to do."

"There's nothing else to say then." She wrapped her arms around his neck. She could feel the warmth from his breath. How his heart raced as fast as hers. She was not going to miss this moment. Not again. She stared into his eyes then threw the last bits of doubt from her mind. Their lips touched. Gently at first. His lips were soft and fit perfectly with hers. It was their moment.

Red lights flashed overhead. Accompanied by an automated voice. "Warning. Proximity alert. T-minus sixty minutes until the Obsidian Trench. Initiate avoidance maneuvers immediately."

Josie looked at the office and took Miles's hand. "Let's do this.

The office looked just like it had when she had been in it last. In no time she was sitting behind the desk of the First Vicar. The doors closed behind them, blocking out the cycle of warnings and flashing lights. She felt the wall underneath the portrait.

She smiled when her fingers slid over one of the symbols that had a small indentation in it. One exactly the same size as the Heart of the Dawn. Relief washed over her. Her hunch had been right.

She held the necklace out, letting the inner warmth from the pendant seep into her palm. She was about to change their lives forever. She only wished her dad and Felix were there so they could see the future that was only possible because of them. Nothing would ever be the same.

She took a deep breath. Then pressed the Heart of the Dawn into the socket.

Nothing happened.

Several seconds passed. Pressure crept up the back of her neck. Was it broken?

Then a worse thought crossed her mind. Did it ever work?

A low and rhythmic rumbling from the floor vibrated her whole body and interrupted her thoughts. It was different than the shaking when the legs smashed through rock formations. This felt like it came from the deepest parts of *November's Dawn* itself.

Flickering lights emanated from newly revealed lenses in the walls. A figure slowly emerged in the center of the room, blue and ghostly, just like the lights. It took her a moment, but she recognized the shimmering face in the hologram. The same figure hung behind her high on the wall. Cornelius Graham's pale eyes were fixed right on her but also through her at the same time, like she was a ghost to him like he was to her.

His voice was cold and distant, almost resigned. "The deepest depths of the oceans were supposed to be mankind's salvation. A haven in the dark where we might wait out the storms and terrors that ravaged the surface and come together once more. Here, amongst the endless dark, we would learn and grow and prosper. We would be unified in a way never seen before in human history. And we would be better for it. Then once the surface settled and the waves calmed, the true purpose of *November's Dawn* would be revealed, and we would rise again from the depths and reclaim our true place in the world. For on the surface above, as well as in the darkness below, *November's Dawn* shall provide. That was my vision and now it is yours. The ascension process will take two days to complete now that it has finally been activated. Use this time to prepare for your new future. A better future for all mankind."

He stopped, as if he had not yet come to terms with everything. Josie didn't blink and hung onto every word.

The hologram fluttered and then it was over. The Heart of the Dawn detached from the slot and landed on the shelf beneath it.

Josie grabbed the necklace then sunk back into the chair as a sense of calm settled over her, but she couldn't fully let go of the tension that drove her. She had been so consumed by her mission that the thought of it now being over was like losing a piece of herself. Was this truly it? She took a deep breath and tried to put it in perspective. She had done it. She had fulfilled her dad's legacy and brought peace to everyone who died to make the new future possible.

But why did she feel it had been too easy? Like Cornelius Graham should have had some trick or safeguard. She tried to block the thought from her mind and just be in the moment. She hadn't failed. Her demons would not keep this victory from her.

The giant metal legs of the ark stopped and so had the familiar gentle movement she had lived with her whole life. The stillness was eerie.

Miles paced around the office, switching between broad smiles and laughter. He sat on the desk next to her and took her hand. "You did it, Josie. You actually did it. You're incredible."

Josie couldn't help but smile. His happiness was infectious and made her forget her doubts. "No, Miles. We did it."

A growing rumble spread throughout the ark. Not loud enough to be distracting but enough to always be present. Like a final countdown to whatever might lie ahead.

November's Dawn was preparing to rise to the surface.

"Josie, we're going to see the surface. We're going to see the sun. And feel the breeze. It's all ours."

"I know," she whispered. "This changes everything."

"We should go tell Adrian and your mom. It feels like time to celebrate to me!"

She nodded and took his hand as they left the office. She felt Miles's warmth beside her. He felt safe. He felt like home. There was no one she would rather face the future with than him. She turned to kiss him, but a loud scream startled them.

Josie spun around to identify the source. At the far end of the hallway were the last two people she ever expected to see.

Odette and Nila ran toward them. Josie braced herself. The last time she had seen them she had been betrayed and captured. Her jaw clenched as they neared.

"You!" Odette sneered at Josie. "What're you doing here? You should be in jail."

Nila turned to Odette and frowned. "What do you mean Josie should be in jail? You said a random patrol found her."

Odette's face flushed as she stammered for an answer. "You wouldn't do it. I know you wouldn't have. So I had to turn her in."

"Tell me you didn't," Nila whispered. The horror of the realization flashed in her eyes as she glanced between Odette and Josie.

Josie stood still, unable to fully process what Nila had said. She'd thought Nila had been part of betraying her. Hearing that Nila had no idea about Odette turning her in sent a torrent of different thoughts through Josie's mind, thoughts she didn't have the time to untangle.

Adrian stormed out of another suite with Commander Rexus right behind him.

"What's going on here?" Commander Rexus demanded.

That only made Odette more angry. "What did you say to

me? Do you know who I am? Anyway, don't you have somewhere better to be? There are lower deck people running all over. Somebody has to stop them!" She took a self-confident step forward.

Commander Rexus's arm snapped up and blocked her way. "I suggest you rethink that action and go home, Miss Reyes." He looked at Nila. "You too, Miss Clarke."

Josie gasped at the last names of Odette and Nila. Of course she had known them before but never put two and two together. It was only in this moment that she realized who their fathers were. She could not help but feel sorry for them. They clearly had no idea. She especially felt bad for Nila. Part of her hoped at some level she could rekindle that spark with her, the only question was how. But she couldn't hide the surprise on her face now. She felt like someone had punched her in the stomach.

Odette picked up on it right away. "What are you looking at? Just wait till I see my dad." She looked at Adrian. "Why haven't you arrested her?"

"Enough!" Adrian grimaced and put a hand over his wound. His patience gone. "Both your fathers are traitors. Leave. Now."

"What? My daddy isn't a traitor," Nila said.

"Consider yourselves lucky I don't have you both taken in just to see if you knew anything about their insidious plans."

Odette's initial surprise faded. Then her face flushed. She redoubled her focus on Josie. "You did this! You must have framed them!"

Josie shook her head. She could see the two girls' worlds collapsing and felt especially bad for Nila, who had been kind to her in the past. Even after everything Odette had done to her, seeing them suffer didn't make her feel good. "No, Odette, I promise you I didn't."

Odette didn't seem to care. She shrieked and lunged toward Josie with her arms outstretched. Josie jumped backward. Just in time for Miles and Commander Rexus to close in from either side. Together they caught Odette and pushed her back. Odette fell to her knees, panting wildly.

Adrian motioned toward the P&C officer down the hall and pointed to Odette and Nila. The officer nodded and closed in on them, then lifted his holorifle just enough so the girls understood his meaning.

"Get them out of here," Adrian ordered.

Rexus took one last look at them then nodded. He started to walk with the other officer down the hallway, Odette and Nila positioned safely in front of them.

Adrian sighed. "I'm sorry about that, Josie. You shouldn't have to worry about them anymore."

Josie looked down and shrugged. "It's okay. I feel bad for them really. They have no idea what's coming."

"You did it? You were able to find the controls? I felt the ark stop moving."

Josie smiled and glanced at Miles. "We did it, Adrian. We're going to see the surface again."

Adrian took both Josie and Miles's hands. "I knew you both would figure it out. You're our future. I'm just so sorry it took me so long to see it."

"We're here now. That's all that matters," Josie said. "Where's my mom?"

Adrian pointed far down the passageway to another suite. "Let's go see her."

Serena sat on the edge of a wide bed. Her eyes were red and puffy. Rose stood off to the side, clutching Lewis with a smile on her face. Josie's throat clenched seeing her little sister safe and happy.

Both of them jumped when Josie, Adrian, and Miles came in.

Josie ran over and pulled her mom and Rose into a hug. Tears stung in her eyes. "It's over, Mom. We're finally safe."

"Your dad would be so proud of you, Josie," her mom whispered in her ear. "You've become everything we ever could have imagined."

Adrian put a hand on Josie's shoulder. "You've given your sister a chance at a life your dad only dreamed of. And I don't like the thought of it—or admitting it out loud—but you saved me, Josie. My path was shrouded in darkness. Then you came along."

Josie swallowed to choke back a sob. Then she got up and looked at the group. Her heart hammered. "I'm not good at making speeches, but I just wanted to say I love you all. You're the family I never knew I needed. And I know that together we're going to build the world we always dreamed of."

Adrian added, "Josie's right. We must have faith in ourselves and the ark. In the darkness below, *November's Dawn* will provide."

They looked around silently. The phrase held new meaning for each of them in the room. Even though they all—Josie, Miles, Adrian, and Serena, in their own way, held some doubt about the words, hearing them now was oddly comforting and gave them a sense of security.

It was a feeling that even though their futures were now shrouded by the unknown, they still had each other and the ark they called home. And if they held true to each other, they would have hope and a chance that the future would be better.

Josie pulled Rose close in front of her and held her tight. Adrian and Miles stood on either side of them. Adrian rested his hand on Serena's shoulder. In some way Josie felt like her dad and Felix were with them too. After all, this was the future they had given so much for. Her whole life Josie had felt alone, but it was different now. She was surrounded by people who loved her as much as she loved them, and the surface would offer a new start for everyone. She was stronger with them then she ever could be by herself.

She reached for Miles's hand and squeezed it gently. The one thing she knew for sure was that whatever the future had in store for them, they would face it together.

In her world where everything was changing, nothing would ever change that.

EPILOGUE_

THE OFFICE of the First Vicar was shrouded in an eerie gloom. Josie sat at the First Vicar's desk as she scanned through years of records in the holoterminal. Adrian had given Josie full access to everything aboard *November's Dawn* as part of her new role as one of the People's Leaders of the ark. An informal title and position for now, but one she took very seriously. As always, the eyes of Cornelius Graham watched over her from the portrait hung behind the desk. A conspicuous location meant to unnerve those who met with the First Vicar and remind those who sat at the desk of their burden.

Josie didn't mind that though, she had a duty to the people aboard *November's Dawn* now. They had put their trust in her.

Their very lives depended on her.

The last thing she was going to do was fail them now.

Every few minutes, a sequence of red lights flashed in warning, a constant reminder of what lay ahead for the great ark once they reached the mysterious world above.

Ever since Josie had activated the ascension process, a strange calm had settled over the people. It was as if they hadn't decided how they felt about leaving the depths that had kept them safe for decades. At least, no one had voiced a strong opposition, for which Josie was thankful for. The last thing they needed was for fear and dissension to spread right as they were on the cusp of a new future. The feeling was emphasized even more by the fact that when Josie started the ascension process, *November's Dawn* diverted all non-essential power sources toward the effort of rising thousands of meters out of the depths.

The entire ark was mired in the same gloom as the First Vicar's office, with only sparse emergency lighting and the red warning lights as a companion. Thankfully, there was only one day left until the ascension process was complete.

Part of her wished they had more time though. There was no telling what the surface would hold, what dangers might be there. If the air would even be safe to breathe. The Order of Scientific Discover had sent probes to the surface decades ago, but that project was shelved for fears of heretical thoughts spreading amongst the people.

Now things were different.

The ark was built for this purpose, but Josie couldn't help but worry. In the end it didn't matter though. *November's Dawn* had been forced out of the depths of the ocean by the computer virus that crippled its navigation systems and retaking the surface was their only future. There was no other choice but to succeed.

And Josie did everything in her power to make sure they were ready.

"Have you found anything surprising in the records?" Adrian asked from across the office where he was sitting.

Josie jumped, half forgetting he was with her. "There're thousands of data files here. I could spend weeks looking through it all."

Adrian opened his hands to her. "Well, you'll need to be

faster than that. You're a leader now. The people are expecting you to have answers. And you'll sometimes find you don't have those answers. You need to be ready to talk them down from the ledge if need be."

Josie held her head and groaned. "It's just all so much. We haven't even had a chance to breathe since the ascension process started."

"I know how you feel, Josie." Adrian lowered his voice. "Better than most. You're not alone. You have me, and your mom, and Miles too. I will prepare you as best I can, but in the end, it is your voice that will speak for us."

"Thank you, Adrian. Really." Josie meant it. It was still hard for her to believe that only a few days ago she considered Adrian her worst enemy and now he was one of her closest advisors. But she had never been more thankful to have his advice and support than she felt now.

Adrian smiled and picked up a holotablet to sift through more files. "Speaking of Miles, where is he?"

"On Aegean Deck," Josie said without missing a beat, even if she felt Miles's absence all too well. "He wanted to make sure his mom was okay after everything that happened."

"I pray she's okay. I'm sure she will beat the sickness."

Josie nodded and was about to echo the sentiment, but something caught her eye on the holoterminal display. A file subgroup buried between layers and layers of other domains titled, *Restricted Access Register: CG.*

"Adrian, what is this? Something called Restricted Access Register. Then the initials CG. I assume that's Cornelius Graham?"

"Your guess is as good as mine," Adrian said and sighed. "But I think you're right. It's a heavily encrypted data vault from before my time. I never could get into the files, only the cryptic names of some. I'd forgotten all about it."

Josie's curiosity was bubbling over now. She double clicked on the file. Several new files appeared. One stood out among the rest, *CG The Finality of it All*. A status symbol flashed next to the name indicating that the file recording was still in progress and that Cornelius Graham had never finished whatever work he was doing on it.

She moved the curser over the name. A thousand thoughts rattled in her mind as her heart raced even faster. She was about to see something that Graham himself wanted nobody else to see. Something he would not even share with Adrian, his handpicked successor.

She took one final breath and double clicked. A surge of hope coursed through her as a loading symbol appeared.

This was it. Her face was a nose length away from the display. Her excitement was running wild.

Red error messages flashed across the display. The change in brightness burned into her eyes and made her yelp.

Adrian came closer to see the display as well.

Then a string of text appeared, *Present that which is at the center of it All*. The only other option was to close out of the file directory.

Josie frowned and slumped back in her chair.

"See," Adrian said. "You can't get in. I tried. You clearly need a password."

"Yeah, yeah. I just needed to see for myself." Josie stopped as a thought hit her. What could possibly be at the center of it all? She smiled and looked at Adrian. "Or a key. Or maybe even a Heart."

Adrian scoffed at himself, understanding her meaning. "The Heart of the Dawn, of course."

Josie pulled the Heart of the Dawn necklace from around her neck. Leaving her chest feeling naked and bare without the heat that the necklace radiated. Immediately the office was bathed with its golden hue, cutting through the shadows, and making her forget the normal lights were unpowered.

She brought the necklace closer to the holoterminal, and a new string of text appeared.

Access granted. Welcome, Cornelius.

Josie and Adrian exchanged looks. He knelt beside her as they prepared to access a file that hadn't been seen in decades. A soft grunt escaped Adrian as he put pressure on the bandage wrapped around his abdomen from where Commandant Reyes had shot him. A bullet he took to save Josie's life.

"I'm okay," he said and motioned to the display. "Go ahead."

Josie did as she was told and opened the file recording, *CG The Finality of it All.*

The holoterminal dimmed as the same projectors reappeared that had given Josie and Miles the message Graham had recorded for when the ascension process started.

Now they lit up once more and showed a man who looked much older and more weathered, beaten almost. But still with the unmistakable poise of Graham himself. His voice carried a depth of sadness it had not before.

"The time has finally come. I know it in my heart. I can feel it in the very iron of the ark. I will soon pass into the watery abyss I fought to save so many from. But I will go carrying the terrible truth. *November's Dawn* is not alone on this earth. There is a second ark, a twin. Built in secret and kept away from the world. A choice I made to give humanity the best chance at survival I could. Together, *October's Fury* and *November's Dawn* were meant to be the pinnacle in human achievement. And they would have been save for the wayward leaders of *October's Fury* who went against my orders and activated the mechanism to bring their ark back to the surface only two years into our voyage. Once the sequence was activated, I lost contact with *October's Fury*. The technology was unproven. I should have stopped it. The science and engineering behind a feat such as this were extraordinary, and I had no way to test it, the smallest miscalculation could have ended in catastrophe. I tried to reestablish contact with *October's Fury* for years, or at least find whatever wreckage might remain of them, but to no avail. It was as if they vanished without a trace. I buried the truth, fearing the worst and what might happen should *November's Dawn* try to follow her sister back to the surface, so that we would remain under the waves forever but at least we would continue to live. I could not face the notion of being the harbinger of humanity's end, not when I had devoted my life to our preservation. But it matters little now. Perhaps one day someone will find this log of my failure. Perhaps someday we will learn to be better than we were before."

The hologram recording flickered and cutoff, leaving the room dark once more. An automated voice questioned if they wanted to rewatch the recording. Josie quickly hit the command to back out.

Adrian put his head on the desk and took several deep breaths.

Josie felt a wave of nausea creep through her. She had started the ascension process for *November's Dawn*. She had done the very thing that led to the disappearance of *October's Fury*.

"Adrian," she whispered. "What are we going to do?"

"I don't know. It doesn't make any sense. I was the First Vicar. I should have known about—"

Static from the overhead speaker system interrupted them. "First Vicar? First Vicar, are you there? It's Helmsman Ido."

"Yes, Helmsman. What is it?" Adrian answered.

"You wanted a report right away. About why the navigational computers malfunctioned. I isolated the signal that activated the dormant virus."

Adrian looked visibly relieved. "Go on."

"Well, the thing is. It doesn't make any sense. The signal makeup looks exactly like those we use on *November's Dawn*. Only this came from outside the ark. As in thousands of kilometers away in the oceans. I don't know what to think, First Vicar, but I'm going to keep trying to clean it up to be sure."

"Thank you, Ido. Contact me the moment you know more." Adrian flipped a switch leaving them in silence again.

They stayed quiet but Josie was sure they were thinking the same thing. The signal could have only come from one place.

October's Fury.

The second ark was still out there somewhere. And they had been the one to use a computer virus to disable *November's Dawn*, the same virus that had almost killed them all. It meant the second ark was willing to do whatever necessary to get what it wanted. Josie couldn't assume anything anymore. *October's Fury* could be a sign of hope of what the surface offered, but it could also mean danger. It could mean the end of everything they ever knew.

JOIN THE CURSED DRAGON SHIP NEWSLETTER_

Want more just like this one? Sign up for our newsletter so you don't miss out on the adventure. You'll get:

- A free book for signing up
- Advanced notice of new releases
- First word of books on sale
- Opportunities for free books
- Most up-to-date information on author appearances.

We're busy and know you are too. We won't send more than one newsletter a month.

Register below.

ACKNOWLEDGMENTS_

November's Dawn is the culmination of a number of themes and concepts that have danced around in my head for years now. Seeing that story come to life and manifest itself in something that can be shared with the world is an incredible feeling, and I'm so thankful to be able to experience everything that it involves.

Stories are for the readers. I stand by that concept. Sure, there is a part of it for the writer—an itch that needs to be scratched so to speak. But a story thrives and takes life with its readers and for that I thank you, the reader. For sticking with my words and letting them take you to strange new worlds, for believing I could guide you on that journey. And for trusting me with your curiosity.

I have to thank my editors, Jesse Sprague and Kelly Colby, for believing in me and thinking I had a story worth telling. The team at Cursed Dragon Ship for the grind they do each and every day. My friends, for their feedback and excitement that keeps me going. My siblings, for their support and encouragement. My parents, Ralph and Marlene, for teaching me every lesson, truth, and wisdom I hold close to my heart.

And lastly, thank you to my partner, Vanessa, for sticking with me through everything and always helping me to find my "potato in a pot" moment in every tale.

C.T. Moshage, a Chicago-based author, writes young adult science fiction and fantasy stories. With a degree in International Studies from Bradley University, Moshage infuses his narratives with a global perspective. His stories explore themes of found families, loyalty, and duty, mirroring the complexity of real-world relationships and ethical dilemmas. Outside writing, Moshage is an avid drone enthusiast and tennis player. As a lifelong fan of sci-fi and fantasy, he is committed to crafting stories that not only captivate but also challenge young readers to think deeply about the themes of connection and responsibility. *November's Dawn* is his first novel.

Join his newsletter from his website for a free story: www.ctmoshage.com.

instagram.com/ctmoshage

One mind different from the rest must save her community from itself.

9 781951 445645